THIS SPECIAL SIGNED EDITION OF

HALLOWEEN
AND OTHER SEASONS

IS LIMITED TO 1,250 COPIES.

HALLOWEEN
AND OTHER SEASONS

HALLOWEEN
AND OTHER SEASONS

AL SARRANTONIO

CEMETERY DANCE PUBLICATIONS

Baltimore
❖ **2008** ❖

Cemetery Dance Publications
132-B Industry Lane, Unit #7
Forest Hill, MD 21050
http://www.cemeterydance.com

The characters and events in this book are fictitious.
Any similarity to real persons, living or dead,
is coincidental and not intended by the author.

First Limited Edition Printing

ISBN-13: 978-1-58767-183-8
ISBN-10:   1-58767-183-2

Cover Artwork © 2008 by Alan M. Clark
Interior Design by Kathryn Freeman

To Alan M. Clark:
Great Artist and Good Bud

TABLE OF CONTENTS

SUMMER

IT WAS A SUMMER day that was all of summer. Dry heat rose from the cracks in the sidewalks, brushing the brown grass that grew there as it shimmered by. There was a hush in the stilted air, high and hanging, the sun like a burnt coin frozen in the pale and cloudless sky, the trees still, green leaves dried and baked, panting for a breeze.

Rotating window fans moved hot air from outside to inside. Newspapers rustled on kitchen tables, their pages waving until the artificial breeze moved on, then settling hot and desultory back into unread place. The breakfast plates sat unstacked, forgotten; lunch plates with uneaten lunch—curling pumpernickel, wilted lettuce, an inkblot of mustard dry as paper—sat nearby. Morning coffee milled in two mugs, still tepid from the afternoon warmth.

"My Gosh, Mabel, has it ever been this hot before?" George Meadows said from his easy chair; he sat arranged like a man who had eaten a great meal, with his shirt and trousers loosened, but only against the heat.

His wife Mabel, prostrate on the nearby couch, the faded sunflowers of her house dress clashing and merging in a wilted riot with the worn daisies of the sofa print, tried to say something but failed. Her right hand continued to weakly fan herself with its magazine and she tried again.

"Hot as it's...ever been," she managed to get out in a croak, and then closed her eyes and ears, discouraging further comment.

"Yep," George managed to answer before closing his own eyes. He couldn't resist, he never could, getting the last word in. He rallied to add, even though Mabel was already perfectly aware: "Man on the radio said it might get hotter still."

◆ ◆ ◆

Three twelve-year-old boys hated summer.

They hadn't always. At one time, summer had belonged to them. From the first day of school letting out, until the dreaded bell sounded again, they had ruled summer as if they owned it. There had been baseball and bad tennis, and miniature golf and marbles in the hot dust. There had been butterfly hunts with orange-black monarchs big as pterodactyls and just as difficult to catch. Trips to the secret pond with jars, and pond water drops under Lem's microscope to watch the amoebas within. And their own swimming, from dawn to dusk some days, emerging at the end waterlogged beings, raisin boys, to dry and unwilt in the setting sun. And Monk's telescope at night, the fat dry cold moon sliding across the eyepiece like a pockmarked balloon; Saturn hanging silent and majestic with its golden split ring. Backyard campouts, the walls of Shep's pup tent lit from within not with fireflies but with the flashlights of boys with comic books, the smell of Sterno and pancake batter the next morning, the metal taste of warm water in boy scout canteens.

Summer had been their time—the time away from schoolbooks and parents' waggling fingers, the time to be boys. And this year it had started the same—the banishment of black-and-white marble notebooks, pencils thrown under beds spearing dust bunnies, school clothes in the backs of closets.

And out with the baseball glove! Oiled, smelling like new wet leather, sneakers that smelled of dirt, short pants, the dewy morning giving way to a fresh hot feeling and late afternoon thunderstorms scattering the ballplayers with warm wet drops big as knuckles and the temperature dropping and making them shiver. And swimming, and more swimming, and more swimming still, and the cool-warm nights, the sharp cold taste of ice cream, of a bottle of cola drawn from an iced bucket, of a hot dog steaming, hiding under hot sauerkraut. A drive-in movie in Uncle Jed's pickup truck: two hiding under the tarp until they were in.

Morning noon and night it was summer.

Real summer.

Until:

Something...

...began to change.

It was Shep who noticed it first: in the dangerous tree-house on a mid-August afternoon. They had finished trading baseball cards, arguing over how many cards (always doubles!) to attach to bicycle spokes to make them clack, and were halfway through another argument about who was prettier, Margaret O'Hearn or Angie Bernstein, when Shep's head went up and he sniffed, just like a hound dog might. His leg, swinging through one of the hut's many floor holes, pendulumed to a frozen stop.

"What's wrong?" Lem asked, and Monk looked up from his new copy of *Vault of Horror* with a frown.

"Turn off your brain, Shep," Monk growled. "It's summer."

"Just because you don't want to talk about girls or leg hair or b.o.—" Lem began, but he stopped dead at the look on Shep's face.

"Something's different," Shep said, and he still held that pointer-at-a-bird look.

Lem tried to laugh, but stopped abruptly, a hiccup of seriousness at the look in Shep's eyes.

A whisper: "What do you mean: different?"

Shep spoke without breaking his concentration. "Don't you *feel* it?"

Monk shook his head with finality and went back to his comic, but Lem's face had taken on a worried look.

Shep was never wrong about these kinds of things.

"I...don't feel anything..." Lem offered mildly.

Idly, still scanning his *Vault of Horror*, Monk kicked out his sneaker and caught Lem on the shin. A scatter of orange infield dust, dislodged from the sculpted sole, trickled down the other boy's bare leg.

"You feel *that*, Lemnick?"

"Be quiet—" Shep said abruptly, and it was not a request.

The other two boys were silent—and now Monk sat up, his butt easily finding the structure's largest hole, which they inevitably called "the crapper."

Something like a faint hiss, something like the eerie castanet sound cicadas make, passed by his ears and brushed him on one cheek, but there was not so much as a breeze in the early hot afternoon.

"What was—"

"It's getting hotter," Shep said simply.

"Maybe it's because of Hell Cave," Monk laughed, but nobody joined him.

✦ ✦ ✦

That afternoon it was too hot to swim. It stayed that way the next three days. They abandoned the tree-house, leaving its lopsided openwork collection of mismatched boards and tattooed, badly nailed orange crates, and moved into Monk's cellar, which was damp but cool.

It had never been too hot to swim before:

Never.

They perused Monk's comic book collection, which after banishment to the basement was on the verge of mold. Monk had built, from boards too useless even for the tree-house, a lab table in one corner, and they fiddled with the chemistry set, trying to make things that were yellow and then turned red, others that made smoke. They toyed with the rabbit-ear antenna on the ancient television, a huge wooden box with a tiny black-and-white screen the size of a TV dinner tin—for a while they brought in the monster movie channel, and watched, in a snowy and line-infested picture, the Man from Planet X rampage through the Scottish moors. Monk brought down a bowl of grapes, and they ate some of them, and spit the rest at each other out of their mouths, pressing their cheeks for cannonade.

But their eyes kept drifting to the cellar windows, and the heat and light outside.

"Maybe we should go swimming anyway," Monk said, finally, on the second day.

They made it halfway to the secret pond, and turned around, dripping and panting.

Overhead, the sun looked hotter, if not larger.

They played darts in the cellar, and set up plastic army men and knocked them down with marbles and rubber bands.

Lem and Shep talked about body odor and shaving their upper lips while Monk scowled.

And always, for three days, they kept looking to the cellar windows, up high, filled with light, and closed against the summer heat.

✦ ✦ ✦

That night they took Monk's telescope to the secret pond, and Shep's pup tent, and Lem's dad's battery radio.

The radio played music, and talked about the heat. The air was dry as the insides of an oven. There was a cloudless sky, and a smile of moon tilted at an amused angle, and, after a while, there were stars in the dark but they looked faraway and dim through the hot air. The telescope went unused. They swam for a while, but the water, over the last three days, had taken on the temperature and feel of warm tea. Inside the tent it was as hot as outside, and they shifted uncomfortably as they tried to sleep. When they tried to read comics by flashlight, the flashlights dimmed and then went out.

In the dark, Lem tried to talk again about Margaret O'Hearn and Amy Bernstein, and about Shep joining the track team when they all started Junior High in the fall, but Monk told them to shut up.

Later Shep said, out of the blue, "What do you think about Hell's Cave?"

"What about it?" Monk sneered. "You think it leads down to hell?"

"That's what they say."

Lem was silent, and then he said, "You think that's why the heat won't end...?"

"I wonder," Shep replied.

"You really think—?" Lem began.

"Go to sleep!" Monk demanded.

In the morning it was even hotter.

The sun came up over the trees the color of melted butter. Monk set up the griddle over two Sterno cans, but no one was hungry so he didn't even start breakfast. They spit out the water in their canteens, which tasted like warm aluminum.

It was getting even hotter.

"Ninety-nine today," the radio chirped, "and who knows how hot tomorrow. It only went down to eighty-nine last night, folks. Hope you've got those fans on high, or your head in the fridge!"

He went on to say the weather bureau had no idea why it was so hot.

"What does that mean?" Shep said. "Isn't it their job to know?"

As if in answer the chirpy radio voice said, "Apparently, folks, this heat has little to do with the weather! According to meteorological indications, it should be in the middle eighties, with moderate humidity! Fancy that!"

"Fancy *that!*" Monk nearly spat, in mocking imitation.

The radio voice, again as if in answer, chirped just before a commercial came on: "Hey, folks! Maybe it'll *never* be cool again!"

Shep looked at his friends, and there was a suddenly grim look on his face.

"Maybe he's right," he said.

It didn't rain over the next ten days. Thunderheads would gather in the west, dark mushrooming promises of cool and wet, and then break apart as they came overhead, dissipating like pipe smoke into the blue high air. The grasses turned from moist green to brown; postage stamp lawns changed color overnight and died. In town, the few places with air conditioning—Ferber's Department Store, the Five and Dime with its brand new machine perched over the front door, dripping warm condenser water from its badly installed drain onto entering customers—were packed with customers who didn't buy anything, only wandered the aisles like zombies seeking cool relief. The temperature rose into the low hundreds, dropping into the nineties at night. On the roads, automobiles like ancient reptiles sat deserted at angles against curbs, their hoods up, radiators hissing angrily. Buses, looking like brontosauruses, passenger-less, stood unmoving, their front and middle doors accordianed open, yawning lazily at empty white bus stop benches.

Birds stopped singing in trees; the morning dawned as hot as midday. Dogs panted in their doghouses. There were no mosquitoes, and houseflies hung motionless on window screens. Spiders crawled into shadows and stayed there.

Cold water came out of taps almost steaming.

It was getting even hotter.

Three twelve-year-old boys made one more pilgrimage to the secret pond. They were sick of Monk's cellar, had done every experiment in the chemistry manual, had recklessly mixed chemicals on their own until one produced in a beaker a roiling cloud of orange choking gas that drove them upstairs. It had become too hot in the cellar anyway, with the windows closed or open. In Monk's kitchen the refrigerator whirred like an unhappy robot, its doors permanently open to provide a tiny measure of coolness to the kitchen. Milk had spoiled, its odor battling with the sour stench of rotting vegetables. Dishes, unwashed, were piled in the sink. The radio was on, a background insect buzz. Monk's parents had gone to the five and dime for the air conditioning.

"And even hotter, with record temperatures reported now not only around the United States but in Europe and Asia as well, in a widening area..." the radio said, though the announcer sounded less chirpy, almost tired. "Locally, state authorities are warning anyone prone to heat stroke..."

Monk and Shep and Lem took whatever dry food was left, found Shep's pup tent, inexpertly rolled and abandoned in a corner, and set out for the pond.

"...forty deaths reported in..." the radio voice reported unhappily as the screen door banged behind them.

✦ ✦ ✦

It was like walking through a bakery oven. The heat was not only in the ground and in the air, but all around them. They felt it through their sneakers, on their knees, their eyelids. Their hair felt hot. The air was dry as a firecracker.

Shep looked up into the sun, and his eyes hurt.

"I don't care how hot the water is," Monk said, "it can't be worse than this."

It was. When they got to the pond and stripped, there was vapor rising from the surface of the water, and fish floated dead, like flat plastic toys.

"I don't care," Monk said, and stepped in, and yelped.

He looked back at his friends in awe, and showed his retracted foot, which was red.

"It's actually *hot!*" Monk said.

Lem sat on the ground and put his head in his hands.

Monk was putting his clothes back on, his hands shaking.

Shep said with certainty, "Someone stole summer, and we're going to Hell's Cave to get it back."

"Ungh?" a weak voice said from the kitchen table. George Meadows sat staring at his half-empty coffee cup, watching the coffee in it steam. He had poured it an hour and a half ago, and it was still hot.

He lifted his hand toward it, looked at the sweat stain it left in the shape of a hand on the table and lowered it again.

"Mabel?" he called in a raspy, whispery voice. The sound of fanning had stopped and when George Meadows made the extreme effort to turn his head he saw that his wife's housedress looked as if it was melting, with her in it, into the sofa. Her right hand, unmoving, still gripped her magazine and her eyes held a fixed, glazed look. Her chest barely moved up and down.

"Oh, Lord..." he breathed, closing his eyes, getting the last word in though she hadn't said anything. "Gettin' hotter still..."

Three twelve-year-old boys stood in front of a cave opening buttressed with rotting timbers. With them was Monk's rusting Radio Flyer, bursting like a Conestoga wagon with their supplies: the battery radio, two new-battery-filled flashlights (one of them worked); three boxes of cereal; six comic books, no doubles; a large thermos of hot ice tea; four cans of warm cream soda; a length of clothesline pilfered from Lem's mother's backyard; a mousetrap, over which they had bantered incessantly ("What if we meet up with rats?" Lem debated; "Why not a gorilla?" Shep shot back; in the end Shep got tired of the argument and threw it on the pile), a B-B gun, a kitchen knife with a broken handle, a crucifix, a bible. The last two had been added by Shep, because, he said, "We're heading down *there*," and would listen to no argument.

They headed in.

It was dim, and, compared to outside, almost cool in the cave. But as they moved farther in it got even dimmer and hot and stuffy. Their bodies were covered with sweat, but they didn't notice. There was a twist to the left, and then a climb that disappointed them, and then a sudden drop which brought them real darkness and a halt.

Lem, who was pulling the wagon, rummaged through the pile and pulled out the bad flashlight, and then the good one, which he handed to Shep.

Shep switched it on and played the light over their faces.

"You look scared," he said.

"Can we stop here for the night?" Lem asked.

Shep consulted his watch with the light beam. "It's two in the afternoon!"

Behind them, they saw how steeply the floor had dropped; there was a circle of light leading out that looked hot and far away.

"I'm hungry," Monk said.

"Later," Shep answered, and turned the flashlight beam ahead of them.

There was darkness, and a steep descent, and Monk and Lem followed as the beam pointed down into it.

After twenty minutes that seemed like a day, the black wagon handle slipped out of Lem's sweaty hand and the wagon clattered past him.

"Look out!" he called, and Monk and Shep jumped aside as the wagon roared down the steep incline ahead of them.

They heard it rattle off into the bowels of the earth, then they heard nothing.

"Why did you tell us to get out of the way?" Shep asked angrily. "We could have stopped it!"

"We'll catch up to it," Monk shot back.

"Sorry..." Lem said.

"No matter. Monk's right." The flashlight beam pointed ahead, and down they went.

❖ ❖ ❖

Two real hours went by. Lem was thirsty, and Monk wanted to stop, but Shep kept going. If anything it was hotter than above now, and Lem finally panted timidly, "You think we're almost...there?"

"You mean *hell*?" Shep replied, and then added, "If we are, we don't have the crucifix anymore to protect us. It's in the wagon."

Monk snorted, and Shep spun angrily toward him with the flashlight, which at that exact moment went out.

"*Ohhh*," Lem mewled.

"Be quiet," Shep ordered, "it's just stuck." They heard him shaking the flashlight in the dark, but the beam didn't come on.

"Maybe the cover's loose—"

There was the rattle of loosened metal, a *twang*, and they heard flashlight parts hitting the floor of the cave.

"Uh oh," Monk said.

"Help me find them—" Shep ordered, but now there was a note of desperation in his voice.

"I hear rats!" Lem cried, and they all went silent.

Something was skittering in the dark ahead of them.

"Get down and help me find the parts!" Shep said, and for a few minutes there was only the sound of frightened breathing and the pat and slide of hands on the floor of the cave.

"I've got the lens!" Shep cried suddenly.

"And here's the reflector!" Monk added.

"What if there are *rats* on the *floor!*" Lem said, but Shep ignored him.

"All we need is the cover, and one of the batteries. The other one is still in the body."

"I've got the battery!" Monk exulted a moment later.

"I can't find the cover!" Shep said desperately.

"I'm telling you there are rats!" Lem whimpered.

"I can't find the cover either!" Monk.

There was fumbling in the dark, heavy breathing.

A bolt of light blinded them, went out, blinded them.

"I don't need the cover—I'll hold it on," Shep said.

He pointed the flashlight, clutched together by the pressure of his hand, at his friends, Monk on the cave floor, still probing, Lem with his back against the wall, eyes closed.

The beam shot to the floor, moved crazily this way and that, then froze on a round red piece of plastic.

"The cover!" Monk yelled, and pounced on it.

"Give it to me!" Shep said.

There was more fumbling, darkness, then bright light again.

They stood huffing and puffing at their exertion.

Their breaths quieted.

The scrabbling sound was still ahead of them.

"*Rats!*" Lem cried, and then let out a wail.

The flashlight beam swung down and ahead of them, and caught the crashed remains of the red wagon on its side, a chewed-open box of cereal, and the long fat gray-brown length of a rat as it put its whiskered, sniffing nose into the mouse trap.

There was a loud *snap!* which made the light beam shiver, and then, in the darkness behind Shep, he heard Lem laugh nervously and say, "See?"

SUMMER

✦ ✦ ✦

They stopped two hours later for the night. By Shep's watch it was ten o'clock. The flashlight had gone out again, and this time it was the batteries but Shep took the batteries from the other non-working one. They were tired and hungry, thirsty and hot. The wagon was serviceable but now made a loud squeak with each turn of the front wheels. The handle had been bent, but Lem forced it back into shape. They'd found everything but one can of pop, which Monk promptly stepped on when they set out. He smelled like cream soda, and his friends didn't let him forget it.

"We'll need the batteries for tomorrow," Shep said solemnly. He had found a flat, wide place to stop, a kind of hitch in the slope. Ahead of them was only darkness.

It was hot and close and sticky, and they felt a vague heat drifting up at them from below.

"What happens when the batteries run out?" Lem asked.

"We'll have to conserve them," Shep said.

"But what happens—"

"Be quiet," Shep said, at the same moment Monk snapped, "Shut up, Lem."

They ate in darkness, and drank warm soda and un-iced tea, and listened, but there was nothing to hear. No rats, no nearby roasting fires, no dripping water, no sound of any kind. Just the silent sound of heat getting hotter.

"I hope we're close," Lem said. "I want to go home."

"Home to what?" Shep answered. "If we don't find something down here..."

The rest went unsaid.

They sat in a circle, and moved closer, the flashlight in the midst of them like a doused campfire.

Shep laughed and said, "We never finished talking about Angie Bernstein, did we?"

Lem laughed too. "Or how your pits smell!"

"Or your mustache!" Shep shot back.

Monk was silent.

"Hey, Monk," Shep said, "you shaving your lip yet?"

"And using 'B-Oderant'? You smell like cream soda, but do you also smell like a *horse*?"

Monk feigned snoring.

"Hey Monk—"

The snoring ceased. "Leave me alone."

Lem hooted: "Cream soda boy!"

"Horse pit boy!" Shep laughed.

Monk said nothing, and soon he was snoring for real.

Shep woke them up at seven o'clock by his watch.

At first he couldn't move; it was hard to breathe and so hot he felt as if he was under a steam iron. He knew it was growing impossibly warmer. He could feel and smell and taste it, just like he had in the tree-house.

"We have to find the end today," he said, grimly.

They ate and drank in the dark, just like the night before. Now there was no talking. Lem was having trouble breathing, taking shallow ragged huffs at the air.

"Feels...like...we're...in a...barbecue..." he rasped. "Hard...to...breathe..."

They turned on the battery radio and there was hiss up and down the dial until the one strong local channel came on. It was the same announcer, only now all of the chirp had gone out of his voice.

"...hundred and ten here this morning, folks," he said. "And it's September first! Local ponds are steamed dry, and the electricity was out for three hours yesterday. Same all over, now. Ice caps are melting, and in Australia, where it's the end of wintertime, the temperature hit 99 yesterday..."

They snapped off the radio.

"Let's go," Shep said.

✦ ✦ ✦

Lem began to cry after a half hour.

"I can't *do* this!" he said. "Let's go home! I want to swim in the pond, and get ready for school, and look at the fall catalogs and feel it get chilly at night!"

"It's not much farther," Shep said evenly. He was having trouble breathing himself. "This is something we've got to do, Lem. If we do it maybe we can have all that again."

Shep pointed the flashlight at Monk, who was trudging silently, straight ahead.

✦ ✦ ✦

The flashlight began to fail as they reached a wall of fallen rocks. Ignoring the impediment for the moment, Shep used the remaining light to rip the battery cover off the back of the radio and pull the batteries out.

They were a different size, so he put the radio on and let it stay on, a droning buzz in the background.

The flashlight went out, then flickered on again.

"Quick!" Shep shouted. "Check to either side and see if there's a way around!"

Lem shuffled off to the left, and Monk stood unmoving where he was.

Shep pushed impatiently past him, flicking the flash on and off to pull precious weak yellow beams out of it.

"There's no way around here," Lem called out laconically from the left.

Shep blinked the light on, off, punched desperately around the edge of the barrier, looking for a hole, a rift, a way through.

"Nothing..." he huffed weakly.

He turned with a last thought, flaring the flash into life so that the beam played across Monk.

"Maybe there's a crack! Maybe we can pull the wall down!"

"There is no crack," Monk said dully, "and we can't pull it down." His legs abruptly folded underneath him and he sat on the cave floor.

Shep turned the light off, on again; the beam was dull, pumpkin colored, but he played it all over the rock barrier.

"Got to be—"

"There is no 'Hell's Cave'," Monk said dully. "It's just a myth. My father told me about it when I was seven. This is just an old mine that played out and then caved in."

"But—"

"*I* made it all happen," Monk said hoarsely, without energy. "The heat, the endless summer. It was me."

"What?" Shep said, moving closer. On the other side, Lem sank to the floor.

"It was me..." Monk repeated.

Lem began to cry, mewling like a hurt kitten, and the flashlight beam died again. In the dark, Shep flicked it on, off, on, off.

"*Me*," Monk said fiercely, an agonized hiss.

Shep hit the button one more time on the flashlight, and it flared like a dying candle, haloing Monk's haunted face, and then faded out again.

"I didn't want it to end." In the darkness Monk spoke in a whispered monotone. "I didn't want it *ever* to end."

"Didn't want *what* to end?" Shep asked, confused.

"This summer," Monk answered, sighing. "The three of us. I wanted it to last forever. I didn't want us to...change. Which is what we were doing. Talking about girls instead of baseball cards, hairy legs instead of monster comics, body odor instead of swimming and telescopes. We used to do everything together and now that was going to change. When we went to Junior High Lem was going to try to date Angie Bernstein and you were going out for track. Then you would go out with Margaret O'Hearn, and the baseball cards and comics would go in the back of the closet, along with the marbles and the pup tent and the canteen and butterfly net. The chemistry set would collect dust in the corner of the basement. I could see it coming. It was all changing, and I didn't want it to."

"But how...?" Shep asked.

In the dark, he could almost hear Monk shrug and heard him hitch a sob. "I don't *know* how I did it. I just wanted it, I fell asleep crying for it at night, I prayed for it every day. Every time you and Lem started talking about girls and body hair and growing up, I prayed for it louder. And then, suddenly, it happened. And then I couldn't make it go away..."

Lem cried out hoarsely, then settled into low rasping sobs.

It had become even hotter, and then hotter still. The radio, still on, blurted out a stifled cry of static and then was silent.

In the sweaty, close, unbearably hot cave, the flashlight went on with one final smudge of sick light, illuminating Monk's crying face.

"I'm so sorry..." he whispered.

"Mabel?" George Meadows croaked. He could barely talk, his words fighting through the heat, which had intensified. His wife lay unmoving on the sofa, her desiccated arm hanging over the side, fingers brushing her dropped magazine. Her housedress was now completely part of the couch's pattern, melded into it like an iron transfer. The window fan had given up. The sky was very bright. Puffs of steam rose from the floor, up from the cellar, from the ground below. Somewhere in the back of his nostrils, George smelled smoke, and fire.

"Mabel?" he called again, although now he could not feel the easy chair beneath him. He felt light as a flake of ash rising from a campfire.

His eyes were so hot he could no longer see.

He took in one final, rasping, burning breath as the world turned to fire and roaring flame around him.

And, even now, he could not resist getting in the last word, letting his final breath out in a cracked whisper even though there was no one to listen: "Yep. Hottest ever."

SLEEPOVER

CHICKENS WERE GREEN," HE said.

"They weren't," she answered. "They were yellow. Frogs were green."

"That's the sky," he said, grinning slyly to himself. He had a secret grin even when his lips didn't smile. "The sky was green. Grass was blue."

She shook her head back and forth, almost violently. "You got 'em mixed up, Ty. It's the other way 'round. Grass was green, sky blue."

"It was the way I say," he replied, and his eyes were hard enough that he meant it.

"No, little brother, it was the way I remember." Her voice dropped to a whisper, and she looked at the ground. "I think..."

They were on a plane of black smooth glass. Where the sky—which was maroon and devoid of clouds—met the horizon there was a faint curved thin fuzzy line, like a charcoal-drawn heat wave. The temperature never seemed to change, though sometimes Ty complained of being cold at night. Willa pressed up near him when this happened, but always reluctantly. There was a part of her that was sure he claimed cold just to get attention.

Ty was seven, as close as Willa could remember. He had been seven when they woke up one morning in this place which had, during the night, replaced the second floor bedroom of cousin Clara's big white house with the white picket fence. Sometimes Willa had trouble remembering some things about the white house now—such as if the garage doors had needed painting or not, or if the mailbox post at the road was crooked or straight. But there were other things that Willa did remember—the sharpness of the red metal flag on the mailbox, which felt like it might cut your finger when you raised it to tell the mailman there was mail to be taken, or the tart ammonia smell of the cat litter box when it hadn't been cleaned, or the way Aunt Erin and Uncle Bill's smiles lit up their faces when cousin Clara said something clever. She remembered Clara's science project, the working windmill, with its gold first-place ribbon hanging from it (it had been gold, hadn't it?—Ty would now say it had been tan, or orange)—that was displayed prominently on the fireplace mantle.

But she couldn't remember if the fireplace bricks had been red or white.

"I'm hungry again," Ty said, and this time Willa knew he was looking for nothing but attention. They hadn't been hungry since they had found themselves here. They hadn't gotten dirty, or had to brush their teeth, or even had to go to the bathroom.

Which had led Willa to conclude—

"And we're not dead!" Ty said, reaching over to jab her in the ribs. "We're just...*here!*"

"And where is that?" Willa responded.

Ty began to cry, true frightened sobs, which made Willa pleased and then, instantly, sorry. She reached over to brush the hair away from his forehead. "It's all right," she whispered, "We're not dead."

But he was consumed by one of his out-of-control times, and clung to her, shivering. She could feel the wetness of his tears against the skin of her arm, soaking into the upper cuff of her nightdress.

"Ty, it's all right—"

"No it's not, it's not! We're dead, we're *dead!*"

"I was only joking—"

"You were right, you were right! We're *dead dead dead!*"

The arm that wrapped around Ty began to tremble, and Willa felt her own tears rising, though she kept them down.

"There's only one other thing we could be," she said in the faintest of voices, and only to herself.

A while later the light show began, as it did every night before sleep came.

First came the yellow streaks, which crossed in parallel pairs overhead, cutting the maroon sky in half. Then the maroon sky split into two parts, like an overhead dome opening, and the darkest sky Willa had ever seen met the black glass plain and they could see nothing. But this lasted only a moment, not enough to keep them in darkness: for the lights of what looked like a billion stars came on overhead, coming brighter and brighter like novas until their light merged into one overwhelming brilliance like the Sun. They were blinded by the light and closed their eyes, seeing a round retinal afterimage against the insides of their lids, and when they opened their eyes again the world was as it had been, with maroon sky and black glass underfoot and the fine line of fuzziness at the horizon.

"I'm sleepy," Ty said, and curled up on the black glass and closed his eyes, which is what he always did after the light show. Willa fought it but also found herself tired, and then they slept, and always when they woke up they expected to find themselves back in their sleeping bags in cousin Carla's bedroom in the white two story house that, Willa was almost sure, needed painting and had an old clock in the kitchen that had a crack in the face and was a little fast.

But always, for nine sleep periods now, they found themselves here.

After this, the tenth sleep period, the same thing happened.

Only—

Something was different this time.

They were not alone.

In the near distance were two shapes huddled on the ground, one of which began to wail.

Ty roused himself and looked at them wide-eyed. "The sky was blue, I'm *pretty* sure..." he whispered.

"Yes," Willa said, though she wasn't positive anymore. In her own dreams the white house had been gray, the clock in the kitchen a minute slow.

SLEEPOVER

The two figures saw them and began to approach, at first tentatively, then running.

"Help us!" the one in front sobbed.

Willa held on to Ty, and the two of them stood waiting.

The two figures stopped ten feet away.

They were children: two girls, younger than Ty. One had blonde hair and the other's hair was red, curly all over.

They stared at Ty and Willa, then looked up at the sky, then back at Ty and Willa.

The red-haired one began to moan, but the other one got out: "Where *are* we?"

"Where *were* you?" Willa asked. "Before you came here?"

"In bed!" She had a breathy, annoying voice. "Asleep!"

"Where?" Willa demanded.

"*At Janna's house!*" Seeing the probing look on Willa's face, she rushed on desperately: "In Kentucky! In the U.S. of A.!"

"What were you doing at Janna's house, in Kentucky?" Willa persisted, almost unkindly. "Why were you there?"

"We were having a sleepover!" the breathy girl answered, and then she too began to cry.

Ty joined them.

"Be quiet!" Willa shouted, staring sharply at Ty, and then at the newcomers.

All but the red-haired girl complied.

Willa looked at Ty. "They were in Kentucky. We were in New Hampshire. That means nothing."

Tears threatened again, but Ty kept them down. "The sky *was* blue," he insisted quietly.

33

"You're sisters?" Willa asked the breathy girl.

She nodded, studying the sky with frightened eyes. She said, "How do we get back?"

Willa gave her a long, steady look. "You don't." She turned to Ty, her back to the two new children, and said in a whisper, so only he could hear: "I know what happened."

There were pooling tears in Willa's eyes, which frightened Ty more than anything up till now.

The nightly light show was ending. Willa opened her eyes, still seeing a vestige of fading sun image. The two little girls, Eva and Em, were rubbing their own eyes, sitting Indian style twenty feet away where Willa had ordered them to be. Willa watched Eva, the blond-haired one, curl up on the floor and then Em nest into her like a sleeping cat.

In a few moments they were both breathing shallowly, eyes closed.

Willa waited another full minute, fighting the urge to sleep, and then shook Ty gently awake beside her.

He stirred, sought continued sleep, then rubbed his eyes and sat up.

"All right," he said, yawning and stretching. "Tell me."

"This is the truth," Willa answered. She had decided not to cry, and kept her voice steady and low. "Do you remember the night we sneaked down after bedtime, and spied on Mother and Father through the stair rails while they sat at the dining room table with a bottle of wine?"

Ty was concentrating, his brow furrowed. "The dining room was brown."

"It was *white*," Willa said. "Do you remember holding your hands over your ears, because you didn't like what they were saying?"

"The dining room *was* white," Ty abruptly agreed, and then a further amazed spark of remembrance touched his face. He put his hands to his ears for a moment, then lowered them. "They said..."

"They said that some people should never have children."

His eyes widened with a faint catch of breath. "I *remember*..."

"They talked about how good it had been before we came along, how much they missed those days."

Ty's mouth dropped open in wonder. "*Yes...*"

Willa said sharply, with conviction: "They found a way to send us here."

Sudden anger boiled up in Ty's face. "That's not true! They would never do that!"

Twenty feet away, the two little girls stirred, and Willa said calmly, "If you don't quiet down I won't tell you the rest."

Ty fought to hold his rage: he made fists, counted to ten, but at the end of it he still wanted to scream and cry.

Willa warned, "Be quiet."

Another count of ten, and Ty snuffled. "Tell me."

Willa took a halting breath. Her eyes held a faraway look, as if she was staring at a place she didn't want to believe had existed, but knew had been real. "They wanted to be alone again. They would never kill us, or drive us out into the country and abandon us, or put us on a bus with no identification and just enough money for one-way tickets. But in the back of their minds, they knew that if they ever had the chance to make us go away without hurting us, they would take it."

Willa was gazing over Ty's head, her voice flat with shocked belief. "And they found a way…"

Ty's anger returned. He stood up, yelling, "They would *never* do that to us! Dad would never do that to *me*! He helped me build a model airplane! He taught me how to throw a baseball! And mother taught me how to tie my shoelaces!" His face was livid with anger and fear. "They *loved* us!"

The two little girls were awake, holding on to one another.

Willa said, "They loved us because they *had* to. But I'm talking about what people really want, in the center of their hearts. Haven't you always felt it, Ty? When they went away on vacations together and left us at cousin Carla's? The way they looked at each other even when we were with them?"

Willa's eyes were haunted. "Haven't you always felt that the two of them had no room for four?"

"*I don't believe you!*"

Em, the one with red hair, began to wail, and her sister, the breathy one, sobbed, "Stop talking! It's time for sleep!"

Willa continued, "Did you ever watch the way Uncle Bill and Aunt Erin looked at cousin Carla? They never had those thoughts. They were *meant* to have children. Their hearts were big enough."

"*Sleep!*" the breathy one insisted, curling down to troubled slumber beside her sister.

Willa ignored them. She was staring hard into a place of remembrance that was fading. "That night," she said to Ty, "when you put your hands over your ears, Mother's face got a strange look on it, and she told Father she'd found a way."

"*You're lying!*"

Willa gave a single, strangled sob. "And when she brought us to the sleepover at cousin Carla's, she had that same look on her face."

"*I won't believe you!*" Now Ty clung to her, and closed his eyes, and shivered. "I'd rather be dead..."

Suddenly—so suddenly it made her gasp—Willa wasn't sure if Aunt Erin's kitchen had had a clock in it after all.

Or even what a clock was.

Ty moaned, "*No...*"

And then he closed his eyes.

Willa whispered, stroking his hair, "We'll have to make a new life here."

She stifled an abrupt, overpowering yawn.

Beside her, Ty was asleep, still trembling. This time he wasn't looking for attention. Willa lowered him gently to the hard obsidian surface and lay down beside him.

She looked over at Eva and Em.

"And now, other parents know the way..."

She snuggled close to her brother, and closed her eyes.

She awoke to a wailing moan to transcend the sadness of Limbo, and a world filled with children.

Beside her, Ty sat up and rubbed his eyes.

"Chickens were green," he said.

Willa answered, without hesitation, "Yes."

EELS

THEY WERE OUT ON a mirror of green ocean. The land, save for a jetty of sharp rock a hundred yards to the east, a single pointing finger of the island, had disappeared into the hazy distance. At the far curves of the horizon mist squatted, but closer in the air and sea-waves were as sharp as knives.

Davy's father baited two hooks, whistling between his teeth, but Davy sat with his hands folded in his lap. Despite the warmth of the noon sun, and the brine tartness of the salt air, he felt cold: as if this were early morning and the mists had not yet retreated. He wore his jacket buttoned over his sweatshirt, and clenched his hands together as he turtled his ears down into his jacket's collar.

The boat rolled gently in the swells. His father, still whistling, now looked at him and suddenly scowled.

"What is it, boy? You sick?"

Davy shook his head no.

His father's scowl remained; he looked impatient to be back to his baiting of hooks, his whistling.

"What, then? You didn't have to come, you know; I would have been happy out here alone."

"Mother wanted me to."

His father's scowl deepened. "Your mother..."

For a moment a cloud hung over the boat. But then his father went suddenly back to his tackle, and began to whistle again. Davy was left to contemplate his cold clenched hands, his rolling stomach.

"Father, I'd like to go back..." he said weakly.

"What's that?"

Davy took one hand away from the clenched other, and pointed toward the finger of rock eastward. "If you could take me..."

"I won't!" his father snapped. "I told ye before we came out to either come or stay. I won't be rowing back now. 'Twould be near two by the time I rowed myself back out. That's not enough time to make a day of it." His coarse, unshaved face turned away from Davy, his eyes back on his hook. "You'll stay, and be content with it." He added, "You know what I think of you anyway, boy."

Davy's hands joined again. If he had had anything in his stomach he would have emptied it over the side.

The sun inched upward. A wheeling pair of seagulls appeared, complained loudly over the boat and circled up and away, disappointed. Davy thought of home, the house on the island, and the chair by the large window in the family room. The hearth fire there was warm. It was dry in that corner of the room, there was no sea-smell in that dry corner...

"Here," his father said abruptly, thrusting a fishing rod into his hand. It was one that barely worked, with a sticking reel. Davy's hands opened in benediction to take the rod, but already his father had turned away from him, tending his own two good rigs. With a plop his father dropped one sinker into the water, snugging this untended rod into the oarlock before dropping the other rigged line into the ocean. Davy heard the thin scream of the filament and then its sudden stop as the weighted end hit wet sand far below.

His father turned around and said, "Well? You going to fish it or not?"

Davy nodded and then looked away, out at the tip of his fishing pole. An old sinker was tied there like a rutted lead teardrop, the thin green filament of the hook's line angled sideways and then curled down to the barbed hook imbedded in the struggling red bloodworm thrashing this way and that—

Davy lay the pole down and heaved his empty stomach. He held his straining face over the side of the boat. A thin acidic line of bile dripped from his mouth into the water.

"Christ's sake!" his father said behind him. Davy felt the hard dry hands on his shoulders as he was pulled back, his teary eyes looking into the angry red face above him, the hard hand now pulled back as if to strike.

"I'm...sorry, father—" he blurted out, between sobs.

His father's hand stayed, then lowered, and his father turned away, shaking his head.

"Nothing to be done about it now," he said, ignoring the boy once more, but pausing to grab the old rig and let out the bail, dropping the sinker and thrashing worm over the side of the boat and into the blank cold waters, before thrusting the pole into Davy's hands once more.

"Ho! A good one I'll bet!" his father cried, straining against the sudden fight in his pole. He began to turn the reel's handle furiously, half standing to stare over into the water, watching the tightened line for signs of the caught beast.

"A fighter!" he laughed—but then the line went abruptly slack. He sat down, scowling once more.

"And you, boy?" he called back, not looking around. "Checked your bait?"

Davy stared at the rod tip, saying nothing, and in a moment his father had forgotten about him, whistling once more, as he pulled his own hook from the water and cut a fresh blood worm in half to replenish it.

Off in the distance, at the hazy edge of the world, Davy heard the long, sad call of a foghorn. In the sky, the sun had turned a sour lemon color as it now sank toward the growing fog. At the limits of vision, gulls wheeled out on the water, diving one after another to hit the waves and then rise again. One of them clutched something long, black and struggling in its beak. Davy turned to stare again at the tip of his own fishing rod.

His father spat over the side of the boat. "Damned fog'll be here in a half-hour or so. Thought I'd get the whole day in but it was not to be."

Without another word, he went back to his own equipment, checking the extra rod that lay in the oarlock before turning his full attention to his other pole.

EELS

A sudden tremble shot through Davy's hands. The edge of his fishing pole flicked, and then the pole end bent down, straining toward the water.

The pole nearly leapt out of Davy's hands before he tightened his grip on it. His fingers fumbled for the bail as line unraveled with a thin high screech. "By God, boy, you've got something!" his father shouted. "Keep the tip up, dammit! And don't let so much line out!"

Abandoning his own pole, the old man made his way back to Davy, his face flushed with excitement.

"The way you're holding that pole, he'll get away, damn you!"

His father reached out angrily to take the rod from Davy's hands.

At that moment the bale caught and the tip of the pole bent down into the water, lost in the waves. His father's face flushed in surprise as he tore the rod from Davy's hands and fought with the line.

"By God! What have you got on here, boy?"

Standing in a crouch, his father managed to get the pole out of the water and then loosened the bale to let out a bit of line.

"She's deep, that's for sure!" his father said. A smile came onto his features as he battled, one eye turned to the approaching fog and late afternoon.

"It'll be close!"

Humming fiercely through clenched teeth, he began to inexorably reel the line in, letting the catch run when it needed to, but gradually drawing it up from the depths and closer to the boat. The sour-yellow sun was edging the horizon; the mists began to caress the rowboat with their tendrils. Davy shivered and drew deeper into his coat, but his father seemed oblivious now to everything save the thing on the end of the fishing line.

"She's almost up, boy! Get the net!"

Roused from his chill, Davy moved to his father's abandoned spot on the boat and lifted the wide net by its handle.

"Hurry, damn you!"

He turned back. His father's angry face motioned him to hold the net over the side of the boat.

"Damned beast's about up!"

Kneeling, Davy dangled the net over the side. Now, in the late afternoon, the water's surface was a sickly, deep, impenetrable green. It smelled of salt and overly wet vegetation.

Bile rose in Davy's throat, but he held it down.

"Here it comes, boy—here it comes!"

From the soupy depths something became visible, twirling as it reluctantly rose. Davy held the net ready. The shadow became more distinct: a long, slender shape, heavy in the water.

His father peered over the side, squinting.

"Can you see what it is, boy?"

"Yes..."

The thing broke water. Its black, thin, slick head rose out to stare up at Davy with leaden eyes—

"Snatch it with the net, boy! Can you see—?"

His father's voice suddenly turned full of disgust. The black thing's head held suspended for a moment, mouth opening to show the embedded hook in its jaw, its head now seeming to expand in the air, to change shape, before there was a snap and it dropped back down into the sea. It's shadow held for a moment, as if it might rise again on its own. But then it sank toward indistinction, the curl of its long sinuous length essing once before it was gone, back into the deep.

EELS

Davy turned to see a look of abhorrence on his father's face. In one hand he still held the tip of Davy's fishing pole; in the other, his long fillet knife.

"'Twas nothing," his father said, before turning away. "Just an eel."

The fog closed in on them then, and, without another word, his father weighed anchor, and rowed for the island.

◆ ◆ ◆

Davy's mother waited for them at the pier's end, at the base of the jutting finger of rock, near the small second boat, a dinghy. Wrapped in a shawl, her worried look made her a specter in the early evening.

"I was worried you—" she said, putting a hand on Davy's father's shoulder as the old man brushed by her. "Bah," the old man said, continuing on, arms laden with fishing tackle as he went up to the house.

In the unseen distance, the foghorn cried out again. Davy's mother opened her shawl to enclose Davy within it, within herself. He felt her warmth through his clothes, through the damp, salt wetness.

"Come to the house and sit by the fire," she whispered into his ear, stroking his hair.

He nodded and, soothed by her words and warmth, followed her to the open doorway, a dim rectangle of orange light against the chill and dropping night. In a while he sat in his chair in the warm corner while his mother prepared supper, and his father smoked his pipe and drank his rye in silence, staring out through the open doorway at the storm that grew and battered the island.

✦ ✦ ✦

Later, Davy lay in bed and listened to them argue. Outside, the night wind had picked up. A spray of cold, salt-scented rain hit periodically against the side of the house, washing the single window in Davy's dark room.

A thin line of firelight flickered beneath the closed door. Beneath his pile of quilts Davy felt cold and damp. His body felt leaden, empty, numb. A dull chill went through him remembering the cold supper that had been eaten in silence, his mother's barely disguised, frantic fear as she hovered around him shielding him from his father's arctic mounting rage.

"It's not like I ever wanted 'im," his father said now, out in the main room beyond the door. His voice was gruff, tentative. He sounded like he was treading careful waters, knew it, but had decided to proceed anyhow. "And it's not like he'll ever be a help to me."

"But he's *mine!*" his mother answered, her voice a choked cry.

His father grunted, and a few moments, in which Davy could almost feel his mother's fear through the door, passed.

"He's no help to me at all. And no comfort," his father continued.

"I *wanted* him! You agreed!"

Again his father grunted.

"'Twas a mistake, then."

"No!"

Now anger was creeping up into his father's voice, mingled with frustration.

"You should have seen him out there today, Ellie! Useless! Sat unhelpful the entire time. Like a pile of wet stones. Couldn't bait his own hook, or carry his weight.

He's little better around the house, here. Nothing more than a burden to me."

His mother was weeping now, and suddenly his father's tone softened.

"Now, Ellie, don't be like that. You know our bargain was a fair one. For your sake I met it. And now it's time…"

"I won't let you! I won't! He's all I have!"

"What of me?" his father shot back. "Do you forget that it was I who took you to myself? The boy should never have come in the bargain." Again his voice softened. "It's my own fault for not doing better by you from the beginning. In the future, I promise I will. I know now how lonely you must have been. Nearly as lonely as I was here before I had you. I promise that when things are like they were in the beginning—"

"I won't hear of it!"

"My mind is set, woman."

"No!"

There was a sharp, quick sound, hand against face, and then Davy's mother began to weep.

His father said, his voice strained: "You'll see it clearer when it's over." He tried to soften his voice again, but it only sounded harder. "When it's over."

After an hour of silence from the outer room, the door to Davy's bedroom opened. He tried to hide within the quilts and covers.

"Get up, boy," his father said sharply. "We have business to attend to."

Through an opening in the folds of material, Davy watched his father, outlined by orange light, approach the bed.

"I said rise, boy."

The quilts were pulled back. Davy looked up into the pained but hard face of his father. He smelled sweet alcohol, a warmth of the breath.

His father's rough hand poked at him. "Rise up and get your slicker on."

Without another word, his father turned and walked out.

As Davy dressed, he watched his father, stoney-eyed, shrug on his own oilcloth coat, and take a final drink, emptying the bottle which sat on the dinner table.

Salt and rain lashed the island, the night.

The storm had risen high, driving sheets of water across the rock path to the pier. Overhead, angry banks of low, spitting clouds drove one another on. Out on the water, walls of water seemed to have risen out of the chopping waves, forming a bridge between cloud and ocean.

The rowboat rocked furiously against its mooring, roughly tapping at the dinghy beside it. His father battled with the rope, undid its knot, then fought to keep the boat steady while Davy climbed in. Davy thought he felt his father shudder when they were thrown together for a moment in passing.

His father climbed in after Davy, and cast off. He rowed furiously from the outset. Davy sat in the bow seat, ahead of the oarlocks, staring unspeaking back at his father, who concentrated on fighting the waves.

EELS

Behind them, the dock pulled away into the finger of rocks and then, abruptly, the ocean surrounded them.

Davy felt his lately eaten supper begin to churn in his stomach.

Far distant, the foghorn bleated, hidden and muffled by the roar of rain and wind. Water pelted them in sheets. Off in the direction of the foghorn, a single bolt of silver-yellow lightning struck at the wet horizon.

"Bail, boy!" his father shouted, pausing in his rowing to indicate the bottom of the boat filling with water. His father pointed a sharp finger at the bailing bucket next to Davy, who made no move toward it. "Bah!" his father cried, suddenly stopping his rowing and moving in a crab's crouch to lean over Davy and pick up the anchor.

Their eyes met for a moment, and Davy saw the fear in his father's face. Then his father looked away and dropped the anchor over the side.

It made a splash, dropped, and the line played out nearly to its length before it found purchase.

"It's done, then!" his father said, seemingly to himself.

Behind them, off through the sheeted rain, the slapping waves and roar of the storm, came a sound from the finger of rocks: the wailing cry of his mother calling to them.

Davy's father stood, squinting back into the storm.

Now Davy could see the tiny yet growing image of the dinghy, his mother's tiny form huddled within, rowing.

"Damn her," his father spat, then turned to look down at Davy.

"I said 'twas done." His father loomed over him, lashed by rain. He seemed diminished as a man. He seemed to have shrunk into his oil cloth, hands dropped limply at his side. Davy looked into his face. There was anger and fury and determination in his eyes, but defeat, shame, and, that bolt of fear, too.

"Go ahead, father," Davy said. "I'm not afraid anymore."

"This should never have happened to begin with," the old man said, his words leaden, and then he grasped Davy in his two hands, tightening his grip, and lifted him up unresisting and threw him into the water.

At that moment, off through the rain, Davy heard his mother call out to him.

The ice-cold hands of the sea enclosed Davy for a moment before he rose. As his head broke the surface, he saw his father straining at the oarlocks, turning the boat around toward shore. His father's eyes stared down into the boat, then up quickly at the dinghy, which approached through the lashing rain and rising waves.

"*What have you done!*" Davy's mother demanded.

Davy cried out once before the sea took him down again.

The world became as seen through green glass. His body, head to toe, was cold and wet.

He looked down; below him, long slow shapes moved deep in the water, blacker against cold darkness, moving one over another, making and unmaking shapes. Davy's numb hands felt suddenly oiled. And now, beneath his clothes, he felt his body bump and squirm, as if alive in its parts. His bones moved painfully against their sockets; it was as if his arms would yank free from his shoulders, legs from his thighs. His neck felt slick and alive.

The squirming shapes pulled up closer.

EELS

With a sudden kick and spasm of unmouthed protest, Davy fought against his sinking, and began to claw and drive his way back up to the surface.

"*No!*"

He broke free into the roiling waves. The rain felt oddly warm against his face.

He gulped, spit water, focused his moist eyes on the twin boats twenty yards away, bobbing together as if wedded. His struggling father was trying to climb from the rowboat into the dinghy.

His mother's defiant form stood straight in the smaller boat, her eyes blazing with hatred.

"Then you'll lose me, too!"

"Ellie! No!" his father beseeched, his hand seeking to reach Davy's mother.

Davy tried to call out. His raised his hand but it went unseen as the sea began to weight him down. His limbs became cold lead, his mouth filled with water, his grasping hands now found only water.

He sank. He went inexorably down. Off through the darkening cold, he saw the roped straight line of the anchor on his father's boat. It made a line linking heaven and earth, disappearing into the depths below.

Davy looked down. The roiling black shapes were growing closer.

Beneath his clothes, he slowly began to break free.

His arms became black oily things, squirming like wet thick ropes. Up under his armpits the pulp of their live flesh thumped against his arm sockets in little pulses, even as his torso lengthened, pulling his head and face into a thick, snakelike shape.

His legs and arms broke away, swimming from his clothing, which floated off.

The boiling, excited, living, vast plateau of eels was just below him.

He dropped into their midst.

Flat welcoming eyes turned to look at him.

And, somewhere far above, he heard a splash, then heard his mother's voice assuring him that she would soon be there.

LETTERS FROM CAMP

DEAR MOM AND DAD,
   I still don't know why you made me come to this
dump for the summer. It looks like all the other summer
camps I've been to, even if it is "super modern and
computerized," and I don't see why I couldn't go back
to the one I went to last year instead of this "new" one. I
had a lot of fun last summer, even if you did have to pay
for all that stuff I smashed up and even if I did make the
head counselor break his leg.
   The head counselor here is a jerk, just like the other
one was. As soon as we got off the hovercraft that
brought us here, we had to go to the Big Tent for a "pep
talk." They made us sit through a slide show about all
the things we're going to do (yawn), and that wouldn't
have been so bad except that the head counselor, who's a
robot, kept scratching his metal head through the whole
thing. I haven't made any friends, and the place looks
like it's full of jerks. Tonight we didn't have any hot
water and the TV in my tent didn't work.

Phooey on Camp Ultima. Can't you still get me back in the other place?

✦ ✦ ✦

Dear Mom and Dad,
Maybe this place isn't so bad after all. They just about let us do whatever we want, and the kids are pretty wild. Today they split us up into "Pow-wow Groups," but there aren't really any rules or anything, and my group looks like it might be a good one. One of the guys in it looks like he might be okay. His name's Ramon, and he's from Brazil. He told me a lot of neat stories about things he did at home, setting houses on fire and things like that. We spent all day today hiding from our stupid robot counselor. He thought for sure we had run away and nearly blew a circuit until we finally showed up just in time for dinner.
The food stinks, but they did have some animal-type thing that we got to roast over a fire, and that tasted pretty good.
Tomorrow we go on our first field trip.

✦ ✦ ✦

Dear Mom and Dad,
We had a pretty good time today, all things considered. We got up at six o'clock to go on our first hike, and everybody was pretty excited. There's a lot of wild places here, and they've got it set up to look just like a prehistoric swamp. One kid said we'd probably see a Tyrannosaurus Rex, but nobody believed him. The robot counselors kept us all together as we set out through the marsh, and we saw a lot of neat things like

vines dripping green goop and all kinds of frogs and toads. Me and Ramon started pulling the legs off frogs, but our counselor made us stop and anyway the frogs were all robots. We walked for about two hours and then stopped for lunch. Then we marched back again.

The only weird thing that happened was that when we got back and the counselors counted heads, they found that one kid was missing. They went out to look for him but couldn't find anything, and the only thing they think might have happened is that he got lost in the bog somewhere. One kid said he thought he saw a Tyrannosaurus Rex, but it was the same kid who'd been talking about them before, so nobody listened to him. The head counselor went around patting everybody on the shoulder, telling us not to worry since something always happens to one kid every year. But they haven't found him yet.

Tonight we had a big food fight, and nobody even made us clean the place up.

◆ ◆ ◆

Dear Mom and Dad,

Today we went out on another field trip, and another stupid kid got himself lost. They still haven't found the first one, and some of the kids are talking about Tyrannosaurus Rex again. But this time we went hill climbing and I think the dope must have fallen off a cliff, because the hills are almost like small mountains and there are a lot of ledges on them.

After dinner tonight, which almost nobody ate because nobody felt like it, we sat around a campfire and told ghost stories. Somebody said they thought a lot of kids were going to disappear from here, and

55

that made everybody laugh, in a scary kind of way. I was a little scared myself. It must have been the creepy shadows around the fire. The robot counselors keep telling everyone not to worry, but some of the kids—the ones who can't take it—are starting to say they want to go home.

I don't want to go home, though; this place is fun.

Dear Mom and Dad,

Today we went on another trip, to the far side of the island where they have a lake, and we had a good time and all (we threw one of the robot counselors into the lake but he didn't sink), but when we got off the boat and everybody was counted we found out that eight kids were gone. One kid said he even saw his friend Harvey get grabbed by something ropy and black and pulled over the side. I'm almost ready to believe him. I don't know if I like this place so much anymore. One more field trip like the one today and I think I'll want to come home.

It's not even fun wrecking stuff around here anymore.

Dear Mom and Dad,

Come and get me right away, I'm *scared*. Today the robot counselors tried to make us go on another day trip, but nobody wanted to go, so we stayed around the tents. But at the chow meeting tonight only twelve kids showed up. That means twenty more kids disappeared today. Nobody had any idea what happened to them, though I do know that a whole bunch of guys were playing outside the perimeter of the camp, tearing things down, so that might have had something to do with it. At this point I don't care.

Just get me out of here!

✦ ✦ ✦

Mom and Dad,

I think I'm the only kid left, and I don't know if I can hide much longer. The head counselor tricked us into leaving the camp today, saying that somebody had seen a Tyrannosaurus Rex. He told us all to run through the rain forest at the north end of the camp, but when we ran into it, something horrible happened. I was with about five other kids, and as soon as we ran into the forest we heard a high-pitched screeching and a swishing sound and the trees above us started to lower their branches. I saw four of the kids I was with get covered by green plastic-looking leaves, and then there was a gulping sound and the branches lifted and separated and there was nothing there. Ramon and I just managed to dodge out of the way, and we ran through the forest in between the trees and out the other side. We would have been safe for a while but just then the robot counselors broke through the forest behind us, leading a Tyrannosaurus Rex. We ran, but Ramon slipped and fell and the Tyrannosaurus Rex was suddenly there, looming over him with its dripping jaws and rows of sharp white teeth. Ramon took out his box of matches, but the dinosaur was on him then and I didn't wait to see any more.

I ran all the way back to the postal computer terminal in the camp to get this letter out to you. Call the police!

Call the army! I can't hide forever, and I'm afraid that any second the Tyrannosaurus Rex will break in here and

✦ ✦ ✦

Dear Mr. and Mrs. Jameson:

Camp Ultima is happy to inform you of the successful completion of your son's stay here, and we are therefore billing you for the balance of your payment at this time.

Camp Ultima is proud of its record of service to parents of difficult boys, and will strive in the future to continue to provide the very best in camp facilities.

May we take this opportunity to inform you that, due to the success of our first camp, we are planning to open a new facility for girls next summer.

We hope we might be of service to you in the future.

ROGER IN THE WOMB

WHEN MRS. J'S PREGNANCY came to term and nothing happened, the doctors told her not to worry. Mr. J was instructed to keep a firm eye on her, and to rush her to the hospital as soon as labor pains began. Assurances were given that this was not an uncommon thing.

When, after a further month passed and the baby, by all accounts still healthy and active in the womb, refused to be born, Mr. J truly began to believe something was not right. The doctors, however—more of them, now—still held the opinion that there was no reason to be alarmed, and after a complete examination Mrs. J was returned home to her bed and Mr. J given instructions to keep an even firmer eye on her and to call the moment any sort of labor pains, no matter how tentative, began. This time, there seemed to be a bit of worry and clinical interest mixed in with the reassurances.

At the twelfth month of pregnancy, when the possibility of Mrs. J's body being poisoned by the continued presence of the fetus became acute, she was installed in the hospital and artificial inducement of labor was attempted, but to no avail. One doctor made the wry observation that the baby had "set up shop in there." Another doctor, not at all wryly, remarked that the baby did indeed seem to be resisting with unnatural vigor, and that preparations for Cesarean section should be made. The fetus was still judged to be in perfect health.

Cesarean section was attempted, but the doctors attending were startled to find the abdominal area completely resistant to incision. After two scalpels were broken, radical measures were instituted, but the area surrounding the womb was impervious to violation. After five hours of continued frustrated effort the doctors retired to consultation, and a completely exhausted Mrs. J was awakened and given assurances. Mr. J was sent home, his box of cigars yet unopened.

Repeated attempts were made during the next eight days to enter the womb and remove the baby. Numerous specialists were flown in from all points on the globe, various exotic and revolutionary methods employed—all to no avail. The baby continued to thrive, however, and Mrs. J, despite the mental fatigue resulting from constant questioning by the doctors and nurses, remained in good health.

On the ninth day after forced birth had been attempted, an orderly interrupted a volatile meeting of all personnel on the case to announce that some sort of communication had been established with the fetus. The meeting immediately adjourned to Mrs. J's room. On arriving, the staff was informed by the nurse on duty that, while making a routine medical check on Mrs. J, she had detected a series of tappings with her stethoscope that seemed to emanate from the womb. They appeared, she reported, to form some sort of pattern, although she had no idea what that pattern might be. The chief surgeon, on examining the womb area with his own stethoscope, quickly substantiated the nurse's claims by announcing that he, too, could hear what sounded like a series of measured tappings. A discussion ensued over what this could mean; the discussion quickly grew into a heated argument. Physical violence had nearly erupted when a young intern suddenly thrust his way to Mrs. J's bed and, after a few moments of concentrated listening with his own stethoscope, let it be known that the tappings were nothing more than a message communicated in Morse code. The message, he said, was simply, "I am staying in the womb."

A furor broke out. Within the hour, representatives from all the media were present at the hospital. Mr. J, not having been notified in the confusion, learned of the situation on the evening news.

After this breakthrough an attempt was made to contact the fetus as the chief surgeon proceeded to ask, in Morse code translated by the young intern, a series of complicated questions, to which there was no reply. After failed attempts by other high-placed doctors and officials, the young intern was put in charge. He immediately asked the fetus whether it was comfortable, and received the answer yes. The fetus then declared it needed time for thought and would answer no more questions at the present time.

Despite constant attempts by the young intern to regain rapport, the fetus was entirely uncommunicative for the next several months. There was constant monitoring, and any potentially communicative sounds that were recorded outside the occasional sounds the fetus produced when it stretched or shifted to make itself more comfortable, were scrupulously studied for a Morse code pattern, or even for the emergence of a new code. A four-day period of frantic activity, during which the monitoring team was sure they had recorded a message in new code, turned out to be nothing more than the sounds made by the fetus suffering through a particularly noisy intestinal disorder.

During these months of silence the doctoral and professorial committees, which had naturally formed, grappled furiously with new theories and ways to handle the various dilemmas that had arisen. There were uncountable social and religious implications in the event, as well as scientific and medical questions to be answered. There was continued debate on how to handle the problem medically. Papers and theses abounded.

Meanwhile, the fetus continued to develop. Remarkably, Mrs. J sustained no discomfort during this period of fetus growth; though her midsection swelled to elephantine size she retained good humor and exhibited no signs of stress. She now inhabited a spacious suite in a little-used wing of the hospital, complete with a fluid-mattressed bed that was acoustically attuned to counteract the least ache and pain. Having been accustomed to little more than housework before her sudden notoriety, she found her present quarters comfortable and even preferable to home life. Constant entertainment was provided by a large-screen television over her head. Any food or beverage she required was instantly prepared. Mr. J, now fully cognizant of the situation, offered no resistance or complaint; he found his time taken up with various endorsements which had resulted from his family's celebrity. He also found himself burdened with the management of an income of considerable amount.

ROGER IN THE WOMB

Finally, two days before the deadline that had been imposed on the young intern by the chief surgeon, contact was re-established with the fetus. In a short message the fetus stated that it wished to be called Roger, and that there would be a statement the following Monday at 1:00 P.M. It—or rather, Roger—refused to elaborate, and repeated questioning was met with silence.

At 1:00 P.M. there was an expectant hush; the fetus' statement began, and the young intern translated the tappings through Mrs. J's abdominal wall. The statement ran:

"I want to thank all of you for your constant diligence and continued goodwill, and most especially for providing me with the necessary accoutrements for my continued development. My hat is tipped to you all.

"No doubt you wonder what I am doing in here, and most especially why I have refused to come out. These are valid points to raise and I intend to answer them.

"Though you may have trouble believing me, and may scoff at my reasoning, or call me coward, the simple reason why I have not left the womb—and one that should have been immediately obvious to you—is that I do not want to leave. Life is safer and more secure here.

"Now these are well-known facts about life in the womb. All of you went through the experience I continue to go through, and all of you were thrust from that security after nine months and made to stand on your own against the cruel environment—physical and psychical—of the outside world. You thought there was no choice. You didn't know better.

"Soon after gestation I discovered that outside impressions experienced by my mother, Mrs. J, were filtering down to me in an understandable form. It may be that I was specially suited to receive these impressions but I think not; rather, I suspect that all embryos and fetuses take in, to some degree, the sights, sounds, and even smells experienced by their carriers. I suspect that due to some quirk of development or abnormally high intellectual sophistication for my age, I was able to better interpret the deluge of sensory data flooding into my form. Thus I learned of the world.

"During the first few weeks of pregnancy my mother, Mrs. J, began to read romantic novels and watch violent television programs. Little of value was learned. For a period of time—from the fourteenth week through the twentieth—she embarked on a reading program covering all areas of birth and child care, a few popular medical and scientific works, and one psychology text of questionable merit. In the course of reading one of the popular medical texts she (and I) came upon the case of one Roger deCovernaire, who resisted birth so successfully that he was not born until ten weeks after labor began. When birth finally ensued, his mother—the Countess deCovernaire—succumbed, but Roger entered the world in perfect health and lived to the ripe age of ninety. As a sidelight, it is interesting to note that his life's work was in the architectural design and building of railway tunnels.

"It is from Roger deCovernaire that I take my name, at best a symbolic gesture since I have resisted birth far more successfully than he was able to. The fact is that the bleak medical views espoused in the literature read by Mrs. J coupled with the world view presented by the romantic novels, television programs, and newscasts she assimilated, strengthened my resolve to prevent, if at all possible, my expulsion into the outer world. By yoking the knowledge gleaned from those few books with a few reasonable chemical and biological deductions, I was able to successfully prevent my release.

"I will continue to do so.

"I think you will agree with me that I have chosen the safer course. Since I may be considered a scientific and medical curiosity, it would be to your greater interest to continue to treat Mrs. J with the utmost deference and to provide her with every comfort. I intend to devote myself to the study of my environment—the womb— and to the processes that surround the conception and gestation of the human fetus.

"I do have one request. At the completion of my nine-month term, my access to Mrs. J's information and sensory systems was severed—a natural occurrence, no doubt, since at that time the fetus would normally be thrust into the outside world and begin to use its own sensory systems. Though this may be a natural and predictable event, it leaves me, as it were, in the dark. I would ask that at the time in my physical development when I am able to accommodate certain aids for my continued study, these items be provided; I will make ample provision for their passage to me. I thank you in advance.

"There will be periodic communications from me; I will work out some sort of schedule with the young intern who has formed such an accommodating relationship with me—I'd like his superiors, if they are here, to take note of his achievements and to grant him the courtesy and advancement he deserves.

"According to the neurologist Freud, whom I'm afraid I consider to be something of a buffoon, most if not all of you suffer from a repressed wish to return to the womb; if there are any truths in this belief, I find it significant to note that I should therefore be able to avoid most, if not all, traumas of human existence since I have not left the womb in the first place.

"That's all for the moment, if you'll excuse me. I'm tired."

There was a moment of stunned silence, and then a sudden collective cheer went up from all those present. They were so delighted by the fantastic, carnival-like spectacle that they had witnessed that it took all of the security people, aided by a good number of hospital staff, to keep the crowd from lifting Mrs. J up over their head, fetal burden and all, and parading her around the room and out into the street. The media representatives were especially happy about the episode, given the bountiful reportage possibilities it presented.

The young intern was, of course, immediately promoted and given a staff of his own. Things proceeded smoothly for Roger in the womb, and every four weeks thereafter, he gave a short report and new observations. Mrs. J, who was now completely content with watching the television that was over her head, was providing more than enough materials than Roger needed to maintain his health and foster his growth; she was maintaining a huge protein and fat-rich diet that Roger had developed, and had assumed balloon-like proportions.

Despite constant and growing pressures from religious, cultural, political, medical, scientific, and media groups, Roger's privacy was strictly maintained by the young intern. Every two months a statement based on Roger's periodic reports was released to the press. The first few of Roger's statements were relatively pedestrian dealing with such matters as the format for future pronouncements and the correct procedures involved. Then there followed a number of statements dealing with the womb itself, its structure and characteristics. An occasional message dealt with a physical characteristic of Roger: at the age of one he discussed the impossibility of crawling in the womb; at the age of two-and-one-half the frustrations caused by the urge to walk counteracted the inhibiting characteristics of the placenta.

At the age of three Roger made his first request for materials, asking that a small reading lamp along with a copy of Spinoza's *Ethics* be passed in to him. Roger made room in the womb for these items that had been waterproofed to resist the effects of amniotic fluid and made provisions for them to be passed in; he did not, however, allow the young intern (now, young doctor) a view, even brief, of the womb. Other texts, among them works by Blake and a novel by Henry James (which was immediately passed out again) were soon requested; before long a constant supply of books flowed in and out of the womb. Roger went so far as to solicit a small pillow to prop his head up in order to make reading for long periods easier. It was discovered that Roger was a bit far-sighted and reading glasses were designed through a long and complicated process, though the glasses, in the end, worked perfectly.

By the age of nine Roger found himself completely absorbed by the problems of conception, gestation, and birth; and he provided his young doctor-companion with long philosophical tracts on the nurturing, as well as the expulsion from the womb, of the human fetus. He also provided detailed drawings, rendered in a somewhat cramped style, of the interior of the womb. He began to keep a notebook of his studies (waterproofed, of course), and spoke glowingly of his progress.

Due to the secrecy surrounding Roger, as well as to his meditative way of life, the phenomenon of Roger in the womb had the status of a cultural event of ever-expanding and ever-distorted proportions. The Cult of the Womb, a rapidly spreading movement which had formed shortly after Roger's first message was released, held Roger in near-deitic esteem; its members lived most of their lives in artificial, self-supportive womb structures, unhindered by thoughts of or contact with the outside world. Another cult, the Rogerists, a purely religious sect, declared Roger the unborn second son of God, and devoted their lives to a truly Byzantine set of devotions. Political, medical, and publishing groups were putting ever-increasing pressure on him for time and attention.

A growing anti-Roger group was in evidence at this time, also. This company encompassed a wide spectrum of types. The general consensus among them was that Roger was either the devil (in a supra-fetal form) or at least an unworthy leftist coward unable to face the world as it is. An attempt on Mrs. J's life was even made by one of the more bizarre sectors of this assemblage.

During all this time the young doctor had successfully kept Roger shielded from the media and other groups, and had even resisted quite large sums of money in doing so. The press found themselves unable to meet a rabid demand for news and comment concerning Roger, and were resorting to ever more imaginative and devious means to attempt to feed the public craving for information. One television celebrity even made his way into Mrs. J's room and attempted to deceive Roger by telling him in Morse code that he was the young doctor and that there were several matters that had to be dealt with immediately, among them the imparting of such information as Roger's views on a recent election and his favorite color.

ROGER IN THE WOMB

Roger's monthly reports became increasingly esoteric. Suddenly he announced that there would be no more monthly communications, that he had embarked on a new and radical course in his studies involving the womb, and was searching for a synthesis of mystical and metaphysical concepts. The flow of books stopped, and the pillow and reading lamp were passed out of the womb. Roger kept only his notebook and a pencil, citing that whatever few notes remained to be made could be made in the dark. He was very excited about the "new direction" in which he was heading. The young doctor, despite frantic attempts, was unable to regain communication; he was particularly interested in making Roger understand that there had been increasing funding problems for the project and if the public was not fed with more accessible information there was a danger of the project being discontinued. But only silence ensued.

The doctor continued to inform Roger of the pressures against him for the next few weeks, but was met only with silence. At the cessation of the monthly reports and bimonthly press releases the public outcry was well in evidence; stock in Roger-related merchandise markedly dropped, and some hospital officials began to murmur about the good uses that the wing Mrs. J was occupying could be put to. The young doctor developed an ulcer.

The media, who had been casting around frantically in search of a way to force Roger to make himself public, suddenly found their outlet when a woman in Delaware brought suit against Roger (and Mrs. J as his legal guardian), claiming that her unborn son had communicated with her through a series of kicks, telling her that he would not be born, and that Roger had somehow influenced him in making his decision. Though the full weight of Roger's fortune was thrown into resisting his appearance in court, a subpoena to testify was upheld and Mrs. J was forced to part with her overhead television console for the first time in a decade. Needless to say, the courtroom was filled to capacity.

The woman from Delaware quickly lost her case when her baby was born in the courtroom on the opening day of the trial. Though Roger's intention not to speak remained untested in court, his privacy had been violated and the dam which had been cracked now burst.

Roger refused to speak after the trial, and the anti-Roger movement quickly gained support. More questions were raised about the use of public hospital facilities and funds to house and protect Mrs. J, and to support the project that the young doctor still maintained. Mr. J, now close to bankruptcy due to bad business investments and decreasing stock value, sought to gain complete control over Mrs. J, Roger, and the investments that had been made in their names by the young doctor. The young doctor, seeing things begin to crumble and concerned about his own health, embarked on an extensive and lucrative lecture tour, leaving the project to younger and inexperienced aides who shortly began to allow anyone with a working knowledge of Morse code to badger Roger.

A few weeks after the young doctor's departure the budget for the project was suddenly terminated and Mrs. J's television console went blank, giving her time to think about how nice it would be to be thin and able to walk, go to the market, and possibly even make love again. She reached the conclusion that she wished Roger would be born. She communicated this to the doctors at the hospital, getting quite hysterical in the process. Due to her dangerous condition a firm decision was made to try once more to forcibly remove Roger from the womb. This intention was passed on to Roger in code. The doctors were afraid that Mrs. J's hysteria, coupled with his continued presence in the womb, might endanger the health of one or both of them. The young doctor returned from his lecture tour to supervise.

A massive effort was mounted to enter the womb employing every new technological technique of the past decade, but the entire, vast surface area of the womb was still found impenetrable. The young doctor was close to a tearful breakdown and communicated his frustration to Roger in strong language. He was being led from the operating room when a short series of taps were heard from Roger. The young doctor quickly translated them as saying, "I am leaving the womb."

An immense sigh of relief was heard in the operating room and the young doctor immediately answered, "We'll be right in to get you." Preparations for birth were resumed. However, there was no movement from within the womb, no labor pains began, and the appointed operating areas were still found impervious to penetration. It was deduced that Roger would give some sort of indication when he was ready to come out. Mr. J, who had undergone a tearful reunion with his estranged wife, resolving to reform a happy family unit when Roger was expelled from the womb at last, was sent home to wait. His same box of cigars, unopened all these years, remained in that condition.

The doctors waited all that night and into the following day, but still there was no indication from Roger that he was prepared to emerge. The media, which had been alerted to the impending event, stood constant vigil in and out of the operating room. Another full day went by with no change.

On the morning of the third day a flurry of activity was heard in the womb, and the doctors immediately came to attention. The young doctor could plainly hear Roger moving about, but his repeated queries of "Are you ready now?" went unanswered. Then suddenly, just before noon, the movement stopped.

There was a sudden intake of air, and Mrs. J's womb slowly began to deflate, like a punctured hot air balloon. The doctors were horrified. The young doctor desperately tried to signal Roger through the rapidly shrinking abdominal wall, but could not obtain any answer. Mrs. J was apparently suffering no ill effects other than a pronounced tickling sensation.

The deflation continued for almost forty-five minutes, until Mrs. J's midriff had returned to preconception size. Once a stable condition had been reached, the doctors found that the womb area was now able to be violated. They operated immediately, and lost no time entering the womb to see if anything at all could be done for Roger.

The womb was empty. A thorough search was made, and the media was even allowed to examine the womb area to substantiate the doctors' observations. All that was found to indicate that Roger had been there was a severed placenta and a note, scribbled in a childish scrawl and torn from a page of Roger's notebook, which read, "Do not follow me."

THE RETURN OF
MAD SANTA

THE WHOLE MESS BEGAN on the afternoon of Christmas Eve. I was in the sleigh shed talking with Shmitzy, my chief mechanic, about some minor problems he'd been having with the front runners of the sleigh. Shmitzy's a little guy—about two-and-a-half feet tall, a good foot shorter than me—a solid, reliable elf with a grease-stained beard. The sleigh sat polished and clean in the center of the room, and Shmitzy was leaning against it with his arms folded, throwing unintelligible technical terms at me. I'd just gotten him to tell me in English what the heck was wrong with the sleigh when the doors to the shed burst open and Santa Claus bounded into the room.

"Gustav! Shmitzy!" Santa boomed. "How are my favorite helpers?" He was fat and pink, his beard fluffed, his eyes twinkling. He leaned over, patted our backs playfully, and brought his rosy cheeks down close to our faces.

I gave him the thumbs-up sign and rapped my knuckles on the side of the sleigh. "A-okay, Santa.

Everything's right on schedule, and Shmitzy tells me he'll have this boat ready to roll by tonight."

"Good, boys! Good!" Santa threw back his head and gave us a hearty "Ho ho ho!" I was sick of that laugh—it usually started to get to me around this time of year, though I have to admit I'd have walked off a cliff for Santa, annoying laugh or no—but I gave him a big smile anyway. He patted us gently again.

"See you later, boys! I just came by to see how things were coming along. I'm supposed to be helping Momma with her baking for dinner tonight." His eyes sparkled. "Special cakes for everybody! Ho ho ho!"

I winced, then quickly gave him a grin and the thumbs-up sign as he turned to leave.

And then a strange thing happened. He was halfway out the door when he suddenly froze in mid-step. He stood locked like that for a few seconds. Then, just as suddenly, he unfroze. He turned back to us with a strange, confused look on his face.

"Boys," he said. But then he shrugged. "Oh, never mind. It was nothing." He turned and took another step.

Again he froze. Shmitzy and I started toward him to see if he was all right. All of a sudden, he gave an ear-piercing roar and spun around, plucking Shmitzy up off the floor beside me and tossing him through the air. Shmitzy gave a yell and sailed like a shot put about thirty feet, hitting the floor in the corner of the shed with a groan.

Santa turned to me, his hands reaching for my neck. There was a horrible look on his face—his eyes bulged whitely from their sockets, and he was beet red above his beard. "Gustav," he said, his voice a cold growl.

He opened his mouth in a gaping cartoon grin, grasped my neck with his white-gloved hands, began to squeeze...and then suddenly returned to his old self. It was like someone had flicked a switch. He dropped his hands and looked at me, completely mystified.

"Gustav, what happened?"

I was shaking like a belly dancer, but I managed to open my mouth. "I don't know, Santa. You...didn't look so good for a minute."

There was an expression of helplessness on his normally jolly face. "I don't know what came over me," he said. He turned to Shmitzy, who was sitting on the floor across the room, touching his head tenderly. "I'm sorry, Shmitzy. I...just don't know what happened."

I took Santa gently by the arm. "Don't worry about it," I said. "Why don't you go back to the house and lie down. Have Momma fix you something hot to drink. The rush must be getting to you."

He brightened a bit and let me lead him to the door. "Yes, I suppose I should. Now that I think of it, Momma has seemed a bit irritable today, also." He paused, trying to think of something. "And I remember something...a long time ago..."

"Well, don't you worry about it, Santa. Go in and take it easy. You've been working too hard." I smiled and patted his arm, nudging him in the direction of the house. "Leave everything to me."

"Yes, I will. Thank you, Gustav." He smiled and patted his belly.

I watched him walk across the snow-covered courtyard to his cottage, open the door, and go in. I thought I saw him freeze again for a moment as he stepped through the doorway, but I couldn't be sure. He really must be working hard, the poor guy; I'd never seen him get mad before, never mind toss an elf across a room. I considered going over to the cottage and having a talk with him and Momma to make sure everything was all right, but then Shmitzy, now recovered, called me over to explain one more time what he was going to do with the front runners on the sleigh, and I soon forgot all about Santa.

That night everybody came marching into the dining room at the usual time for our special Christmas Eve dinner—a little celebration we have every year before all the craziness and last-minute work. They were all there: the wise guys from the Toy Shop, tripping each other and giggling and sticking each other with little tools; the gift-wrappers, lately unionized; the R&D boys with their noses in the air (big deal, so an elf can get a college education); the maintenance men; and assorted others. The dining room was decorated for the occasion: holly and tinsel, and red and green ornaments all over the walls, a "Merry Christmas" sign hung crookedly over the big fireplace behind the head of the table, fat squatty candles hanging from the low-beamed ceiling giving the place a warm, cheery glow. Though I know it sounds mushy, I have to say that getting that dinner organized always left a warm glow in me and was one of the high points of the year.

When everyone finally sat down I rose near the head of the table in my place as chief elf and raised my glass of wine to give the traditional toast to Mr. and Mrs. Claus, just as my father had done before me and his father before him. Every year it was the same thing: a simple toast, Mr. and Mrs. Claus come in, they bow, we bow, everybody drinks the wine, everybody sits down, we eat a great meal prepared by Momma Claus, we all eat too much, we all eat some more, and then we work like crazy getting ready for the big ride. All traditional. Smooth production. End of story.

This time I stood up and made the toast, and Mr. and Mrs. Claus entered, and everybody dropped his wine glass and gasped. Santa and Momma swaggered into the room like a couple of movie gangsters. Santa had a big cigar clamped in his teeth, and that evil grin I'd seen on his face that afternoon was now painted on both of them. I couldn't believe that the always-sweet, round-faced, bun-haired Momma Claus could ever look like a prune-faced dockworker, but she did. In the glow from the candles, they both looked pretty nasty.

Momma Claus stepped to the head of the table and raised her fist. There was a toy bullwhip in it. "Santa's going to talk to you now," she snarled, "and you'd better listen. Anybody who doesn't gets *this*." She cracked the whip down the length of the table, over our heads. It knocked Shmitzy's cap off, revealing the large bump on his head.

Momma stepped aside, and Santa took her place. He pounded on the table with a fist, then looked up, glaring into each of our faces up and down the table. "I like you boys," he growled, "so I'm going to keep you around." He opened his mouth in a horrid, toothy smile. "But from now on we're going to do things a little differently."

The heavy table shook from all our trembling.

Santa grabbed a full bottle of wine from the table and drank half of it in a gulp. He wiped his mouth with his sleeve. "Come on!" he roared, and, waving the bottle like a banner, he stomped out of the room into the courtyard.

We all sat rooted to our seats, eyes wide with terror; then Momma cracked her whip and we scampered out.

As we marched out into the snow, old Doc Fritz, the physician here at the North Pole, a solemn fellow with the body and face of a miniature Sigmund Freud and a professorial manner to match, edged up to me. He leaned over unobtrusively and whispered into my ear.

"I believe I know what is happening," he said. "This has occurred before."

"What?" I said.

He nodded slowly and scratched at his beard. "It was a long—"

Just then, Santa came screaming down the line, waving his arms madly in the air. "Everybody to his station!" he shouted.

Fritz opened his mouth to continue, but Santa came charging toward us. We quickly separated. Fritz shambled off toward the infirmary, and I scooted to my office.

I sat drumming my fingers on my desk for a few minutes, and then decided I had to talk to Fritz again to find out what was going on. There was a lot of howling and yelling outside, but I climbed quietly out of my window and made my way to the infirmary, a small, neat cottage at the edge of the village.

The door was locked and the windows dark. As I stepped off the porch I nearly bumped into Santa as he ran wildly around the corner of the building, a wine bottle in his hand. "Gustav!" he yelled. "Come with me!" And, dragging me along behind him, he went on a rampage.

He drank two and a half bottles of wine, and stumbled from building to building, department to department, shouting and breaking things. He started in the maintenance shed, went through the dining room and kitchen, and eventually made his way to the Toy Shop. There he told one of the master craftsmen that he didn't like the face on two thousand just-completed toy soldiers, lined them up in rows, and stomped them to sawdust.

At that point, one of the apprentices tried to shoot him with a replica Winchester rifle. Santa snatched it, batting the apprentice aside. He stumbled out into the snow.

"Where's Rudolph!" he roared. "I want to see my Rudolph!" Barely able to stand, laughing drunkenly, he found his way to the stables and threw open the wooden doors. "Rudolph!" he shouted, swaying from side to side. The interior of the stable was illuminated by moonlight. Rudolph, still in his stall, looked up and blinked, his red nose flashing. "Red-nosed bastard," Santa said, and as I watched in horror he raised the rifle, fumbling for the trigger.

As I leapt for him, he pulled the trigger, but as he did so he fell over backwards, out through the doors. He lay laughing in the snow, kicking his feet and howling, and firing the rifle at the moon and the weather vane on top of the stable. Then suddenly he stopped shooting, gave one long wolf-like howl, and instantly fell asleep.

The moment this happened, I gave a signal, and Shmitzy and a couple of other guys ran and got a long rope. We jumped on Santa and started to tie him up, but just as we got the rope around his waist, Momma Claus burst out of the Toy Shop and came running toward us, swinging a headless doll over her head and shouting, "Get away from him! Get away!" We scattered, and from a safe distance I watched as she dragged Santa's snoring body across the courtyard and into the house. Apparently he woke up, because a few minutes later all the lights in the house went on and I heard them laughing and breaking things.

I looked for Fritz but couldn't find him anywhere, so for the next couple of hours I tried to organize clean-up crews and estimate the damage. For all intents and purposes, the North Pole lay in ruins. There wasn't one building with its shingles and shutters intact, and the infirmary and elves' quarters were burned to the ground (Momma and Santa had danced around them as they blazed). The only structures left reasonably unscathed were the sleigh shed and the Toy Shop. I had no idea what we were going to do. There didn't seem to be any way to stop him, and I couldn't possibly let him make his Christmas Eve ride in his condition. It was almost too late to start, anyway. It looked as if there wouldn't be any visits from Santa this year.

As I was walking out of the Toy Shop I heard a commotion going on in the courtyard, and was just in time to see a great cheer go up as Santa walked out of his cottage. He looked like the old Santa we all knew and loved. He had a bright clean red suit and cap on, his cheeks were rosy and his beard was brushed and fluffed, his boots were polished to a high gloss and he was rubbing his belly. He even had a sack flung over his shoulder. Tough guy that I am, I almost started to cry for joy; but suddenly my eyes went dry and the cheer died in the middle when he got closer, because the wild look was still in his eyes and that twisted grin was still stuck to his face. When he opened his mouth and growled, we knew nothing had changed. He still looked like a bleached bluebeard.

"Get ready to roll!" he shouted.

We all looked at one another, mystified. Was he going to make his rounds looking like that?

"*I said get ready to roll!*"

Shmitzy stepped meekly out of the crowd. He was trembling like a leaf. "B-but Santa—"

Santa thundered, "Do what I say, or I'll string you all up like sides of beef!"

Five minutes later I had them buffing up the sled and loading piles of empty toy sacks onto the back of it, as per Santa's instructions. The Toy Shop remained untouched. The reindeer were groomed, the harness cleaned and rigged.

When all of this was finished, Santa assembled us by the sleigh, which had been pulled out into the courtyard. "Okay, boys," he said, chuckling sardonically. "It's time to make our rounds."

Momma was laughing, too.

Poor little Shmitzy stepped out of the crowd. He was still trembling uncontrollably. He pointed at the Toy Shop and the empty sacks in the sleigh. "S-Santa, we—"

Santa reached out and picked Shmitzy up by his feet, turning him upside-down. He brought him up very close to his face, and opened his mouth wide. For a moment it looked as if he were going to bite Shmitzy's head off. Then he put him down.

Shmitzy hurried back into the crowd.

"Gustav," Santa said in a low, mellow voice, rubbing his hands together and smiling evilly, "get your crew into the sleigh."

I was so scared I hustled the three elves nearest to me into the back with the empty bags. Santa threw his own half-filled sack into the front and climbed in after it. He cracked the reins.

"Ha ha ha," he said.

The take-off was fairly smooth, given the circumstances. Rudolph was still a bit shaken by almost having his nose blown off, but we got off the ground in one piece. It was a clear night with a bright moon, and I looked down as we made our turn over the North Pole.

The jolly, festively painted little village of a few days before now looked like an abandoned amusement park: wreckage and near-wreckage everywhere. None of the Christmas trees along the perimeter had been decorated; none of the remaining decorations had been polished. None of the last-minute work had been done. The scene would have made a disheartening air-photo. I shook my head and put up my collar. It was cold in that sleigh.

Santa laughed diabolically and straightened the sleigh out for the ride south. I was depressed, and the three elves huddled back there with me surrounded by empty sacks didn't look too cheerful, either. I looked closely at them now: two shivering apprentices, and a third elf bundled up like a mummy with his face covered. I glanced up front; Santa was waving his arms madly, cracking the reins fiercely over the poor reindeer. I wondered what he was going to do.

The bundled-up elf inched over to me and pulled down the muff covering his face. I almost shouted; it was Fritz!

He motioned for me to be quiet, and leaned over to whisper in my ear. "Don't raise your voice, my friend," he said. "If Santa finds me here I'm sure he'll throw me overboard." He whispered that we should move carefully to the back of the sleigh, and we did so. We piled up empty canvas sacks to form a sort of wall.

"I've been in hiding," Fritz continued. "I'm the only one who knows what's wrong with Santa and Momma Claus, and he knows that I know. I concealed myself in the basement of the infirmary, and, after the infirmary burned down, I hid in the Toy Shop trying to puzzle this out and come up with some sort of solution. Gustav," he said, stroking his chin thoughtfully, "to tell you the truth, I never believed the tale."

THE RETURN OF MAD SANTA

"Tell me everything," I said.

He nodded sagely. "Well, in summary form, this is the story. On Christmas Eve, eight hundred years ago to this night, when Santa and Momma Claus and their helpers still lived in Myra, in what is now southern Turkey, Santa and Momma lost their minds. It happened very suddenly. According to the story, they carried on like madmen all of Christmas Eve. The elves—my great-great-grandfather was the physician at the time—tried to stop them, but could not. They destroyed the village.

I was dumbfounded. "Why didn't I ever hear of any of this?"

"I'm coming to that. After the destruction, on Christmas Day, Santa went to sleep, and when he awoke it was as if nothing had happened. He could not believe what he and Momma had done. At that time, St. Nicholas was just a local phenomenon. He hadn't made his Christmas Eve visits, but they were limited at that time to poor children in the area, so excuses were easily made and the local furor eventually died down. No one outside the village ever knew what had really happened. The following year, Santa moved to the North Pole. A solemn vow was taken among the elves that only the physician would ever be tainted with the knowledge of what had occurred. The story was passed down to me by my father. I thought it was just a nasty fairy tale; even my father told me he didn't really believe it."

"Did they ever figure out why it happened?"

Fritz sighed. "No. The only explanation my great-great-grandfather came up with was that Santa had been possessed by a demon, and that the demon had been driven out by Santa's extreme goodness." He paused. "Very backward of him, don't you think? But now I have my own theory."

AL SARRANTONIO

I looked at him expectantly, and after some thoughtful beard-stroking he went on.

"I believe that after eight hundred years of extreme, selfless, total goodness, something happens within Santa's subconscious mind. I think there is a kind of reaction against all this goodness which builds and builds, a kind of ego-force, and when it has built to a sufficiently high point it bursts through to the surface volcanically. A similar reaction occurs in Momma Claus, also. That reaction is what we are seeing now." He paused, shook his head quickly, resolutely, and reached inside his coat. "But no matter what the cause," he said, producing a syringe, "we must now do something. Santa's actions have now taken an even wilder course than they did the first time this occurred. We have no idea what he will do, and we cannot allow him to continue. I decided today that if he tried to carry his violence beyond the North Pole he should be stopped at all costs. We must give him this strong sedative and turn the sleigh back."

"Should we get the two apprentices to help?"

"They are obviously in no state to be of assistance. We must—"

"Having a nice chat, boys?" Santa's demonically smiling face looked down at us over the little wall we had constructed. He reached over and pulled Fritz up by the collar, taking the syringe from his hand and throwing it overboard. I looked up front: the two apprentices were frantically trying to control the reindeer, and were being bounced all over the front seat by the reins.

For a terrible moment, I thought Santa was going to pitch Fritz over the side after the syringe, but after shaking him a few times he put him down. He held him with one hand while he reached up front between the bouncing apprentices and rummaged in his sack,

84

producing a length of rope. He tied Fritz up and gagged him, then let him go and grabbed me by the collar. "And you, little Gustav, will be my special helper, just like always. Hold this," he growled, thrusting the sack into my hands. "And if you make one wrong move I'll toss you out like a sandbag." I threw a helpless look at Fritz, who was wriggling in his ropes, trying to tell me something, and followed Santa up front.

He retrieved the reins from the two apprentices and frightened them into the back. We made a long, slow turn and came in over North America.

Santa turned and showed his teeth. "And now," he said mockingly, "it's time for our Christmas visits. Ho ho! Ha ha ha!" He snapped the reins, and we swooped down to a landing on a snowy rooftop.

He bounded out of the sleigh, and drove me and the two apprentices toward the red-brick chimney. I took a quick look in the bag I was struggling with; it was filled with all kinds of tools. I groaned silently. Santa hustled us down the chimney.

We found ourselves in a cozy living room. There was a lot of comfortable-looking furniture, and the fireplace was big. I brushed past four small stockings as I stepped into the room. A Christmas tree was decorated and lit in one corner.

Santa grabbed the sack from me and opened it, removing a set of fine jeweler's tools, a heavy monkey wrench, a hammer, and a flashlight. He gathered them all into his arms, then turned to us. "Now let's be quiet, boys," he whispered, grinning. "We wouldn't want anyone to disturb us, would we?"

Santa Claus, the gift-giver, then set about taking everything of value and stuffing it into the empty bag. Whatever was fastened or bolted down, he lifted with the wrench or the back end of the hammer. He dragged me along beside him, making me hold the sack open as he dumped in all sorts of stolen goods.

When he was through with the furniture and the other valuables in the room, he tiptoed through the rest of the house looking for money and jewelry. He found a wall safe in the den, and chuckled sardonically when it popped open under his sensitive fingers, revealing a small horde of gems and gold jewelry to his flashlight beam. When we came back to the living room he hoisted the stuffed sack and drove us to the fireplace. The room was completely bare. We'd even taken the lights and ornaments from the tree, which now stood naked and forlorn in the corner.

Before hustling us back up the chimney he turned to the living room, put his finger to the side of his nose, and said, in a grotesque parody of his normal self, "Happy Christmas to all, and to all a good night—ha ha."

We loaded the sleigh, and with a slap of the reins we were off to the next rooftop. Santa took a fresh empty sack with him, and we went through the same routine.

We finished with the last house at about three in the morning. My arms ached from transporting stolen property. I dragged myself into the front seat, and we rose, the reindeer straining against the load, from the last snow-covered roof.

Santa kept an eye on me for a while, but as the sleigh turned up toward the North Pole he finally forgot about me. He sat with a bag filled with the biggest diamonds and silver pieces he'd taken, and after telling the reindeer he'd "roast them alive" if they didn't find their own way home, he put the reins aside and sat with all the precious stuff in his lap, scooping big handfuls up and letting it run through his fingers.

THE RETURN OF MAD SANTA

I slipped silent as a shadow over the seat into the back. Fritz was wedged between a sack of paintings and a bag filled with patio furniture that Santa had spotted piled up on someone's back lawn. The two apprentices were exhausted, snoring in odd positions on top of two bags filled with bar stools. I pulled the gag out of Fritz's mouth and said in a low voice: "Is there anything we can do?"

He nodded. "There is in my left coat pocket another syringe which I brought for just such an emergency. If you could somehow give him an injection, we might still do something. But you must hurry." I took the syringe from Fritz's pocket and made my way back up front. Santa was still drooling over the jewels. I leaned over to push the needle into him, but as I did so my foot came down on a champagne glass that had rolled out of one of the bags.

He whipped around at the grinding noise. "More tricks!" he said, grabbing me and lifting me off the floor. I hid the syringe behind my back, but he saw it and his face went red with anger. He reached around me with his free hand, and I kept it away from him by squirming this way and that. He stood up to get a better hold on me, and the sudden movement panicked the reindeer. They started weaving crazy patterns in the air. Santa lost his balance for a moment, and I gave him a kick in the belly. He said "Ooof!" and dropped me. I ran into the rear of the sleigh and hid behind a sack.

Santa came after me, blubbering and huffing, and climbing over filled sacks as I darted between and around them. The reindeer were still flying out of control. The apprentices woke up; they started screaming and tried to crawl up front to calm Rudolph and the rest down. Santa bounded over one sack and came down inches from Fritz's head; he was close behind me, his hands almost around me when I suddenly saw a tiny opening between two bags. I dove through it, scooting around to the right.

I found myself face to face with Santa's rear end.

I froze there in surprise, the needle held out before me, when suddenly the sleigh lurched ahead and I fell into Santa and the needle hit the bulls-eye. He yelped once, went stiff as a board, and fell over backwards.

I quickly untied Fritz as the two apprentices managed to calm the reindeer down and get them flying in a straight line again. Fritz examined Santa, nodded his approval, and then, at his instructions, we took Santa's suit off and tied him up with the rope that had bound Fritz.

When he finished, Fritz looked up into the night sky. "We have about two and one half hours of darkness left, Gustav," he said. "I suggest that if we are to save Santa's good name you put this suit on and go up front and take over." He then told me his plan, and I balked and screamed, but finally gave in. The suit was forty sizes too big, but I put it on anyway and climbed into the front seat; we were soon heading at top speed back to the North Pole.

When we touched down in the courtyard everything was dead quiet. We were expecting the worst from Momma Claus, and while Fritz ran over to try to find another syringe in the wreckage of the infirmary I climbed out of the sleigh and cautiously began to look around. My feet kept getting tangled up in the too-long legs of Santa's suit, and I kept falling down. I looked in the toy shed, but found no one. When I tip-toed into the sleigh shed, hiking the suit up around me like a skirt, twenty-five elves jumped out of every crack and corner in the place, yelling like bandits and pummeling me with rubber toys. They wrestled me to the ground and had wound about two hundred feet of rope around my neck before one of them saw my face and shouted, "It's Gustav!"

They helped me to my feet, and I stood panting for a few minutes before I told them to go out and get Santa. They carried him off like triumphant hunters bearing a huge wild boar. I found Momma Claus already bound and gagged in their cottage; she'd passed out after drinking an uncounted number of bottles of claret while making everybody dance the rumba out in the snow. Good old Shmitzy had then rounded everybody up and set up the ambush for Santa's return.

After making sure the two of them were safely salted away, I got everyone together and quickly told them what had to be done. Their eyes all went wide, but they moved like jackrabbits. In fifteen minutes the sleigh, already packed solid, was piled twice as high with great sacks filled with toys. The Toy Shop was emptied. We harnessed a couple of back-up reindeer—Dentzen and Pintzen—to the rig for extra power. Fritz informed me that we had about an hour and a half to succeed. I pushed Shmitzy and the two apprentices who'd gone with me the first time into the front seat, and we made our take-off.

It was quite a ride. Everything went by in fast motion. The reindeer, though obviously straining under the mountainous weight, didn't offer a squeak of complaint as they moved like lightning from rooftop to rooftop. We hauled two bags down each chimney—one filled with toys and one filled with stolen goods.

I'm almost sure we got all the stolen stuff back in the right place, though somebody probably ended up with an extra golf bag or can opener. If something looked like it didn't belong in a particular place, I put it with the Christmas presents.

The only time we came close to being caught in the act was in one of the very last houses when a little girl walked sleepy-eyed into the room where I was madly stacking gifts. She took a long look at my baggy suit and dark beard, and stared suspiciously at me. "I've been dieting," I said, and darted up the chimney.

We finished as the first crack of orange sunlight broke on the horizon. I tumbled into the sled, and the reindeer just barely managed to pull off the last roof and into the sky. Shmitzy and the two apprentices fell dead asleep in the rear, and I had to fight to keep my eyes open to guide us home.

When we touched down at the North Pole there was a cheering welcoming committee waiting, but I stumbled through them with a tired smile on my face and went to my office and fell asleep on top of my desk for twelve straight hours with the red suit still on, the legs and arms draped over the desk like a tablecloth. When I awoke it was broad daylight, and the North Pole had been pretty much cleaned up—at least, all the wreckage had been swept into high piles. I was proud of my elves.

Santa and Momma Claus, just as Fritz had predicted, awoke late in the day in apparently normal condition and were appropriately astounded by what they had done. Santa seemed quite depressed for a while, but I gave him the thumbs-up sign a few times and kept patting him on the back and before long he was rubbing his belly merrily once again and giving booming "Ho ho ho!"s that made me cringe. We drew up tentative plans to rebuild the North Pole.

THE RETURN OF MAD SANTA

We had a long conference with Fritz, who explained all the psychological implications and convolutions and repressed reasons why all of it had happened. None of us had the faintest idea what he was talking about, but the upshot was that he thought he understood why it had happened—why it *had*—and that there was nothing wrong with Santa and Momma Claus. He assured us that according to all the scientific data he had it shouldn't happen again for at least another eight hundred years; he even said it might be possible to offset its happening again by the use of encounter sessions, mind expansion, and other ego-soothing measures.

"I am positive the effects are not cumulative, and that once this so-called volcanic gush of bad feelings is expelled, it will not build up again for centuries. And I believe that by using precise psychological techniques we can bleed off these feelings before they build. I am certain of this."

His lecture finally ended, Fritz gathered his notes together and prepared to leave.

Momma and Santa had sat very still through all of this, but when it was all over they nodded slowly in understanding. I saw them turn to one another and smile sheepishly, and this was all very touching until Santa's smile suddenly widened into that horrible toothy grin and both their eyes went big and white. I could swear I heard Santa say "Heh-heh-heh." But it was all over in a second, and Fritz missed it, and the two of them were as normal and healthy as one of Momma's pies again. The sheepish smiles were back, and they even kissed and held hands.

I thought I'd imagined it until we were all leaving and Santa suddenly turned to me and winked, flashing his fangs. "Everything back to normal for another eight hundred years. Right, Gustav? All in my head, eh?"

I gulped, gave him the thumbs-up sign, and scooted by him as he whacked me on the can. His smile had turned back to normal by then.

That's why I'm getting out of the North Pole tonight while the getting's good. I've told Fritz and the rest of them, but they just won't believe me. They think everything's back on track.

Maybe I'll buy a house in Florida.

Wherever it is, it won't have a chimney.

BABY BOSS AND THE UNDERGROUND HAMSTERS
A FEATURE-LENGTH CARTOON

REEL SEVEN

"Stop drooling!" Baby Boss snapped, in a fierce whisper. "You're always drooling! And keep quiet!"

"*YES, BOSS!*" Squirmy screamed at the top of his lungs. "*I'LL BE QUIET FROM NOW ON!*"

Squirmy cowered in fear as the hairy flat of Baby Boss's right paw caught him flush on the head. He dropped to his knees, reeling, but continued to slobber and mewl.

"I said—!" Baby Boss began, then suddenly his rage turned to alarm and he pressed Squirmy tightly against the cavern wall.

"*Someone's coming!*" he hissed.

Squirmy continued to whimper, and Baby Boss covered the slavering hamster's mouth with his paw as he studied the cave gloom ahead.

From around the cavern corner came a happy clucking sound, and Doozy the Chicken appeared, her feathery dugs prominently displayed before her as she twirled her Magic Umbrella, which gave a sparkly luminescence to the dank, dreary cave.

"Cluck-CLUCK! Cluck cl-cl-cluck…" Doozy sang, until she spied Baby Boss and stopped dead in her tracks.

"You—!" she clucked.

"Yes, me!" Baby Boss snarled, jumping out into the center of the cave. Behind him, Squirmy's drool-covered, asphyxiated body sank to the floor.

"I knew it would come to this…" Doozy averred.

"By all the chittering chipmunks in heaven, you're right!"

Doozy twirled her umbrella, whose lights dimmed to a soft green glow. A target sight and trigger materialized from the instrument's handle.

But Baby Boss's twin six guns were already blazing, and Doozy disappeared in a cloud of brown feathers.

"CLUUUUUUUCK!" she cried, her last word cut off by the rain of deadly lead.

The walls of the cavern trembled and collapsed around Baby Boss's ears.

"Oh, shit," he muttered—

REEL EIGHT

"Ha!" Baby Boss cried, brushing dirt from his furry hamster torso as he stood in Hamster Central, the largest of all the underground caverns. "That was close!"

BABY BOSS AND THE UNDERGROUND HAMSTERS

He strode with purpose to the Underground Hamster Alarm, and pushed the large, brightly lit button. Instantly the call went out, a high chirrupy squeal, and before long the Underground Hamsters were assembled before him expectantly.

"Hamsters!" Baby Boss shouted, throwing his paws into the air. "Our day of triumph has arrived! Doozy the Chicken is dead!"

"Not so fast!" came a clucky voice from the rear of the assembly. The sea of hamsters parted and there stood Doozy, unfeathered but alive. A neat line of bullet holes traced through her bodice above her massive dugs.

"But—" Baby Boss sputtered in disbelief.

With a grand gesture, Doozy drew a wing across the front of her body, which fell to the floor. Behind what had been an impenetrable shell, containing her false dugs and the line of bullet holes, each still containing the bullet which had never reached her, was her real chicken chest, brown feathers and all.

"Everyone knows chickens don't have tits!" Doozy cried, and drew out her Magic Umbrella, already glowing green in weapon-mode.

Pandemonium, and the cries of frightened hamsters, filled Hamster Central until the roof, with a massive roar, suddenly caved in.

"Oh, shit," Doozy clucked.

BABY BOSS AND THE UNDERGROUND HAMSTERS HOLIDAY SPECIAL...LIVE FROM HAMSTER CENTRAL...!!!

Scene: Hamster Central, a huge, dome-ceilinged cavern, and the underground rallying point for all hamsters. It is Christmas Eve. Hamster Central has been decked out in holiday colors, greenery and red bows, twinkling Christmas lights—it is a veritable Fezziwig's Ball. From somewhere, the muted sounds of Christmas music is heard, Nat King Cole's "Christmas Song". A massive sideboard is crowded with food and drink: a glistening moist turkey, two huge pink hams, a punch bowl as big as a child's swimming pool lapping waves of spiked eggnog.

In the center of Hamster Central, alone, two figures dance slowly: Baby Boss and Doozy the Chicken. Their happy voices murmur and coo; amidst their whispers of affection the sound of contented laughter. We listen in:

DOOZY (sighing): I wish this evening could go on forever, Baby. I wish this could always be (sighing again) *our* Christmas Eve.

BABY: Me, too. It's a mystery to me how one magic evening could change everything. Yesterday we were bitter enemies, and now...

DOOZY (blushing): Yes, now...

BABY (sighing himself, a regretful sound): But soon the Underground Hamsters will be back, and the promised party will begin. (gazes lovingly into Doozy's eyes, his eyes glittering with a sudden thought): Our special night will be a night to be shared by all!

BABY, SUDDENLY SHY, PUSHES DOOZY GENTLY AWAY AND THEN ABRUPTLY GETS DOWN ON ONE KNEE. HE FUMBLES SOMETHING FROM HIS FUR, SOMETHING WHICH SPARKLES WITH THE CAUGHT REFLECTION OF A THOUSAND TWINKLING CHRISTMAS LIGHTS—

DOOZY: A ring!

BABY: (holding the knuckle-sized diamond up toward Doozy, while placing his other paw over his heart) Doozy Chicken, will you marry me?

DOOZY: Will I? This is a dream come true!

THERE ARE SOUNDS FROM THE MANY CAVERNS LEADING INTO HAMSTER CENTRAL, AND NOW THE UNDERGROUND HAMSTERS APPEAR, LAUGHING, JOSTLING ONE ANOTHER, IN GOOD SPIRITS AND LOOKING FORWARD TO THE PARTY TO COME. BUT, AS ONE, THEY HALT AND GASP AT THE SIGHT OF THEIR BOSS AND DOOZY.

SPIFFY: It's Baby Boss! And he's in the clutches of Doozy!

ALL HAMSTERS, AS ONE: Let's get her!

BABY (his voice drowned out by the roaring torrent of screaming hamsters around him): Stop!

HE HOLDS UP HIS PAWS FOR SILENCE, BUT IS IGNORED AS THE HAMSTERS, THEIR MOUTHS FROTHING IN FURY, TEAR DOOZY TO SHREDS. FEATHERS FLY MADLY AND THERE IS A SINGLE STRANGLED CLUCK AND THEN SUDDEN, COMPLETE SILENCE.

BABY (staring in horror at what is left of his beloved: a pile of bloody feathers, a beak, two wrinkly feet): What have you done! This was the last chance for reconciliation between hamsters and chickens! *And...I loved her!*

HE BEGINS TO WEEP AS THE CEILING SUDDENLY COLLAPSES, SENDING TONS OF ROCK, SOIL AND SNOW FROM THE WHITE CHRISTMAS ABOVE DOWN UPON THEM.

HAMSTERS (as one): Oh, shit—

BABY BOSS AND THE UNDERGROUND HAMSTERS

REEL EIGHTEEN

Baby Boss awoke at his desk with the sour taste of bourbon in his mouth.

How long had it been? Two weeks? A year?

He groaned, as memory, along with the desk calendar in front of his face, told him the real story: it had been only a week, for today was New Year's Day.

"Oh why! Why!" he cried, throwing his paws out, knocking the empty Jim Beam bottle from his blotter to the floor, where it crashed atop a pile of three-dozen others. "Just when happiness was in my grasp!"

He looked up at his paw, which closed into a furry fist—and then a bout of weeping overcame him and he covered his face with his paws and lowered it to the desk. "Oh Doozy, my love, you are gone!"

There came a sound behind him in the doorway that separated his office from the cave beyond. A tentative knock followed.

"Baby, are you in there?"

The voice was a soft cluck.

Could it be?

Baby sprang from the desk and ran for the door, which flew open to reveal...Doozy Chicken!

"You're safe!" Baby cried.

Doozy smiled—and then pulled from behind her, where it sat waiting in its special hidden holster, her Magic Umbrella, glowing with menacing green light. Her eyes were filled with sudden hate.

"But Doozy—our love—!"

"Did you think I'd send the real me to test the depths of your treachery? That was no chicken you asked to marry you—it was a Cyber Doozy, produced in my secret lab at the Center of the Earth!"

She laughed, pulling the trigger, and the evil light intensified to a blinding flash.

"But Doozy—*ahhhhhhhhhhhhhhh*—!"

Baby Boss disappeared in a sour flit of green smoke, leaving only the smell of ozone behind.

"Ha!" Doozy cried, shouldering her weapon and turning about-face. "Now to deal with the rest of the Underground Hamsters!"

The cave roof, with a tremendous roar, collapsed around her—

"Oh, shit—" Doozy said.

REEL NINETEEN

"Ha! That was close!" Doozy Chicken effused, brushing dirt, along with the remains of a housing project that had been built above the hamster cave, from her sleek brown feathers.

She stood in Hamster Central, the tip of her wing pressing the Underground Hamster Alarm, which would bring all of the hamsters scurrying to what they thought would be a meeting called by Baby Boss.

"A meeting with their own doom!" Doozy amended, throwing her head back to cluck a laugh.

There was the roar of tiny feet, and the many tunnels leading into Hamster Central were suddenly filled with hamsters armed with atomic pistols—the new, and deadly, Platinum Model. Hate glowed in their tiny mammalian eyes.

BABY BOSS AND THE UNDERGROUND HAMSTERS

And there, pushing his way through the furry crowd in the largest cave opening, and armed with nothing less than a golden Hydrogen Rifle, the most powerful weapon in the Universe, was Baby Boss himself!

"But I—" Doozy clucked in stupefaction.

"Yes, you vaporized me—*not*!" Baby Boss chortled. "Did you think I was stupid enough to let the real me ask your Cyber Chicken to marry me? That was a Cyber Baby, manufactured in my secret underground facility on the planet Pluto, that you vaporized, you clucking wench!"

He lowered the yawning foot-wide barrel of the Hydrogen Rifle toward Doozy.

"And now," he cried in triumph, "chicken dinner!"

There came a tremendous roar, and the ceiling of Hamster Central, recently upgraded with what Baby Boss had thought were infallible reinforced concrete arches, providing a dome as smooth as that on St. Peter's Basilica, and on which had been painted by Spiffy beautiful and colorful scenes of hamster life which, in their intricacy and inspired imagination, rivaled those of that great Michelangelo work, collapsed around them.

"Oh, shit!" everyone said.

REEL THIRTY-NINE

Spiffy said, "I think it was a mistake to leave our Underground headquarters."

The steel in the hamster's voice made Baby Boss look away from the port window of Space Station One, where he had been dreamily watching the pinpoint beauty of the stars. "It had to be done," he said at last. "We had to take this war to Space."

"But—"

Baby fixed his subordinate with a cold gaze. "The final battle will be fought in the heavens." He threw a paw out to point through the porthole. "It is here that the fate of hamsters and chickens will be decided."

Spiffy lowered his head and nodded. "It's just that…"

Baby let his paw drift to rest on the younger man's shoulder. "I know. You miss your underground life."

"Yes."

"It can't be helped." Baby's gaze wandered back to the porthole, and the beautiful vista beyond, white tiny diamond chips against a background of black velvet. "Soon," he said, and it was as much sigh as conviction.

Space Station One had been designed to mimic, as closely as possible, the labyrinthine cave lair of the Underground Hamsters. It consisted of a series of steel tunnels radiating from a central hub which, except for its Spartan metal nature, resembled nothing so much as Hamster Central. The dome overhead exhibited a half-finished mural of colorful hamster life.

And, when the Hamster Alarm was sounded, as it was now, the response was no different than it had been on Earth: all hamsters had been summoned, and they ran as fast as their furry feet would carry them to the meeting hall.

Only now when they ran in to Hamster Space Central, they converged on the laughing, clucking figure of Doozy Chicken, who stood with the tip of her wing pressed tightly to the alarm!

BABY BOSS AND THE
UNDERGROUND HAMSTERS

"You!" Baby Boss gasped. "How—?"

Doozy held up her wing for silence, and then covered her form in the tight fitting latex costume which had gained her entrance to Space Station One. With the body mask in place, she looked exactly like Spiffy!

"But—?" Baby exclaimed.

Doozy clucked a hoarse grunt of pleasure, and pointed upward. All hamster eyes looked to the dome to see the dead, splayed figure of the real Spiffy, squashed between two cartoony hamster figures of his own manufacture—it looked as though he was holding hands with them!

"You fiend!" Baby growled.

"I could have killed you at the porthole," Doozy shot back. Her eyes gleamed red fire. "But the rules of Space Battle forbade it! But now—!"

She produced her Magic Umbrella, in green-glowing battle mode, from its hidden holster secreted in the feathers of her back.

Someone behind Baby Boss tossed him his massive golden Hydrogen Rifle, the most powerful weapon in the Universe, and he cradled its smooth lines against his fur-covered ribs as he raised its foot-wide maw of destruction and aimed it in Doozy's direction.

"Yes, now!" Baby said, preparing to pull the trigger.

Space Station One trembled and convulsed, and the domed ceiling collapsed in a groaning, vacuum-of-space—inducing pile of wreckage around them.

"Oh, shit," Baby said—

AL SARRANTONIO

REEL NINETY-THREE

"I can't believe we're back on the planet Pluto," Spiffy said. He waved his atomic paintbrush in the air for emphasis. The night sky, black as ink, the faraway dot of the Sun, a lonely cold beacon, all of it was so alien!

"Yes, and I'm particularly glad that we've been able to reconstitute you in Cyber form, Spiffy!" Baby Boss put a fatherly paw on the younger hamster's shoulder. "You always were one of my favorites—and a heck of an artist!"

They shared a chirp of hamster laughter before Cyber Spiffy climbed back up into the massive rigging of catwalks crisscrossing the Pluto Dome, half finished, which, when completed, would ape both Hamster Central on Earth and the lately destroyed Hamster Space Central. Since the soil of Pluto was rock hard, making it impossible to make an underground abode, it had been decided to build a series of above-ground tunnels, all leading to Hamster Pluto Central. It would be, in effect, Hamster Space Central lain gently on the ground of the ninth planet.

Baby Boss sighed in satisfaction, and prepared to push the Hamster Pluto Alarm.

"Stop!" It was the voice of Doozy Chicken, broadcast from her Chicken Rocket, which now swooped sleekly in through the open ceiling of the dome and settled in a susurrus of smoke and dying fire next to the waiting Baby.

"Bring me my Hydrogen Rifle!" Baby exclaimed, and Cyber Spiffy scrambled down the scaffolding to obey.

"That won't be necessary!" Doozy cried, jumping from the lowering rocket gangplank to stand beside Baby. There was a strange look in her eyes. "The war is over!"

"What!" answered Baby, dumbfounded. He saw that Doozy's holster had been taken from its secret hiding spot in her feathers and was empty.

Doozy suddenly took Baby in her arms, and kissed him!

With shock and relief, Baby found himself kissing her back!

"I love you, Baby Boss! I've loved you ever since our Cyber Selves fell in love!"

"And...I love you too!" Baby replied in wonder.

He jabbed at the Hamster Alarm with authority. "It's time all the hamsters knew this! Time they all shared in our joy!"

"This will mean the end of hostilities, and the friendship of hamsters and chickens forever!"

"Hurrah!" said Cyber Spiffy.

The alarm was sounded, and the Underground Hamsters arrived to see Baby Boss and Doozy pledging their love.

"Hurrah!" all the hamsters cried.

At that moment the scaffolding gave way, along with the badly designed, half-finished dome, and tons of building material, as well as Cyber Spiffy's partly finished mural, came crashing down.

No one said, "Oh, shit," because, this time, they were all dead.

TRAIL OF THE CHROMIUM BANDITS

Ride the Wild West.

Ride the Wild West with the hiss of falling spaceships splitting the sky like comet trails.

Ride the Wild West with justice in your heart and the remembered kiss of a woman on your lips.

Ride the Wild West in a Toyota.

◆ ◆ ◆

MITCH HILLIGAN HOODED HIS eyes to squint into the lowering sunset of West Texas. Something itched at his fingers, then burned; he looked down to see the raw red end of a cigarette gouging into the flesh of his thumb and forefinger. He dropped the cigarette into the dust and ground it out with the toe of his boot.

"What do you think, Sparky—game's gonna start soon?" he said. He tried to bite his words before they came out, knowing how useless they were now, but still not quite used to the way things were. "Come on, Sparky, speak to me." The dog at his feet wagged its tail, its tongue lolling out expectantly. Hilligan cursed shortly and drew a dog biscuit out of the deep pocket of his poncho. He tossed it to the ground and the dog was upon it instantly, making crunching sounds that annoyed Hilligan. He tried to ignore the sound, then suddenly drew his foot back to kick the dog. He hesitated, his anger draining.

"You're a useless weapon, old pal," he said, reaching to pet the dog on the ruined head that had once held Sparky's intact brain. "Not your fault."

Hilligan straightened, and brought his binoculars up to his eyes. He scanned the horizon below, searching for the telltale signs of a campfire, but found nothing. He cursed and lowered the binoculars. Waiting for night to fall before trying again.

They were stupid, in most ways, but incredibly crafty. Here they were, a band of four, leaving their droppings—candy wrappers, empty food cans, milk cartons, beer cans, liquor bottles, pissmarks, piles of shit—and still, Hilligan had barely had a glimpse of them for three days. One silhouette glinting in the sunset two nights ago, a hint of horizon movement the day before. He knew he was close but still they were all but invisible, leaving a trail of crap but it was the Invisible Man's refuse.

"Yep, game's gonna start soon," Hilligan repeated, to himself.

Hilligan made camp twenty minutes later. The sunlight had dropped; the Moon was a weak sickle just cutting up the East. Stars burned into the purple of twilight; burned brighter into the blackness of night.

Sparky tried to piss, seemed to forget how, mewled as the wetness ran ineffectively down his leg followed by a runnel of tepid shit.

Hilligan cleaned the dog, settled him under the rusting rear of the Toyota Corolla and lit another cigarette. The dog, under his blanket, gave a large sigh and then slept.

Hilligan watched the stars, passing his cold gaze from Betelgeuse through Orion's belt and down to Risius. The Milky Way stretched gauzily through the ecliptic, a pointillistic band of millions of tiny, distinct flaming suns.

"Games..." he said to himself, and then rolled into his blanket and lightly slept.

He slept heavily. The heat of day, not the light, awakened him. Sparky was still under the Toyota, awake, tongue lolling, dehydrated but not realizing it. He opened his mouth when Hilligan's eyes met his, and for a moment Hilligan had hope; an aching sense of loss, combined with an overwhelming wish—and need—for the dog the way he had been, washed over him. But only a weak rumbling sound came out. Sparky put his head down on a front paw, still panting.

Hilligan poured water into a bowl and gave it to the dog. By the sun, it was already nine o'clock. It had been stupid to sleep so long; by now the band would be miles ahead.

Hilligan ate a can of beans, washing it down with a warm can of Coors, and then packed the car. The engine resisted, coughing toward death and then suddenly roaring into its bad muffler like a lion. On the seat next to him, Sparky slept. The radio was on, hissing nothingness, the occasional snatch of Country-Western music from a faraway station.

The day, the miles, rolled on.

He found their trail at four. A telltale pile of refuse and body wastes broadcast their direction loudly: west toward Lawrence. He thought fleetingly of Anne; he had left her in Lawrence not four days before, and the salt-taste of her first kiss still lingered on his lips. He saw her amusement at his blush—"Why, *Marshal*, one would think you'd never been kissed before," and her deepening amusement and interest when he asked, "This love thing's sort of a game, isn't it?" and he remembered the look on her face that said, "Come back, come back soon..."

Hilligan turned his attention back to the bandit's camp. If anything, they were even less concerned with his pursuit. They had been reading; he found a pile of *Mad* and *Playboy* magazines in with the chili and tuna cans; on closer inspection, the magazines were smeared with shit, had been used as toilet paper.

Once again, he stood on a ridge and studied the darkening sky with binoculars.

A movement among a group of live oaks.

Them.

A chill crawled up Hilligan's back. He knew they had stopped for him. *The game was about to begin.* The images he had been able to push aside the last three days flashed into his mind, stark and terrible. The town that had been Davidson, Texas, roasted to the ground, the huge trough of their ship nosed into what had been the library; the smell of broiled human flesh left in its wake; black human bodies with open mouths and empty charcoal eyes; smoking ruins that had been buildings, a McDonalds, a five and dime; what they'd done to Sparky, half his head roasted off...

TRAIL OF THE CHROMIUM BANDITS

He remembered the way the people of Davidson had looked up to him when they made him Marshal not three weeks before, after he came walking out of the desert with his dog like a movie hero, tall, sure of himself, unnaturally handsome, what a Marshal should be. They sensed trouble; he said he'd take care of it. "Thanks, Marshal," they'd said, giving him his Toyota to use. He'd believed he could protect them. And now their eyes were burned sockets, their mouths silenced even from screams...

Thanks, Marshal. He'd been on the way back from Lawrence when they'd needed him, seeing the black smoke from the desert through the windshield of the Toyota, roaring back into town just as the bandits were leaving, loading Jud Stern's Plymouth Voyager with tennis rackets and golf clubs and guns from STERN'S SPORTING GOODS, laughing as they did so, turning to regard him with their perfect mirror chrome faces as he'd screamed, perfect human beings covered in chrome, running after them, one of them raising a lazy hand, turning the palm flat toward him but another standing next to the Voyager, smiling lazily, saying, "No, let's make a game of it."

The other shrugged, and lowered the hand to Sparky. The hand glowed metallically, and the dog buckled, then rose unsteadily again and pissed on himself, the look of the dead, the lost, in his eyes.

"Not that you have any choices, but we'll make it a real game," the first one said, lifting a rifle from a pile of guns in the back of the Voyager and tossing it to Hilligan. His metallic head, a perfect replica of a human's head in chrome, smiled. "We'll only use these." He turned his palm toward Hilligan, the threat of death held in check. "Agreed?"

Biting back useless rage and frustration, Hilligan nodded curtly.

The others had laughed, and they loaded into the vehicle and were gone, leaving their laughter behind, the laughter of tourists on holiday, having sort, packing picnic lunches from the ruins of Davidson, taking clothes and guns and food, leaving behind Hilligan screaming and the silent screams of a dead town.

And now it was time for the game to really begin.

They were getting tired and bored. He knew because their toys had begun to be abandoned: the tennis rackets, the golf clubs broken in two. Soon their minds would turn to bigger larks. The town of Lawrence was only five miles to the East. They would head there next. Where Anne was…and continue their fun from town to town, from city to city, until there was nothing left.

Something spat past Hilligan's ear, pinged into the door of the Toyota.

"Shit," Hilligan said.

Crouched behind the fender of the Corolla, he waited for another shot. Raising his head tentatively, he searched the desert with his binoculars. No shot came, and then he saw them: a retreating band of silver glints in the distance, just disappearing behind an outcropping of rock. A careful look at their wake showed the half-buried wreckage of the Plymouth Voyager, half merged with the side of the rock wall.

For the first time in days, Hilligan smiled.

"Shit, we're gonna win," he said.

TRAIL OF THE CHROMIUM BANDITS

He spent the next hour packing and camouflaging the Toyota in a stand of live oaks. The only burden was Sparky's food, an oversize box of dog biscuits, the only thing the dog recognized now and would eat, but he gladly strapped it to the top of his knapsack, cursing not the weight but the bulk. One somber, lost look from the dog made him bite the curses.

"Come on, pal."

He set off at a brisk walk, the dog hesitating, then following mechanically behind, the sight of the dog biscuit box firing some barely connecting relay in his ruined brain.

After two hours, he badly missed the stuttering air conditioning of the Corolla. Salt sweat had nearly blinded him, but he kept on. The sun was like a sieve, arrowing heat down at him. Paradoxically, Sparky didn't seem to mind; as long as the bright blue box with the hungry-looking German Shepherd on it was in his eyesight, he marched resolutely in tow.

They passed the ruined Voyager at noon. It had been plowed deliberately into the side of the bluff and trashed; whatever hadn't been taken was broken. The van was haloed in broken flashlights, dart games, ripped clothing, crushed miniature televisions, portable cassette decks. Nearby, carefully placed to seemingly view the wreckage, was a severed human head, which on closer inspection turned out to be that of Stern, the sporting goods store owner. He had been placed to view the destruction of his own robbed goods.

Hilligan kept walking.

At one o'clock he had to stop. He ate a sparse lunch, sipping at the water canteen instead of gulping, until his thirst was slaked. Sparky ate a dog biscuit, fighting the blurred mechanism of his mouth to work on it.

As Hilligan watched the dog slap his tongue tentatively at the shallow bowl of water, he heard the unmistakable crack of a rifle shot.

The dog tensed momentarily, then resumed drinking as if nothing had happened, completely ignoring the round hole in its left eye.

The dog drank, liquid dripping down its ruined face into its water bowl, and drank its own fluids until its body suddenly collapsed.

The dog shivered and lay still.

Hilligan was already halfway up the side of the outcropping. He hoisted himself between two peaked rocks as another shot rang out below him. "Just had to make sure, *Marshal*," a voice shouted, laughing. This time he saw where it came from.

He took aim at the spot and there, in his sights, was a blinding chromium head.

He pulled the trigger and the head flared in a shower of metal and flesh fragments as the soft pink fleshy head exploded.

The rifle shot echoed, then the tranquility of the desert returned.

Cautiously, Hilligan returned to his pack and removed his binoculars. He climbed the hillock and scouted.

A mere mile ahead was the remainder of the band. They had stopped in the bare shade of a stunted stand of cottonwoods, waiting for their compatriot.

He hoped they had seen what had happened to their scout; and then knew they did because the three of them abruptly walked out into the sunlight, blinding him with the metallic brilliance of their heads.

When his eyes had adjusted, he saw that between them they had two weapons, one of which looked like an automatic rifle. The third carried an inappropriately small red pack, the kind children carry schoolbooks in, stuffed to overflowing; as Hilligan watched the other two tried to load it further until the one bearing the pack suddenly lashed out, knocking the other to the ground.

Hilligan put the high-power binoculars down and tried to sight through the rifle, but they were too far away.

He returned to the desert floor, mounted his own pack, and moved on.

◆ ◆ ◆

When he got to the cottonwoods, the bandits were long gone. A scatter of Ritz Crackers and empty juice cartons attested to their stupidity. He hoped the juice had gone down burning hot.

He went on.

He spotted them forty-five minutes later, as they moved into the low hills. On the other side of those hills was the town of Lawrence. They were moving fast, spread out, twenty or thirty yards between them.

Hilligan sprinted to the nearest rock outcropping, balancing his rifle carefully on the lip of the overhang, and caught the nearest in his finder. It was the weaponless one with the pack, standing at the limits of range. Carefully, using the rock to steady him, he pulled off a single shot, watching the bright metallic head shatter, scattering the sandy ground with cookies, plastic jars of peanut butter, and soft flesh.

The other two glanced around, then broke into a run.

Night was coming, and they had made it to the hills.

AL SARRANTONIO

✦ ✦ ✦

The stars were up. The Milky Way rose like a glowing band. The night was Moonless, but Hilligan could see his way by the blue glow of the Milky Way alone.

He saw with his ears as much as with his eyes. He thought of a novel he had been given by Anne after taking the job of Marshal in Davidson. It was one of the Leatherstocking Tales by Cooper. With the book, Anne had also given him a book by Mark Twain with an essay marked out in it about how lousy a storyteller Cooper was. According to Twain, most of the suspense in a Cooper novel developed when someone made noise by stepping on something while sneaking around. Someone was always stepping on something and giving themselves away.

Up ahead of Hilligan, someone stepped on something.

"Sorry, Twain, Cooper was right," Hilligan muttered.

There was a line of jutting rocks ahead, threaded by a stony path. Hilligan crept to the first outcropping, avoiding any stepped-on somethings of his own.

He waited, and then there was another sound, very close.

Suddenly one of them appeared, the silvery luminescence of his head turning a mere yard from Hilligan.

It was the one with the automatic weapon.

Hilligan was quicker, and as a spatter of lead lined the rock wall to his right he pulled a shot out of his rifle and hit the other square in the chest.

The night flared and Hilligan briefly covered his eyes at the hissing explosion as the thing dropped its rifle, uttering a tiny cry as it was blown apart.

Beyond it, in the night, Hilligan heard the other one running.

Fast.

Hilligan followed. They had entered a desert forest of cactus, up the side of a small hill. The cactus looked like they had been planted, lined up in neat rows up the side of the hillock, each giving the next just enough room to catch any available water.

Hilligan caught a brief glimpse of his prey, heard a scraped tumble of rocks that splashed down past him to the foot of the hill below.

"I'm coming for you, you bastard!" Hilligan shouted up into the darkness.

Only silence greeted him.

In the dark, with the night over him, Hilligan moved upward, from cactus to cactus. Cursing his boots, he knew that he was the one making noise this time as he kicked a scuff of shale that slid down the mountainside.

He stopped, leaned into the curve of a prickly pear without touching it, and waited.

Still nothing.

The night breathed silence.

He felt presence; heard the faintest of sounds—

A silver-white hand appeared from behind the cactus and was on him before he could react.

He was knocked to the ground. A chrome head loomed over him. He heard his rifle slide away down the hill in the darkness. His attacker raised a Colt .45, then tossed it contemptuously away and held his palm downward over Hilligan.

"This game's over," the bandit hissed at him. "Tomorrow I'll play games in Lawrence. And then everywhere else on this miserable planet..."

The palm began to glow with silver light.

Something flashed in the darkness, hovered overhead, dropped on the alien's back.

The alien cried out and fell off into the night.

Hilligan pushed himself up to see the bandit clutching at his ripped-out throat, see it thrash helplessly before lying still.

"That would have been you in another second," Hilligan heard in his head, weakly. There was familiar laughter behind the words.

"Sparky," he said.

The dog lay panting a few feet from the imploded corpse of the desperado. His head looked like a scooped-out bowl, the top completely collapsed, wires and bio-tubes hanging uselessly. But there was the old look of unmistakably intelligent though weakening fire in one of his eyes.

"Should always check to make sure your sidekick has really stopped playing," the dog's thoughts said to him. "That bullet they hit me with fused a couple of the right circuits back together. It was like waking up from a bad dream. And you were gone." There was more humor than blame in the voice.

"Sparky—"

"Don't apologize, Mitch. I had just enough left in me to save your ass and this planet..." The voice trailed off tepidly.

As Hilligan watched, the weak light began to fade in the dog's eye.

"So long, pal..." the dog said in a dying whisper.

Hilligan stood in the darkness for a long time. The Milky Way, a blue glowing ribbon cutting the night, passed overhead toward the west and morning.

✦ ✦ ✦

Finally, as the Milky Way faded, Hilligan picked Sparky up in his arms and headed back to the Toyota. He pulled off the camouflage, lay the dog gently in the back, and headed out.

The morning colored the east purple and yellow. Hilligan smoked a cigarette and thought about his own spaceship hidden out in the desert. He thought about the four bandits he had been sent to catch who had terrorized and destroyed so many other worlds, and about how his race's addiction to games had probably saved himself and this planet. And he thought about Sparky, his only weapon, and how he'd been constructed to look like any Earth dog. Hilligan thought about the thin plastic flesh that covered his own chromium skin.

Hilligan thought about what he would do now. He could go home, but somehow, the remembered kiss of a woman named Anne made him want to stay for a while.

He had a feeling that love was a good game to play.

There was a tool kit out in that spaceship buried in the desert; perhaps he could spend his spare time trying to fix Sparky up. A good sidekick was hard to find.

Perhaps the town of Lawrence needed a Marshal.

Hilligan rode the Wild West in a Toyota.

THE MAN IN THE OTHER CAR

I THINK I SAW his face as we went by. We passed his car as you pass most cars, using peripheral vision and a vague radar sense of distance and speed. I think the car was blue, possibly gray. The plates were green and white, in-state, I think.

My son was the first one to bring it up. "Dad, did you see that guy?" he asked, and my eyes were on the road and my mind elsewhere because I grunted and said, "Why?"

"The guy in the car you just passed—the one that looked like ours—did you see him?"

My first instinct was to glance in the rearview mirror—at Rusty's face, half filling it on the right, the features matching the worried tone of his voice—and then at the car in the right lane, now receding, almost as if it had stopped. It was at least a quarter mile behind me now. I could see the front grill, a lot of plastic chrome, squarish, just like my car and a million others on the road. There was a glint off the windshield.

"What about him?" I asked.

"He just looked..." Rusty left the statement unfinished, and I glanced at him again in the rearview mirror. I moved my head so I could briefly study Mona, sitting next to him. She, too, had a strange look on her face.

"Did you see him, Mom?" Rusty asked.

"No," Debra said, in a clipped tone.

"No need to snap at the kid—"I started, but she cut me off, as always.

"I'll say any damn thing I like," she said, and without looking at her I knew she wore *the glare*.

I took a deep breath and said, "Let's try to keep the trip pleasant."

"Pleasant as you like," she said, only now I was studying the rearview mirror again, my kids in the back seat whose looks had turned stony.

"So what did he look like, Rusty?" I asked, trying to change the subject in the suddenly quiet car.

He shrugged, looking away.

"Whatever," he mumbled.

"Look," I said, in a measured tone, knowing I was using the conciliatory tone they all knew a mile away. "I know the trip has been difficult so far, but I think we should try to get along better."

Debra was silent, eyes closed, leaning back into the headrest. Rusty and Mona were looking out each of their side windows, lips tight.

"Christ," I said, letting out my breath. I almost yanked the car into the right lane and then into the service lane, where I would slam on the brakes, but I had already tried that and nothing had come of it. I briefly studied my hands, tightly gripping the steering wheel.

"*Christ.*"

"Just drive, Harry," Debra said, keeping her eyes closed.

I counted to ten and watched my hands relax on the wheel.

For a while I looked at nothing but the road in front of me. The radio had been turned down during one of the previous fights and I turned the knob back up, flooding the car momentarily with oldies music before turning it back down to a reasonable level.

"Sorry," I said, but still kept my eyes on the road.

Suddenly the music started to annoy me, and I twisted the knob, turning the radio off. I studied the faces on the three people in the car with me.

I counted to a hundred, then said, "Anybody hungry?"

There was a brief silence, then Mona said, not too glumly, "Sure."

"Rusty?" I asked, waiting for his reply.

"Why not," he answered, sulkily.

"Eating now might be a good idea," Debra said, opening her eyes with her head still on the headrest. She was staring at the visor in the up position in front of her. There was a little mirror on it.

"All right then!" I said, forcing cheer into my voice and beginning to study road signs. "Anyone spots a fast food sign, let me know."

A few moments later Mona said, "There!"

Sure enough, a billboard for the golden arches had appeared, as if by magic. TWO MILES UP, it said.

"We're on the way!"

I eased the car into the right lane, then, two miles on, left the highway and we ate.

The meal started well enough; the food seemed to revive everyone's spirits, and Mona and Rusty, between sips of cola, had enough energy to begin sparring lightly. When it looked like it might go past the giggling-pushing stage I stepped in, since Mona wasn't about to.

"That's enough, kids. Save it for the park."

"I still don't think we should go," Debra said, and I knew that we were on the same old path and that the moment of peace had ended.

"We discussed all that before we left," I said, watching myself ball my napkin, squeezing it tighter and tighter.

"I know—" Debra began coldly, but then the kids chimed in.

"You said we could, Mom!" Rusty cried, almost simultaneously with Mona, who reached out imploringly, without touching her mother.

"You said we could!"

Debra was silent, seemingly studying the empty, grease-stained fries carton in front of her.

"Then let's go," she said suddenly, getting up, not waiting for the rest of us to catch up as she pushed through the glass door to the parking lot, where, arms folded, looking away, she waited for me to unlock the car door.

It didn't take long before the fighting began again. Like a virus, it spread from the back seat, where Rusty and Mona continued their giggling and pushing but soon started jabbing and yelling at each other. Then it spread into the front seat where Debra, lips clenched, said so that only I could hear, "I told you this was a bad idea."

THE MAN IN THE OTHER CAR

My knuckles where white on the steering wheel. The road constricted in front of me, and I could feel the blood roaring through my veins and into my temples, where a rhythmic pounding began that I knew might not end until I lay down with a cold, wet, folded cloth over my eyes.

There was a break in the highway divider just ahead to the left, a turnaround for the highway cops, and I nearly twisted the wheel towards it when I suddenly spied a sign, in cool green with white letters and an etching of pine trees above it, for the park.

"Hey!" I said, my headache abruptly vanished, my spirits lifted, "we're almost—"

"Dad!" Rusty cried suddenly, from the back seat, in a voice that sounded as if he had been hurt.

I twisted around and said, "Mona, if you harmed your brother—"

Rusty was looking out the window, his eyes tracking a car that was in the right lane, fading behind us.

I turned back to the road as Rusty said, with worry in his voice, "It was that guy again."

"Who?"

"The one I saw before, in the car like ours—didn't you see him?"

The headache was coming back, a pounding that grew quickly behind my eyes. Again I was gripping the steering wheel hard. Debra was feigning sleep beside me.

I took a deep breath and answered, with my teeth clenched, "No, *dammit, I didn't see him.*"

In the rearview mirror Rusty's eyes were large with fright. Guilt pushed through my rage and I evened my voice. "I didn't see him, son."

Almost as an afterthought, I glanced away from Rusty and, in the mirror, saw the car with the plastic-chromed grille far behind.

I could not make out the driver, but it was definitely the same car, blue-gray, nondescript except for its cheap chrome trim.

"I think we should go home," Debra said suddenly, in the calm, cruel voice she sometimes used because she knew that it cut through my head like a knife.

"*What!*" I screamed, the pounding in my temples accelerating to a beat that made me literally see red for a moment. I yanked the wheel hard to the right, cutting across the thankfully empty right lane and then onto the shoulder of the road, at the same time braking to a screeching, fish-tailing halt.

My vision was slowly clearing, but I could feel my head about to burst as the children in the back seat began to howl.

"*You can't!*" Mona whined. "*You promised us the park! You can't turn around!*"

"*Nooooo!*" Rusty added, making the din complete, his wail circling and tightening around his sister's moaning. There was a roar in my ears that only added to the near-unbearable level of noise in the car.

I fought with myself, tried to control my breathing and then, unable to keep silent screamed: "*ENOUGH!*"

The car quieted, Rusty's wail spiraling down to hitching sobs. I turned to face Debra, who was sitting like stone, lips tightly clenched, eyes staring through the windshield.

"Are you happy now?" I hissed.

"We never should have come," she said, her voice infuriatingly matter-of-fact. "Turn around and go home."

"You should have said that an hour ago. We're two miles from the park!" I replied, unable to speak in a calm tone.

Mona suddenly leaned over the front seat between Debra and I and wailed, "Only two miles, Mom! *Two miles!* Pleaaaaase?"

I kept my eyes on my wife, who sat like a statue in the seat beside me; a vein pulsed in her neck like a separate live thing and her lips remained pursed until she said again, her voice a tight whisper, "We never should have come."

Rusty's mewling began to increase in volume, and then Debra turned her face abruptly to me, blank and unreadable as pond ice, and said quietly, "All right."

"Yayyyy!" Mona said, throwing herself away from us and into the back seat again. Rusty's mewl vanished instantly, as if a switch had been thrown.

"Yayyyy! We're going to the park!" Mona exulted, and in a moment she and her brother were poking and giggling at each other as if nothing had happened.

"You're sure?" I asked my wife, who's face was as impassive as it had been.

"Drive," she said, and I nodded, letting out a long breath, feeling my whole body unclench, and signaling to pull back out onto the highway. I watched a car pass close, and then the road was clear.

"Dad!" Rusty shouted, "That car—!"

I looked and saw the car like ours, the vague outline of passengers through the rear window.

"The same one?" I asked, turning to look at my son.

He nodded, his face pale.

The car was gone, far ahead.

I turned my attention back to the still-empty road and carefully pulled out into the right lane.

"Park, here we come!" I said, with the heartiest of false cheer.

"*Yayyyy!*" Mona shouted, too loudly, making me wince.

Debra was staring out through the windshield again, her statuesque mode complete, even the throbbing vein in her neck absent.

I pushed at the accelerator with my foot, and we passed a sign that said, PARK, ONE MILE.

"*Yayyyyyyyyyyy!*" Mona said, and I recoiled at the way her shout assaulted my ears.

"*Dad!*" Rusty screeched suddenly, making me jump, and I reflexively turned to hit him but he was pointing to the right and ahead of us. "Look!"

I turned my head forward and saw the car with the cheap chrome grille parked in the service lane, its doors open, its emergency blinkers flashing.

"It's—!" Rusty began.

"I know," I replied.

I slowed down, hearing the tires hiss quietly on the roadway, and as we glided by I stared at my car, at the man who was killing his wife and two children on the side of the road.

So I pulled off the highway and did.

HEDGES

I THOUGHT, *Will I finally belong?*

I passed the boy at dawn on my bicycle. He was standing in the middle of the road, his backpack slung over one shoulder, the way students do. He was reed-thin and tall, a little hunched at the shoulders, with a cranberry colored baseball cap on backwards. Grinning slightly, ironically—again, the way students do.

There was no danger of hitting him, but I wondered why he was standing in the middle of the street. Then I saw the school far ahead on the left, set back off the road, in the middle of a cleared field. There were lights on in the windows that looked like they had burned all night. They may have been bright in the darkness but now, with the sun rising behind the school, they looked defeated and dim. After giving me a smirk as I passed, the boy slouched toward the school.

I peddled on.

Before the school on either side was a short packed line of small houses, bordered by a thick hedge. Suddenly the dawn was banished back to night. Overhead were crouching, overarching oak trees, their branches brushing like the fingertips of lovers.

The hedges grew thicker to either side, a wall of April green buds on winter-sharp branches. It was dark gray as midnight, and the air had cooled. I was suddenly tired, and I slowed, and then the bicycle, urged by my slowing, tilted to the right and leaned me over against the hedge.

It held me pricking, a wall of sharp sticks and tiny faintly perfumed wet buds, and I heard a faint voice I could not make out. It sounded like it said, *Yes.* The voice was very close. I pushed myself away from the hedge, my hands sinking momentarily into it, branches scratching, and something else, something that felt almost liquid and very cold, drew over my hand and then away.

I pulled my body back in disgust and fumbled at the bicycle, which caught against my straddling leg and again moved me over into the hedge.

The voice was right next to my ear, whispering, *Yessss.*

I flailed back, pushing my left foot against the bicycle pedal as I straightened the machine with a scrape and pushed off, back out into the road—

A car passed, close by in the gray darkness, horn bleating. Its lights were dimmed, swallowed by the encroaching gray, and a pale oval face, hairless, lit with a green inner light, peered out at me from the rear window as it drew roaring away.

The hedge was next to me again.

I heard the whisper and felt cold pushing toward me and lurched back, dragging the bike sideways, making its tires scrape with complaint. My feet fumbled and found the pedal and then I was off again, straightening the front wheel.

But now in the grayness I saw the hedge narrowing in front of me.

I began to fight for breath.

The oaks had disappeared overhead and the hedge had grown up around into a crowning arbor. The air was chilled, damp, sick-sweet smelling.

The hedge narrowed into a closing dead end; I heard beyond it the fading roar of the car I had seen with the pale green face staring—

I thrust my feet backwards against the pedals, making the bike stop with a screech, then forced it around. Already the hedge had grown down from above, almost touching my head.

It was narrowing on all sides ahead of me, like a closing wedge.

With a shout I hit the pedals hard, keeping low, and shot through the narrowing opening even as it closed. I felt the scrape of budding branches like grasping bony fingers on me, and smelled something wet and lush and fetid, and heard what sounded like a sigh—

Gasping for breath I tore ahead, blinded by sudden sunlight. Ahead of me on the left was the school, its windows filled with rising sunlight now, the field in front of it full of milling students.

The loud blare of a horn made me stop short; in front of me was a school bus grinding to a halt, its brakes squealing. The driver was shouting at me behind the huge windshield set into the massive yellow front.

In a daze, I moved the bicycle off to the curb as the school bus ground into gear again. The driver glared at me as he drove past, then pulled into the long driveway toward the front entrance of the school.

I looked behind me.

The street, dappled in tree-shaded new morning sun, stretched straight behind me, lined to either side by a row of neat houses, cape cods and cute ranches. There was no sign of a hedge as far as the eye could see.

In the far distance was a cross street, a busy one by the look of the traffic at the intersection.

I felt a tap on my shoulder.

"Wha—"

An equally startled face peered back at me: a crossing guard, an older woman with a white cloth bandolier across her jacket holding a small red stop sign.

"I'm sorry," I began. "I'm new here, a Chemistry teacher, I start today—"

"You could have been hit by that bus," she said, concern and scolding in her voice. "You were tearing along in the middle of the street—"

"Can I ask you something?" I interrupted. "Has there ever been a long row of hedges in the street back there?" I pointed to the spot from which I had come.

"Hedges?" She looked confused.

"I'm sorry," I said, and began to pedal away, turning in toward the school. "I'll be more careful."

"Do that," she said, the scolding tone coming back into her voice. "There are children around here, you know…"

"So how did it go?" Jacqueline asked, with, as always, neither concern nor interest in her tone. A fresh vodka tonic in a clear tall glass lay on the kitchen table before her. Beads of cool perspiration freckled the glass. She did not offer me one but instead sipped her own, looking out the kitchen window to the backyard, a riot of green trees and untended bushes.

"About as expected," I answered.

"You mean like all the rest?" There was an undercurrent of venom in her voice now. *I told you so* and *I knew it* and *Here we go again*, her tone said, without her saying it.

I tried anyway. "Have you ever felt, Jacqueline, that you just didn't fit in? The children in this school are even worse than normal. They didn't show any interest at all. It was like I was talking to thirty sacks of potatoes. And the Vice Principal was almost unfriendly. I have the same bad feeling, Jacqueline. Just like all the other times. Like I don't belong. Haven't you ever felt that way?"

She sighed heavily, and turned her near-perfect face, framed in long black hair, slowly away from the window toward me. She pinned me with her violet eyes. "I've *always* belonged, Howard. The only question I've ever asked myself is why in hell I married you."

I opened my mouth but she turned her attention back to the window and her drink.

"The back yard needs tending," she said, tonelessly. "Every one of these houses we've rented, in every one of these rotten little towns, always has an overgrown backyard. This one's worse than the rest. Do something about it."

I said nothing.

As I turned and left the kitchen she called out casually, "I'm going out for dinner. There're TV dinners in the freezer if you want something. And I'll need the car again tomorrow."

✦ ✦ ✦

The next day was no better. When I entered the classroom all the desks were facing the back of the room. The day before, every student had been staring intently at the ceiling, which made me look, too. The boy in the cranberry-colored baseball cap was among them. From that moment on, when they all broke into laughter, they had me. Today was no better. I should have made a joke, but nothing came to mind.

I tried to teach the day's lesson, to ignore them, but instead they ignored me, kept their desks turned around.

Soon they began to talk and joke.

The chalk trembled in my hand. I closed my eyes, leaned my forehead against the cool blackboard and then turned around, trembling with rage.

"This isn't right!" I stammered hoarsely, but they ignored me.

I dropped the chalk and walked out of the classroom.

The Assistant Principal was there in the hallway, and I almost ran into her.

"Having a bit of trouble?" she asked, and I couldn't help but detect the near-disdain in her voice.

"Yes. I—"

She moved around me and stuck her head in the classroom door.

"That's *enough*!" she shouted. "Get those desks back where they belong!"

There was instant quiet, followed by the shuffling of moving furniture.

The Assistant Principal confronted me again in the hall.

"Just treat 'em like animals," she said, giving me a smile that told me what she already knew: that I wasn't capable of treating them like animals, or anything at all.

She turned on her heels and marched off.

When I walked back into the classroom the talking began again. By the end of the period they had all faced their desks toward the back of the classroom once more.

I took a different route home, the same I had ridden that morning. There had been no trouble then, but this time as I left the school behind me, turning my bicycle into a wide street with houses set well back on manicured lawns, a wall of hedges suddenly thrust up in front of me. I drew to a stop. The wall was rushing like a living wave toward me. I turned my bike only to see another behind me. To either side the houses began to disappear, sharp green buds pushing out from their trim fronts, doors and windows and shutters, devouring them. The hedge drew in on me from all sides. I felt cool wet green and smelled rich oxygen.

"*No!*" I shouted in panic.

There was a driveway to my right, still clear of obstruction, and I drove the bicycle that way, the hedges closing in on me as I did so. As the driveway reached the side of the house branches pushed out of the siding toward me. The house disappeared in a blanket of green. The hedges pushed the bike to the right, where another wall of green awaited me. I felt the caress of soft buds and a whisper in my ear.

Yesss...

I screamed, driving the bicycle forward. There was a free-standing garage in front of me bursting into green before my eyes, the hedge closing in from both sides in front of it. But there was a slim opening to the left leading to the backyard and I peddled fiercely at it, pushing through as the branches like cold hands sought to pull me in—

And then I was through the suffocating hedge, the bike shooting forward into the clear backyard and toward a well-separated line of forsythia bushes that marked the backyard boundary between houses.

I stopped, skidding on the grass, and turned around.

The house was as it had been—neat, trim, unblemished by green limbs and tiny leaves.

The hedge was gone from the driveway, from the far street.

I turned and dismounted the bicycle, rolling it through a gap between forsythias and into the abutting backyard and then to a new street and eventually home.

I tried one more time.

"I just don't fit in."

Jacqueline laughed. "You've never fit in," she said, her voice slurred, and then she laughed shortly again. "And I do mean that in every way."

She was disheveled, the front of her dress buttoned incorrectly. She had obviously had much more to drink than the vodka in front of her. Her lipstick was smeared and her eyes unfocused as she bobbed her head around to regard me.

She smiled.

"I'll need the car tomor—"

"Have you ever felt physically smothered?" I asked, ignoring her.

She looked at her vodka tonic. "All the time."

"No, I mean physically. For *real*. Like everything, everything you've tried and failed at, your whole life, all your unhappiness, was literally closing in on you. As if...hedges, actual green hedges, were pushing you in from all sides and wanted to swallow you whole—"

It was her turn to interrupt. She laughed and then hiccupped, then brought her drink to her lips before putting it down again.

"Harold, you *are* a moron." She got unsteadily to her feet, forgot the drink, pushing it aside. It tipped over and fell from the kitchen table, breaking in a pool of clear liquid and glass shards.

She moved past me unsteadily, pointing languidly at the refrigerator.

"TV. Dinner," she said. "I'm...out. Need the car... tomorrow. Ride your bike again..."

She walked to the front door, leaving it open behind her, and in a few moments I heard the car door slam and then the engine start.

In the empty house I looked out through the kitchen window at the backyard, overgrown with weeds and bushes and what looked for a moment like a rising tide of hedges, which abruptly vanished.

I took a third route the next morning. After Jacqueline had left the night before, the Assistant Principal had called and told me the school had decided it wasn't working out and that I should not continue teaching. Would I please come in the next morning to sign some papers and pick up a check for two days' work.

The new route was out of the way but clear. In effect, I was riding in a wide circle to get to the school.

As I turned onto an unfamiliar street that would bring me back in the right direction, the boy with the cranberry-colored baseball cap was crossing the street in front of me.

He leered at me as I went by and shouted, "So long!"

I put my head down and rode faster.

When I brought my head up, I gasped.

"No!"

Hedges were pushing in at me from all sides, and the sky was quickly blacking out from a lowering cloud of green.

Buds burst from the street below me, snarling the spokes of the bicycle and then stopping it dead.

Branches twined around the handlebars, the seat, yanking the bike out of my grasp.

I felt a cold wet touch slide across my fingers, my face.

Yessss.

When I tried to scream, hedge shoots snaked over and up my body and deep into my mouth.

I was pushed onto my back and lifted in a cocoon of branches and leaves.

I gagged, and then the voice sounded close by my ear.

You don't understand.

I continued to thrash, to fight, watching the last glimmer of the world, a tiny hole of blue sky, blotted out above me by a tiny green wet leaf.

Think...

"No—!"

And then, suddenly, as if a switch had been thrown in my head, I did understand, and I stopped fighting.

"Yes!" I cried.

The hedge enclosed me, into itself.

Yesss.

HEDGES

My fingers are cold and wet, with green fresh buds
at the ends.
I belong.

THE SILLY STUFF

No, I TELL YOU I'm on to something, Bill. You *have* to keep printing them!"

The voice on the other end of the line said something nasty.

"Oh, yeah? And the same to you!" Nathan Halpern slammed the wall phone back into its cradle. Instinctively he checked the coin return to see if anything had dropped into it. "Damn," he said, and walked back to the bar.

The bartender smiled. "Almost never works."

Halpern waved him off, taking a sip of his beer. "That's not what I'm mad about," he said. He pulled a crumpled newspaper clipping from the pocket of his equally rumpled sports jacket and pushed it across the bar. "Here," he said, "look at this."

It was a slow Wednesday afternoon in the Golden Spoon Tavern, in the dead center of a killing August heat wave. The lunch crowd, what little there was of it, had long gone, and besides Nathan Halpern the only other customers the bartender had to worry about were two regulars at the other end of the bar, each of whom, like clockwork, drank one scotch on the rocks every half-hour; and since it was nearly twenty minutes until the next round was due, the bartender could afford to socialize. He took the clipping and read:

FISH FALL FROM SKY

Copanah, NY (Aug. 12)—Residents of the small town of Copanah, ten miles northeast of Albany, reported a rain of dead fish yesterday. The creatures, which allegedly resembled cod in appearance, were scattered over an area two miles square, and local residents insist that they dropped from the heavens.

One elderly resident of the town, Sam Driller, whose integrity was vouched for by several neighbors including Copanah's mayor, stated that he had gone out to move some trash cans to the street for pickup when "a whole barrelful of fish dropped right on top of me. I looked up, and the sky's full of 'em—they was dropping right out of the clouds. It ain't natural, but I swear I saw it."

Two local policemen and the daughter of the town librarian also witnessed the event, and local authorities could offer no explanation. A spokesman for Margolies Air Force Base, thirty miles away, reports that none of its aircraft were in the air at that time.

The bartender folded the clipping and handed it back to Halpern. "So?" he said. "Silly stuff like that turns up in the papers every summer." He cocked his head toward the telephone on the wall. "I heard part of your conversation. You wrote this?"

"Yeah." Halpern nodded glumly. "And you don't think there's anything to it either?"

The bartender drew Halpern another beer, setting it down in front of him. "That one's on the house. To tell you the truth, no."

Halpern leaned across the bar and tapped his finger against the wood. "I checked every one of those witnesses myself."

The bartender shrugged. "Doesn't mean a thing. All those people could easily have been lying."

Halpern nearly knocked his beer over. "No way!" he said excitedly. "I know it's supposed to be the dog days and all that, but this stuff is for real. I've checked it out. It goes on all the time, all over the place. Little clusters of reports here, little clusters there. The only reason you see more stuff in the paper in July and August is because there's nothing else to print. But these things actually happen all the time, since before newspapers existed. And this time they're happening here in Albany County."

The bartender still looked skeptical.

"Look—" Halpern took a sip of beer and wiped his mouth with his sleeve. "—have you ever heard of Charles Fort?"

The bartender scratched his head. "Wrote a bunch of paperbacks, right?"

Halpern nodded. "Something like that. Fort was a kind of journalist. Spent over twenty-five years in the New York Public Library and the British Museum collecting stories from newspapers and scientific journals—stories like the one I showed you. He had thousands and thousands of clippings and articles, and he put them into books like *Lo!* and *The Book of the Damned*. He documented all kinds of weird things— wolf children, devil sightings, flying saucers, volcanic eruptions spewing out human limbs instead of lava— you name it. He didn't take all of it seriously, but he was convinced that everything that happens is somehow *connected*; that there is only one unified reality that everything is tied to. One of his favorite quotes was, 'I think we're all property.'"

The bartender laughed. "We are," he said. "We're all owned by the IRS."

Halpern didn't smile. "Charles Fort was no nut. Hell, after he died back in the thirties, a bunch of people like Theodore Dreiser, Ben Hecht, and Alexander Woollcott got together and started the Fortean Society to continue the work he was doing. It still exists."

The half-hour chime sounded on the cuckoo clock over the cash register, and the bartender mixed and delivered two more scotches to the regulars. When he came back, he looked thoughtful.

"So you really think there's something behind it?"

Halpern nodded. "I've checked out too many of these stories to think they're all baloney. I swear there's a pattern to it all, just like Fort believed."

"Well, I'm still unconvinced. From what I've seen behind this bar, you can find patterns wherever you want to."

Halpern leaned close, and a conspiratorial tone came into his voice. "Do you know someone named Rita Gartenburg?"

"Sure," the bartender replied. "I've lived down the block from her for twenty years."

"She a drunk? Or a nut?"

"No way!" said the bartender. "Never seen her in here or any other gin mill in town. And she's no kook. She's a nice, steady lady who grows prize roses in her backyard."

"Well," said Halpern, "prize-winning or not, she told me she saw a bunch of those same rosebushes get up off the ground and walk around."

The bartender's jaw dropped. "You must be kidding."

"That's what she told me," said Halpern, "and that's the way I'm going to report it. She even took a couple of pictures, but the damn things didn't come out."

The bartender shrugged. "I don't know what to think."

Halpern downed his beer and prepared to leave. "You know," he said, "I used to be a hotshot columnist, weekdays *and* in the Sunday supplement. Political reporter." He shook his head. "But I never believed anything as strongly as I believe this stuff. I've been at it two months now, ever since the Fourth of July, when a bunch of kids near my house said they saw a skyrocket land back on the ground and run away." He gave a short laugh and held two fingers a quarter-inch apart as he backed through the door. "I'm telling you, there's something there, and I'm getting closer to it all the time."

SKY GOES BLACK AT NOON
ON SUNNY DAY

Sumptersville, NY (Aug. 20)—According to residents of Sagerstown, four miles east of Sumptersville, the sky suddenly turned black at twelve noon yesterday. Local weather charts showed that the day was cloudless and sunny, with north-northwest winds at six to eight miles per hour, but an affidavit signed by nearly all of the seventy-six residents of the tiny community, known statewide for its annual cornbread festival each September, swore that at exactly twelve o'clock "the sky went completely dark, as if God Himself had pulled a light switch off."

There were no stars visible during the occurrence, which lasted approximately five minutes, and an eerie silence seemed to come over the town. Then suddenly, according to the statement, it was bright daylight again.

Witnesses and signers of the affidavit included six members of the local town council, as well as retired weatherman Jed Burns, who worked for local TV station WWWM for twenty-three years. Reached for comment, Burns said that he was "still in a stunned condition" and had no idea what had happened. He said he has tried to get the U.S. Weather Bureau involved in the matter, but that so far they have shown no interest.

"I tell you, Bill," Halpern yelled into the phone, "I'm real close."

There was silence on the other end for a moment, and then a squawking sound that lasted for a minute and a half.

At the end of it Halpern waited a few seconds. "No, Bill," he said calmly, "I have not been out in the sun too long. I've told you from the beginning of this thing that you should just let me run with it, and I'm telling you again. When I break it open, I'll come back to Albany and be a good boy."

THE SILLY STUFF

There was another short squawk on the other end.

"That's right, a good boy. Cover the state legislature and everything. I promise. But you have to let me follow this through."

Another squawk.

"That's right. Six-headed chickens and all. But that was yesterday, editor mine. Today it was ball-point pens dropping through the ceiling of a supermarket."

Another squawk—actually, more of a screech this time, louder and more insistent.

"Didn't you hear me at all? I said I'm beginning to see a pattern to all this. This could be my chance to be Woodward and Bernstein, Bill."

Squawk.

"No, I haven't actually seen any of it. I always seem to be one town behind, and when I guess where the next thing will occur, I always guess wrong. But I'll break the code. And yes, the chicken *could* have been fake, but it wasn't. Believe me, it's beginning to click."

Silence on the other end; then a low, rasping sound.

"That's right, Bill—Woodward and Bernstein. Sure you got that whole story? Okay, call you tomorrow."

COW GIVES BIRTH TO TWO DOGS

Pokerton, NY (Aug. 23)—Bill Gainesborough, a small farmer in this dairy farming community, swears that one of his cows gave birth to two puppies earlier this week. Gainesborough, who was upset by the event and hesitant to talk about it to reporters, stated that his cow Ilse, one of thirty milk cows on the farm, gave birth to two dogs "right in front of my eyes."

The puppies are cocker spaniels, and there are no cocker spaniel owners within ten miles of the Gainesborough property. Neighbors, who urged the farmer to talk about what had happened, swore that Gainesborough was not the kind of man to pull a hoax. The puppies were given to a local foundling home.

Halpern didn't call his editor back the next day. On Wednesday the twenty-fifth he found himself in Lolarkin, where a group of schoolboys claimed to have seen three moons in the sky. Thursday the twenty-sixth found him in Crater, where two grandmothers and twelve of their kin swore that their house had lifted itself off its foundation, turned around 180 degrees, and set itself back down again. On Friday he was in Peach Hollow, just missing a rain of black tar. Saturday he spent in Cooperville, arriving a scant three minutes after two hamsters had talked in a crowded pet store; he'd guessed right on that location, but had miscalculated as to time. Sunday morning the twenty-ninth he sat in a diner in Reseda, staring at a horribly creased map of the state, when suddenly the pattern rose before his blurry eyes.

He shoved the map under his arm as he dialed the phone. His hands were shaking. He stared back across the room at his eggs getting cold while the phone rang.

"Bill, it's me."

This time there wasn't squawking, but rather a high and steady whine.

"I *know* it's Sunday morning. No, I didn't know it was six o'clock. I've been up all night."

His hands wouldn't stop shaking.

THE SILLY STUFF

"Shut up, Bill," he said into the phone as the whining started up again. He fumbled the map up to his eyes. "It's simple as hell. Crisscross, crisscross. These things have been making little *x*'s all over the county. And you know what that means? Something, some single source, is behind it all."

Silence.

"Did you hear me?"

Silence again. Then a carefully phrased question.

"No, I won't tell you where I am. Wait for me to phone in my story. But I'll bet you even money that I'm in the place where the next thing happens. Just another day or two, Bill. That's all I need."

Silence. Then a sigh.

"Thanks, Bill. If you were here I'd kiss your ugly face."

BOY TELEPORTED FROM
OWN HOUSE TO NEIGHBOR'S

Grafton, NY (Aug. 30)—Ten-year-old Bobby Milestone, who vanished into thin air while playing quietly in his own front yard today, was found an hour later in the home of Grafton neighbor Mr. Fred Warbling. The youth claimed to remember nothing that happened to him between the time he vanished and reappeared. "I was out front one second," he stated, "and the next second I was on top of Mr. Warbling's car in his garage."

The youth vanished before the startled eyes of his uncle, Mr. Eugene Milestone, who was looking out the window when the incident occurred. "It was like somebody yanked him out of the air," Mr. Milestone said.

This reporter was on hand and participated in the massive hour-long search, which was mounted immediately after young Milestone vanished. No explanation has been offered for the youth's disappearance and subsequent reappearance.

Halpern called in the Milestone piece on Monday afternoon over Bill Greener's loud protestations. All the rest of the day he double- and triple-checked his calculations, readying himself for the next day's sighting. He rented a car and was on the road before nightfall, munching periodically on a bucket of fried chicken as he drove. Before leaving he sent a cable to Greener which read: I WAS RIGHT, YOU SUCKER. HAVE REACHED END OF SEARCH. WILL KNOW ALL TOMORROW. BRACE FOR BIG STORY.

He drove for four hours, pulling to a halt well before dawn at his calculated site. There was no moon and the visibility was bad, but he seemed to be on a road at the edge of a vast, rolling valley in the middle of nowhere. He shrugged and went to sleep for a couple of hours, awakening just as dawn broke. When he looked out the window, his eyes widened.

"My God," he gasped, "I was right."

There, a scant fifty yards off the dusty road, sat a machine. It looked like nothing so much as an airship, a dirigible-like structure with a long cabin slung underneath. It bore no identifiable markings.

As Halpern drew closer, he saw that his first impression had been a bit mistaken; the thing was not quite as rickety as it had first appeared. It was smoothly metallic and resembled a conventional cigar-shaped flying saucer.

And as he crept even closer, he saw that there was a doorway in the cabin underneath, and a figure leaning against it with his arms folded. Just as Halpern reached the ship, the figure waved languidly and turned away, disappearing inside. Cautiously Halpern poked his head through the opening—and heard someone say, in an even tone, "Please come in, Mr. Halpern."

He entered the craft, stepping as if he were walking on eggs.

Inside, the cabin was a cluttered mess; stacks of papers and charts lay everywhere. A man was at the front of the structure, bending over a control panel composed of antique knobs and a huge bronze steering wheel. Two globes, one celestial and one terrestrial, were mounted on either side.

The man turned, and Halpern at once thought he looked vaguely familiar. He was strongly built, taller than average, and bore a slight resemblance to Teddy Roosevelt, with a bushy moustache and curling hair parted a bit left of center. He wore a pince-nez, and Halpern was at once taken with the calmness of the gray eyes behind it. He also wore a three-piece woolen suit with a watch-chain and fob attached.

"Please sit down, sir," the man said, indicating a camp stool off to the right. "I'll be with you in a moment." He turned to the control panel, and Halpern spun around to see the door to the craft closing with a smooth hiss. Moments later there was a nearly undetectable bump. They were airborne.

With a sigh the man turned from the control board and confronted Halpern with those calm gray eyes.

✦ ✦ ✦

"I must congratulate you," he said, "on your perseverance. I was happy to see you'd found my little pattern. And that you were clever enough to notice that the last little x in my grid of x's would be completed today." The corners of his eyes wrinkled upward—in mirth or perhaps something else. "Very resourceful. You thought there might be something at the end of my rainbow of crisscrosses, eh?"

Halpern nodded cautiously.

The stranger suddenly thrust out his hand. "Well, you were right, of course. My name is Charles Fort, sir."

The man paused a moment to watch Halpern's jaw drop, then went on: "You've become something of a pest these last few weeks, you know. But I must say you've been an interesting pest." Once again his eyes seemed to twinkle.

"You *can't* be Charles Fort," said Halpern. "Fort died fifty years ago."

The other's eyebrows went up. "Did he? I suppose you need a bit of explanation, eh?"

Halpern said nothing.

"First of all," the man said, "I really am Charles Fort. Or was, anyway, for a time. Actually, you might call me a kind of 'overseer.' I was sent here to Earth a very long time ago, Mr. Halpern. My life here as Charles Fort, from 1874 to 1932, was an enjoyable sidelight to my real task, and so to amuse myself I decided to document some of my own doings."

Halpern's eyes widened. "You mean *you* made all the strange things happen? The trees flying around, the puppies—all that?"

THE SILLY STUFF

Fort smiled modestly. "That's right. Beautifully ironic, isn't it? That Charles Fort not only documented all sorts of bizarre phenomena, but actually *caused* them all!" Laughing, he gestured toward the controls. "I do it all with these little knobs. Flying frogs, double suns, night for day, day for night, invisibility—all the silly stuff."

"I can't believe it!" said Halpern. "*Why?*"

Fort's laughter ended in a sigh. "Well," he said, "I've been here a very long time. Doing a job." He yawned, then glanced behind him out of the port windows, pushing at the rudder wheel a fraction. "Not a very exciting one, I'm afraid. Let's just say my job was to start things rolling on this planet, as far as civilization was concerned, and then to—" A hint of a smile touched his lips. "—help things along, so to speak. *Not* to interfere," he added hastily, "but rather to keep you moving, evolving, keep you on your toes. We're not allowed to interfere directly, you know." He smiled dreamily, fingering his lapel. "I always liked the clothes from the turn of this century best."

Halpern was getting impatient. "But why did you invent Charles Fort?"

"*Boredom*, Mr. Halpern. Flying around in this ship all the time, causing mischief here and there—it all gets exceedingly tiring. So I decided to live among you for a while. I made up a being named Charles Fort. Gave him birth records, a family history, everything he needed. Granted, I was bending the rules a bit. But if all I did was chronicle my own doings, I wasn't *directly* interfering, was I? And my job at the same time—doubly so, since I was not only perpetrating all those 'unexplained phenomena,' but bringing them to your attention at the same time. As I said, beautifully ironic."

"But what's all this 'overseer' stuff? You mean to say you came here just to play tricks on us?"

Fort sighed heavily. "For better or for worse, Mr. Halpern, somebody a long time ago decided that this was the way to bring young civilizations along. The object is, quite simply, to make you *think*. To make you look at the world as a strange and beautiful place with mysteries still not fathomed—which, of course, it is." He gave the rudder another touch. "And the more you wonder about what's behind this weird, wonderful universe you live in, sooner or later you'll begin to realize that everything is rather neatly tied together—that it's all a unity. And the sooner you come to understand that unity, the sooner you can, well, join the club, so to speak. While I was Charles Fort down below I cheated a little by sneaking some of that monistic philosophy into my books. But what's a little cheating in a good cause, eh?" He smiled. "So you see, all my hijinks are really just a teaching tool." Suddenly he came over to Halpern and put his arm around his shoulder. "I bet you can't *wait* to get back and tell your story, eh?"

"Yes..." said Halpern cautiously.

"Well, you must let me show you a few of my little tricks first, and then we'll get you back to your office, safe and sound. You see, I *know* what it's like to be a newspaperman."

Once more the limpid gray pools of Fort's eyes sparkled as he led Halpern toward the back of the airship.

"I have a little confession to make," he said, smiling paternally. "You're the first human being I ever let catch me in the act. That's *really* bending the rules, isn't it? But since I'm getting you back to your office, I guess I'm not interfering all that much."

THE SILLY STUFF

"Sure, why not?" said Halpern, suddenly buoyant, thoughts straying once again to Woodward and Bernstein. He laughed. "That really was a clever line of yours, by the way. 'I think we're all property.' Very clever."

"It was at that, wasn't it?" Fort smiled.

VIOLENT INCIDENT
AT DATA TERMINAL

Albany Complex, NY (Aug. 31, 2082)—An intruder dressed in pre-Millennium clothes and claiming to be an employee of the *Albany Sun* caused minor damage at this station's mid-Complex terminal earlier today. The man, who identified himself as Nathan Halpern, stated in loud terms that he was a top *Sun* "columnist," demanded a "typewriter" (such devices have not been used at the *Sun* since it was computerized over forty years ago), and further demanded to see one Bill Greener, whom he identified as his "editor."

The lone operator at the terminal at the time of the incident, Rupert Popkin, attempted to calm the intruder down, but as Popkin stated later, the man "went into a wild fit, repeating the names Woodward and Bernstein over and over and claiming he had been kidnapped by a UFO and put into suspended animation."

According to Popkin, who suffered minor cuts and bruises, the man then became violent and had to be taken into custody by security personnel, but somehow managed to escape while en route to Albany Complex Psychiatric Center. Witnesses at the scene reported that he ran off shaking his fist at the sky and shouting, "I'll find you if it's the last thing I do!" As of this time, he remains at large.

Curiously, a check of files shows that an individual named Bill Greener did work at the *Sun* in the late twentieth century. However, no record of anyone named Nathan Halpern has been found.

THE NEW KID

THURSDAY

I *hate* being the new kid in school.

Today was the same as it's been ever since I moved here. When I got off the bus the line of bullies, sixth graders with a few fifth graders thrown in for spice, were waiting for me. Chunky Fredericks, the biggest one and the leader, smiled his gap-toothed grin and said, "Nice to see you again, loser!" He slapped me on the back, hard enough to make me stumble, and then the rest of them were on me. When they walked away singing, "New kid! New kid!", I was left on the ground with my books all over the place and my lunch stepped on. A peanut butter and jelly sandwich doesn't taste so good when it's flat.

They got me at lunch, too, and then again as I walked to my bus after school.

I hate this. The only good thing that happened today was that I heard a rumor that another new kid was coming to school.

If only that would happen!

Then maybe the bullies would leave me alone!

FRIDAY

It's true!

Today our teacher announced that a new student would be arriving in our class on Monday. That didn't stop the bullies from beating me up today, but even while they were doing it I could feel the weight lifting from me. Chunky Fredericks even sighed and helped me up after they were finished beating me up at lunch.

"You know, loser, I'll really miss whomping on you," he said. "Next week you'll be one of us." And then he slapped me on the back—but in a friendly way!

I can't believe it!

On Monday I'm saved!

MONDAY

My dream has come true!

For the first time since moving here, I walked untouched from the bus to class, and when I walked into my classroom, shielding my face against spitballs and thrown candy, the strangest thing happened: *nothing*.

Nobody hit me, no one shouted, "Get the new kid!"

Slowly, I lowered my hands from my face.

No one was looking at me.

They were all looking at...*him*.

The new student was in the front row, right in front of the teacher's desk. He was kind of weird looking, with a really thin face and skinny arms with long fingers, and kind of pale, almost light green skin.

He was trying real hard not to be noticed, but of course everybody was staring at him.

"Hey, freak!" Chunky Fredericks said, standing up with a wadded-up paper in his hand. He drew his hand back to throw it, and I flinched—but then I realized that he was going to throw it at the new kid and not at me—

At that moment the teacher, Mrs. Adams, came in, and Chunky sat quickly down.

"Later, freak," Chunky mumbled, as Mrs. Adams started class, and I realized with a sudden feeling of freedom that there was someone in the classroom quaking with fear, and it wasn't me!

At lunch they got the new kid, of course.

I was real quiet, still not quite believing my good luck, slipping out onto the playground to eat my lunch by myself, but after a while I couldn't help noticing the group of kids huddled in the spot where they normally beat me up. There were things flying into the air from the center of the group, a paper bag followed by some kind of food and then a jacket and then a shoe, and when the group dispersed a few minutes later, laughing, there was the new kid on the ground, looking dazed the way I had so many times. He gathered his stuff and crawled off, and for a moment then I got scared because Chunky and his friends were heading my way, still laughing.

But they kept walking past me as I hid what was left of my lunch behind my back.

Then, amazingly, Stinky Peters, who was even bigger and uglier than Chunky, and who always brought up the rear of the gang, stopped as he went by and patted me on the head.

"You know, Bud, you're all right!" he said, smiling, and kept walking, lumbering away to catch up with the rest.

And when I walked to my bus after school, they weren't there, waiting for me, but were instead in front of the new kid's bus, in a circle, laughing, as more books and clothing flew up into the air.

As good as I feel about being left alone, I feel sorry for the new kid.

TUESDAY

The bullies did to the new kid what they used to do to me, stealing his pants at lunch, Chunky Fredericks and Stinky Peters fighting over who got to turn them into rags. Stinky, being bigger, finally won, and I think he tore the legs off with his teeth because when he ran by as the bell rang ending lunch he tossed the trousers at me and laughed, "Here, Bud, a little present!"

I returned them to the new kid, who was cowering on the ground, trying to cover himself up with pages from a ripped up notebook. I've got to say, seeing him close up, that he's even weirder looking than I first thought—his legs are spindly and his face is long and oval shaped, the eyes too big and shaped like dark almonds.

"Here's your pants," I said, giving them to him.

"Thanks," he said, in a thin, almost whispery voice.

He started to say something else but then Stinky was calling to me, "Hey, Bud! Leave the freak alone—the bell rang!" and I ran back to class.

After school, there was a big circle of kids in front of the new kid's bus again, and I went home unbothered.

THE NEW KID

In a strange way, I feel kind of lonely.

Not a bad day for me.

But another bad one for the new kid.

The gang of bullies went after him at lunch again. This time Stinky put his arm around my shoulder and said, "Come on, Bud! Join in the fun!"

I had no choice and went along with him, but I just didn't have the heart to turn the kid's English book into confetti or his lunch into mush.

When the gang dispersed, I stayed behind.

"You look better without pants," I said, trying to cheer him up.

When I held out half of his English book he flinched.

"Hey, I won't hurt you," I said. "If fact, until you came along, I was the one they beat up on."

He looked up at me, his almond-shaped eyes suddenly brightening, and said, "My name's Oort. Want to be friends?"

I hesitated for a moment, thinking that maybe Chunky and Stinky wouldn't like it, but then I said, "Sure, why not?"

At that moment I saw Chunky and the others heading in our direction.

Oort groaned and said, "You'd better leave. Looks like they want to get in a little more fun before the bell rings. See you later?"

"Sure."

I backed away as the gang arrived, Stinky rubbing his hands in anticipation, and watched from a distance as the rest of Oort's books flew to pieces above the laughing circle that surrounded him.

But it looks like I won't be lonely anymore.

THURSDAY

Turns out Oort's a pretty nice guy.

I wish I could do something to help him at school, but he seems to understand what being the new kid's all about and takes it as best he can.

He came over after school today, and after we cleaned him up and got most of the dried mud and peanut butter out of his hair he wasn't in too bad shape. We played video games for a couple of hours and then did our homework, and I managed to sneak some snacks up to my room. Oort really likes potato chips, it turns out, and scarfed them down like he'd never had them before.

"Don't they have potato chips where you came from?" I asked, joking.

"Actually...no," Oort said, a little hesitantly.

"Where's that?" I answered, amazed that there could be anywhere without potato chips.

Oort shrugged, still stuffing his face, and said, "Just...somewhere else."

"I can't imagine a place without potato chips..."

But Oort was still stuffing his face, and shrugged again, so I let it drop.

When he left later I felt like we were real friends, and said, "I really wish there was something I could do for you at school."

Again he shrugged and said, "That's what being the new kid's all about. There's nothing you can do about it. Want to come over to my house tomorrow after school?"

"Sure," I said, and when Oort was gone I knew I'd made a real friend.

FRIDAY

It seemed like school would never end today, and, since it was Friday, and the bullies wouldn't see Oort again till Monday, they really let him have it at lunch.

But he seemed to take it really well, and after we'd found all his clothes, even both of his socks, all he did was ask me if I was still coming over after school.

"You bet," I said, "and I'll even bring a bag of potato chips!"

"Great!" he said, giving me directions to his house, and then staggered off as Stinky headed his way to get in one more pop.

They got Oort again at his bus, but he managed to wave to me as he stumbled out of the crowd.

"Don't forget the potato chips!" he shouted, before they were on him again.

I had a heck of a time finding his house. It's not that Oort's directions were bad, but the house was in a place I'd never been before. There was a street I knew pretty well, and at the end of it there was a right turn I didn't remember, which led to a dead end I'd never seen.

But there was the house at the end, just like Oort said it would be.

A strange place. It was house-shaped, but seemed to have too many corners. Also, it was way too tall. The porch was narrow, and all the windows had boards over them. The shingles were strange, some of them round and some of them square at the bottom; the same thing for the shingles on the roof. But it all seemed to fit together in a weird type of way, except that the whole house seemed to vibrate slightly, and glow in a faint greenish light.

It looked weird enough that I was about to turn around and go home when the front door opened and there was Oort, waving to me and smiling. He was wearing clothes different from his school clothes: really bright green, narrow pants and a thin-collared shirt in blinding yellow.

"Come on in!" he said.

I held up the potato chips.

"Great!" Oort said.

I stepped up onto the porch, feeling the boards give way slightly under my feet as if they were rotten inside.

I was about to say something to Oort when he laughed and said, "Uh...old house!" and brought me inside. He took the potato chips from me, popped open the bag, and began to shove big handfuls of them into his mouth.

"I love these things!" he said.

It was just as weird inside the house as outside. We were in a hallway, and as we went down it each room to either side seemed to be too narrow and had too many walls and glowed faintly. There were paintings on some of the walls, but the pictures were long and narrow. They looked like landscapes, but the trees in them were tall and thin with blue bark and the ground was covered with orange grass.

"What—" I asked, but Oort was still moving down the hallway so I rushed to catch up.

"Want to play video games?" I asked.

"Forget it—I've got something better to do!" he said.

We were in something like a kitchen, and on the table, which had different-lengthed legs and was taller than it was wide, was a jar of peanut butter and a half a loaf of bread.

"Not too much time to shop," Oort explained. He tossed the potato chip bag on the table, and I saw with amazement that it was empty.

"Those were great!" he said.

"Where are your parents?" I asked.

"They're...close," Oort said.

He moved to the back door, which had no windows in it and was barely wide enough to get through.

"Like I said, I've got something better than video games!" he laughed, throwing it open.

The doorway was filled with bright light. When my eyes adjusted I said, "Wow!" and stepped toward it.

Instead of the backyard of the house there was a whole other world, just like the one in the landscape painting, with orange grass leading up a rolling hill, brown flowers and blue trees, and a bright green sky.

"*That's* where I live!" Oort said.

I looked carefully through the doorway. "It looks like another planet!"

"It is!" Oort laughed.

"Can we...go there?"

"Just step through the door!"

"Wow!" I said again, and stepped through with Oort.

Suddenly I was on another world!

"Where is everybody?" I asked.

Oort pointed to the top of the hill. "On the other side is a valley, with a whole city in it. But just over the hill is what I really want to show you. Come on!"

I followed him, still wide-eyed at the world around me.

Orange grass!

Green sky!

Blue trees!

We got to the top of the hill, and suddenly I was looking down on the most amazing thing I'd ever seen. There in the distance, in the wide valley at the bottom of the hill, was a huge city made up of the same kind of buildings as Oort's house—a sprawling cluster of strange, tall, narrow, many-angled structures in wild colors—bright pink, red and purple.

"Unbelievable!"

"And look at *that!*" Oort said, pointing to what lay just below us.

I was speechless.

Sitting on a wide plateau was a tall, narrow, weird-cornered place with square and oval windows of different sizes. It was multi-colored—yellow, tangerine, the color like the bottom of a swimming pool. Off to the side was a play field surrounded by a strange, zigzagging fence and filled with things that sort of looked like swings and crooked monkey bars. The play field was filled with kids dressed in bright clothing just like Oort—and a group of them, big and mean looking, was climbing the fence and marching up the hill toward us.

"Hey, Oort!" I said, suddenly alarmed. I looked behind us—but Oort's house was gone, replaced only by orange fields and blue trees.

The gang of kids reached us, brushing Oort aside as they surrounded me. The biggest of them smiled a green, gap-toothed smile at me and said, "Hey, I wonder who this is?"

He turned to Oort and his evil smile softened. "Guess you're one of us now, loser!"

"Sorry, Bud," Oort said to me, as I went down, and felt someone tugging at my shoes and socks, felt someone else shoving orange grass down my pants, and felt something really sticky and bright blue being rubbed into my hair, "It was the only way I could stop being the new kid in *my* school."

AHEAD OF THE JONESES

January 12

Today I'm a happy man, because the deliverymen installed my new abstract lawn sculpture. I had it set up on the property line, and I could swear that Harry Jones's eyes bugged out when he saw it facing his front porch. The bastard'll have to look at it every day as he leaves for work.

January 30

When Jones called me over to see his new lawn sculpture today I had to hold myself back from strangling him in front of it. It's a silver-plated job, twice the size of mine and with twice as many artsy features. And on top of the fact that he had the nerve to *buy* the thing, the son-of-a-bitch had it mounted on his side of the property line, looming over my lawn sculpture. I put on an appreciative grin as he showed it to me, but we both knew what I was thinking...

AL SARRANTONIO

February 16

Today I called one of Harry's kids over to take a picture of him and his friends with my brand-new holo-camera. Gave little Robby an instant print (gave each of his friends one too!) and I just know the kid ran home to show Harry and ask how come they don't have a holo-camera. I could just visualize Harry yelling at the little lout and telling him to shut his mouth about holo-cameras. Made me feel warm inside all day.

February 21

Harry called this afternoon to tell me about the great buy he got on a holo-moviecamera and to invite Sheila and me and the kids over to help them make their first full-length film. Of course I told him we couldn't make it, but the bastard had little Robby run over later with a print. An hour's worth of color film, with sound—self-projecting cartridge too. Just need an empty space to project it in. I projected it into the garbage, of course; it burns the hell out of me that a jerk like that who can't be making any more money than me could afford something like that. Of course there have been a lot of sales on holo-moviecameras lately, and the prices have come down a bit. It's the fact that he just has to do me one better that makes me feel so rotten...

June 17

Eat your heart out, Harry Jones! The workmen turned on the juice today and left, and I must admit they did quite a job. There can't be anyone in the whole county, never mind this block, with a complete amusement arcade like mine in his backyard. And I mean *complete*. Everything from high-reality-level ride simulator to holographic clowns (4-color, yet!) to a changeable-program fireworks grid to close out the evening light spectacle. The guy at the department store started to give me his whole spiel about how I was getting in on the ground floor of a new revolution in home entertainment and how the prices would never be this low again (I don't see how they could get much higher; luckily, I did have a few dollars put away for my kids' college educations) but I didn't let him finish, I just signed the contract and slapped down the advance payment. He threw in the rifle range, no charge, but if he hadn't I would have ordered one anyway. I *know* how much Harry likes to target shoot on weekends.

June 28

God help me, and I'm a religious man, but I almost went over and murdered him today. I'm calmer now, but the initial shock of coming home from a short business trip to find the finishing touches being put to Jones's outdoor 3-D theater, set on top of his domed vapor-pool, and all of that resting on top of his automated midget racer track and micro golf course (combined with a good-sized arcade and target-shoot in one corner, floating six feet above the ground) was just a bit much. After a couple of hours I stopped trembling. I thought I could cheer myself up tonight by programming a light show, but Jones's heat-lightning extravaganza left the blinking lights in my backyard about a thousand feet below.

I'm desperate.

AL SARRANTONIO

November 11

Every last penny I've got is gone; Sheila's run away with the kids—but none of that matters. After five months I've finally found a research assistant in one of the large consumer appliance companies who could be bought, and I *know*—I'm *positive*, because I checked everything out thoroughly—that what I now hold in my hands is absolutely the only one (and therefore the best!) of its kind in the world. The guy I bribed (he wouldn't even tell me his name, the weasel—he looked like he needed the money, though) said this thing's the *ultimate* consumer device—that it can make all kinds of alterations in the space/time fabric of the universe, that it can do almost anything! He almost chickened out at the last minute, claiming the thing was dangerous and hadn't really been tested (it was under lock and key when he took it); he also mumbled something about it "blowing a fuse and throwing the Earth back into the Paleozoic Era." I think he was worried about getting caught; anyway, when he saw the amount of money I had for him, and the gun in my hand, he shut up and took the bribe fast enough; so much for his scruples. I'm standing here on my front lawn now, facing Jones's house, and as soon as the son-of-a-bitch (I know he's in there now with his Yellow Pages viewscreen, putting in hologram calls to every store in the state, trying to order a better model of what I've got—or at least to find out what it *is*) shows his face I'm going to throw the switch. I don't know what will happen, but whatever it is, no one can outdo it! I've beat you, Jones! Is that his face at the window? Yes! And now—

AHEAD OF THE JONESES

November 14, 400,000,000 B.C.

I move rock. Big rock. Slimy hands mine, and have dirt in mouth. Crawl up from sea. Wet sea. Now on dirt. Hard work to breathe, but I work. I stay on dirt now, for good.

Move rock. Nice rock, smooth on one side, flat on other side. Cool under rock, hide from Sun. Live under rock, on cool dirt. Nice.

I happy.

Other me crawl up from sea to dirt. I watch. He work breath, hard, for long time, and almost turn back to sea, but he stay. He look at me, under rock.

Now he move rock, other rock, bigger, more smooth on one side. Is bigger under, more cool. He move rock next to mine and crawl under, out of Sun. He look at me for a long time.

I mad.

THE ARTIST IN THE SMALL ROOM ABOVE

I

I wait for Bates to make me create again.

He sits in the small circular room above me, resting. I hear him tap at the keys of the console with his fingers, making dissonant, unformed sounds, but he does not continue. I am restless to finish; he has been working almost constantly for two days and I know he has deadlines to meet. The cable pads pulse warmly at my temples.

Finally I feel the urging through the pads.

The console in the room above hums contentedly as Bates urges me on at the usual setting. Impatient, tired, I want to finish; I close my eyes and shout up to him through the ceiling, telling him to increase the setting. I have never done this before and he is surprised, but he does so. He turns it up too high. The console's hum increases to a modulated whine.

AL SARRANTONIO

Suddenly pain bursts throughout my body. My hands clutch at the arm rests of my chair; my eyelids snap tightly closed; my throat convulses.

I begin to scream, hoarsely. Life surges through and out of me. My body jumps and tosses crazily in my chair. The console above drones loudly, and above it I hear the music...

Then abruptly it is over. The work is completed. I sink back, exhausted. Above, the console shuts angrily down and I hear Bates give a small cry of astonishment; he is breathing heavily.

My mind drifts off into blackness.

II

Later, Bates descends the curving staircase to my room and wakes me. He helps me remove the electrodes and pads. He helps me to my feet and says he must take me for a drink. I nod weakly and follow.

It is night, and a low-lying, yellow mist has descended. This world is perpetually covered with thin shifting clouds and sickly fog. As we step into the dark street I turn to look at our working place, a two-room two-floor silo capped with a black dome. The part above the fog resembles an ugly, rimless derby. Other derbys rest on the fog on this street and the streets adjacent—this is the area where most artists live. Bates motions impatiently and we move along.

It is dark and smoky in the drinking place. Bates orders two drinks—tall, slender goblets filled with roiling liquid as yellow as the fog outside—and steers me away from the somber bar to the back room. We find a booth and sit down facing one another.

THE ARTIST IN THE SMALL ROOM ABOVE

Bates looks at me queerly across the table. "You've never done what you did today before," he says. "I didn't know you could." His eyes are two white questioning orbs in the darkness.

"I was tired," I respond quietly; "I thought you could finish the work faster if you increased the setting. But you set it too high."

"But do you know what you did?" he says, raising his voice. "Do you know what I composed?" He pulls a recording chip from his pocket and pushes it across the table at me. "Listen."

"No," I say tiredly, pushing it back at him, but he says again, "Listen."

I bring the chip up to my ear and it activates. It is set near the end of the composition. At first there are only the standard, bland sounds that characterize most of Bates's work. Then suddenly I detect a change, and the music becomes more stately. A theme, low, insistent, tragic, begins to weave itself around and through the blandness, enfolding it and gradually overcoming it. Now the theme begins to fold around itself, the high notes beginning to fight the basses head-on, building in intensity, crashing against itself and climbing—

I pull the chip from my ear and place it before Bates. My stomach has tightened itself into a small knot. "I won't do that again."

He gives me a measuring look. "I...don't know," he says. "You've been contracted to me for three months now, and I never realized you could do this sort of thing. I'm going to have to think about this."

"Let me remind you," I say firmly, "that the contract you have with me states that you will compose only popular forms of music. There's no provision in it for other forms of work."

He looks hard into my eyes. "I'm aware of that," he says, "but don't forget that it was you who deviated from the contract today. I didn't expect to have the end of that piece turned into...well, serious music. There was something there that I may want to explore. If you read the contract carefully, there isn't really any provision restricting me on what type of music I can compose. There's no clear restriction on what I can do."

I look at him coldly. "I wouldn't tamper with the contract. And besides, you know that money lies in what you're doing now."

"I know that," he says, "but there are a few people willing to pay for this sort of thing. There might be money in it. I couldn't afford to abandon the other composing, but it just might be worth my while to make use of your other talents." He smiles across the table; it is an empty smile. "And remember," he says, "I still control the cables and you're still my Muse." His smile widens into a sharp, white grin. "For ten years."

We finish our liquor and leave the drinking place in silence.

III

He is right; I am his Muse. I was brought here from my home planet and, like many of my fellow beings, I contracted myself to an artist. The artists on this world are little more than machines. These creatures have somehow lost the ability to transfer their feelings and experiences. It is as if their fingers have somehow been disconnected from their souls. They seem the most selfish of beings: they possess emotions, but those emotions are land-locked. Each being of this world is an island, a world unto himself, and it is nearly impossible for one of them to even touch another. The only social contact they effect takes place on a formal, businesslike plane; even their meeting places are cheerless, murky and cold. But though these people are alienated they are not dead; each lone mind craves nourishment and pleasure. That is where we, the so-called Muses, come in. We supply the machine-like artisans to which we are contracted with transmutable creative energy for their work. In return we are supported by the writers. There are Muses contracted to painters, writers, sculptors, as well as musicians and other artists. Our contracts range from one to twenty years and can be renewed.

On my home planet things are very bad—there is severe overpopulation and the governments are harsh and restrictive. If I had not become a Muse I would have been judged unnecessary and eventually eliminated. There is a trade pact between this world and my own and Muses are valuable commodities.

Something in me, of me, is being tapped, siphoned out by the cables and utilized. My emotions are being sucked dry, for a price. I have thought of running away but I have seen the crucifixion poles jutting through the yellow fog. I've seen what is done to Muses who run away. If anything, the governments of this world are even more ruthless than those on my home planet. If I did escape, where would I run to? There is, in fact, no escape.

There is much pain within me, but at least I am alive and can express myself, unlike the lonely monsters of this world.

Unlike Bates.

IV

Days have passed; I sit in my gray cylindrical room in my chair and Bates composes above me. He has begun another piece; he has been working at his usual pace at the normal console setting.

Someone climbs the stairs and enters Bates' room and suddenly he stops. I can hear muffled voices through the ceiling. Perhaps it is Trevor, Bates's business contact. The day, as usual, is bleak; sickly yellow mist drifts by the small window.

There are shuffling sounds above me; the visitor departs. Bates leaves his room and hurriedly descends the stairs.

I swivel around in my chair to face him as he enters the room. His silent eyes are bright.

"Trevor was here," he says, holding out something in his hand. "He gave me this—a check for five thousand credits. He listened to the composition and wants me to write more, immediately. He especially liked the ending."

"Bates—" I begin.

"He says that if I write a piece that's like the ending of the other one all the way through he'll double the number of credits I got for this one. He says there's an audience for this type of music at the moment. We must start immediately." His eyes stare through me.

"Bates," I say, "I told you the other night it can't be done. The contract doesn't call for it. It's a terrible strain on me."

"I don't care. If you could do it once you can do it now. I'll make you do it. We'll begin immediately."

"Bates—" I say, but he closes the door behind him.

THE ARTIST IN THE SMALL ROOM ABOVE

I swing around in my chair as he reaches the console upstairs. His stool grunts as he settles himself on to it, and I can hear him strapping the wires from the console to his arms and legs. The cable pads are hot on my temples. He has obviously turned the console to a high setting. He replaces the chip from the composition he was working on with a new one, and begins to urge me through the cables.

I try to hold it down but the console setting is strong. I begin to sweat. The urge increases to a forcible level.

Suddenly the dam breaks and a tide of feeling rushes out of me. The tones of the console above form a harmonic boom and then settle, after a moment of silence, into a slow, ominous crescendo. A theme forms, then another and another, and they begin to grind against one another, each building in intensity and each fighting against the others. I grit my teeth; the strain is unbearable. Tears burn my eyes. The room around me begins to tremble as the music builds to a feverish pitch. The three themes converge into a monstrous, tortured strain as my soul tries to tear loose from my body…

Hours later it is over. The ceiling above me rumbles quietly and I can hear Bates struggling for breath. The cable pads have burned my flesh and my arms and legs are very weak.

Just as I begin to calm down the pain comes again. Bates has put a new chip in. I hear him shout through the ceiling, to himself, "More!" The ceiling shakes; my arms fly about madly, uncontrollably. My head is thrown violently about.

He composes continuously for the next two days. I can barely catch a gasp of breath between cries of pain.

Finally he shuts down the console. I can dimly hear it wind down as the power decreases. I can hear Bates pull the wires from his arms and legs and stumble from his stool to the bed.

The room above me is silent.

V

Bates continues this type of work for the next four months. The days drag by. Occasionally Trevor visits him; after these visits Bates's fervor climbs to an almost manic level. Even the console seems to plead for rest. My mind is driven to emotive heights for prolonged periods of time; I am forced to survive on bits of food and water fed to me by Bates at odd and infrequent hours—he will not even allow me to remove the cable pads in fear that I may do something drastic despite the threat of horrible punishment. I could not leave my chair even if I were allowed, my body is so weak. Bates, above, pauses only for food or snatches of rest. Composition after composition is completed.

One day Bates comes to see me. It is after a visit from Trevor, and Bates bursts into my room. He comes to my chair and stands before me. He, too, is wasted and yellow; nevertheless he smiles.

"Trevor has just left," he says in a low, weak voice. "Everything I've composed has received tremendous acceptance."

I stare at him mutely.

"Look here," he continues, pulling small bundles of credit notes from his pockets. "And there's much more coming. But that's not what I wanted to tell you." He pauses. "I've had your contract amended."

My gaze is unmoved.

"There was nearly trouble. It's been all right up to now, but for what I want to do next I had to be sure. I'm ready to do something larger."

"Bates," I say hoarsely, from deep within me. "Bates, it can't be done. I haven't eaten, slept—"

"I know," he says, "but that can't be helped. It's in the contract and this thing must be done now. Trevor says—"

"To hell with Trevor!" I cry brokenly. "You're destroying me. I can't think anymore, Bates. I can't *feel*. I need rest, time to think, time—"

"Never mind your needs! You work for me. Trevor says the public is ready for a symphonic cycle, something magnificent." His eyes are aflame in his dead, blank face. "We must begin."

"Bates—"

"You're my Muse," he snaps. "Amending that contract cost me a lot of credits; you won't disappoint me. It's time to begin." He turns to leave.

I stare weakly at the curved gray wall framing Bates's back. Words rise and die in my dry throat. Bates shuts the door and goes upstairs.

The pain hits me unexpectedly. Bates has done something to the console—some sort of modification has been made to give it even greater power capabilities. I am not even able to resist; the machine reaches right to the core of my emotions and begins to suck voraciously at them. Upstairs the console announces the opening of the work with a gigantic chord in brasses, and then settles immediately into a wrenching, twisting theme in the strings. There is an ominous percussive beat in the background, insistent, ponderous and funereal. The beat increases suddenly to a pounding, terrifying level, nearly excluding all other sound. The strings begin to lash at the beat, in staccato fashion. Now the horns join in. It is as if a hundred thousand instruments have been squeezed screaming into the console and are fighting each other and themselves to get out. The level increases, and I can hear Bates howl through my own agony. The cable pads have welded themselves to the red, raw flesh on my temples. Being, existence, is torn from me by the machine above.

I don't know how much time passes. Existence itself is one continuous, emotive cry. The cable pads rip into me, and the console level, incredibly, is still rising. The music has become one immense, flagellating note, self-destructive and unstoppable. It is out of control. There is a roar of thunder, a burst of unbelievable pain—

I am thrown back against my chair; there has been an explosion in the room above. The wall shakes; the ceiling cracks and plaster chips flake down upon me. I lay, stick-like, broken, in my chair. There is silence.

Plaster dusts the room.

After a few minutes I am able to pull myself up. The cables break away: the wires are fused. I walk, trembling, to the door. The hallway outside is twilit; I can see the dark outline of the curving stairs against the grayness. I slowly make my way up the steps.

The door to Bates's room is open and unhinged—it has been blown outward by the explosion. Inside all is smoke. There is a sickly smell of burnt meat and wiring. I approach the console.

Bates is slumped over the typewriter, arms outstretched, charred. He is dead. I pull him back, away from the machine. Broken black wires hang from his arms and legs. His huge white eyes are turned up into his head. His fish-like mouth is open in a frozen, lifeless cry. His tongue is black.

Slowly, with effort, I pull Bates from the stool. He collapses and tumbles to the floor, twitching. I sit down, slowly, on the stool.

I am racked with sobs.

VI

Soon someone, possibly Trevor, will come and find me here. I will not be harmed; I am a valuable product. Bates's contract with me will be destroyed and the chip he was working on will be sold—an unfinished work. The wrecked console, the debris, will be cleared out and another artist will move into this silo. A new console will be installed. The new artist may bring his own Muse; if not, he may contract me. Otherwise, I will be put back on the market. There is nothing else for me to do. The quality of my work with Bates will be a factor in my next contract—because of my sudden notoriety I may be able to contract myself to an artist who will allow me to work under better conditions. It is this or death.

Outside the window the day is bleak; the far-away sun makes this world sallow. I place a new chip in the console and turn it on to a very low setting. It coughs, then purrs haltingly. I hold my fingers over the keys and a tear beads in my eye and makes its slow, ragged way down my face.

I begin to play.

THE DANCING FOOT

THE STORIES HAD LITTERED the newspapers for days—YOUNG GIRL, PROMISING DANCER, PUSHED UNDER SUBWAY TRAIN—and Lansing had collected them all, reveled in the large type of their headlines, relished his secret infamy. That the girl was dead did not matter to him; it was the fact that he had done something and gotten away with it, that an entire city wanted to get its hands on him but had no idea who he was that made him hug himself in satisfaction.

He sat smoking on his mattress in his apartment, remembering the crowded platform, the crush of the morning crowds piled four deep; then the roar and clatter of the oncoming train, the press of the mob toward the yellow safety line in anticipation; the train almost there; and then his foot, quick and silent, tripping the girl, causing her to fall over the edge of the platform in front of the metal beast, too late to stop; the scream of brakes mingled with the girl's startled, horrified cry—

Lansing rocked himself and smiled, lingering on the sweet moment of impact, thinking of how he had glided silently away in the confusion after making sure to look down for a glimpse of the crushed body.

The papers had said that if she had fallen a few inches to the right she would have landed on the outside of the tracks and that her foot might still have been severed but that she would have survived. As it was, she landed directly under the train between the tracks, and her right foot had been cut off by the wheels, but her body had been dragged and crushed by the momentum of the front car screeching to a halt.

The papers had quieted down some about it in the past week, moving the stories and wild speculations to the inside pages, and though he had slept undisturbed for the first few days after the deed—working a full day just as he always did—he had begun to have bad dreams. He dreamed about the foot. He dreamed that the foot was following him. And what horrified him most in the dreams was the way it followed him, walking. Like some horrible cartoon appendage—like the way his mother used to walk her hand around him with little doll's shoes on two fingers when he was small, dancing those two little feet before him like a little soldier after he was bad and then suddenly lashing out when he wasn't expecting it, smacking him across the face with the flat part of her hand. She was doing it now, hitting him, smacking him—

He awoke, suddenly realizing that he had dozed off into the dream again. He was covered with cold sweat, and the room was dark now. He made a move to get off the bed and turn on the lights.

As he did so he heard a sound. He knew he was wide awake now, and he heard something moving around in the closet. Something walking around, pushing things aside, *kicking* things aside.

He thought, *It has to be rats.*

He pulled himself unsteadily from the bed, wiping the sweat from his face with the front of his tee-shirt, and lurched over to the light switch. He clicked it on and the sounds from the closet abruptly stopped. He threw open the closet door and there was nothing there. No rats. Nothing.

He slammed the door roughly shut and went to the bed, settling onto the old, creaking mattress. He took a deep breath. I've got to stop this, he thought. He was starting to be afraid to go out, of taking the subway, of doing anything.

This has got to stop.

He thought again of tripping the girl, saw her falling off the platform, and that made him feel better. He looked at the clippings pasted to the wall around the room—YOUNG DANCER CRUSHED—and was even able to smile. I got away with it, he thought. No one knows I did it

He lay down and slept.

And dreamt, screaming, of the foot again.

The next day he arrived at work late. Walking by a shoe store something made him hesitate; there was a pair of dancer's shoes, ballet slippers, in the window, and he found himself staring at them. As he looked they suddenly began to move—

He realized with a start of relief that it was just the shop owner, taking the pair of shoes off their hook to show a customer. But the image of the moving shoes lingered in his mind...

He didn't say hello to Joey, the lobby attendant, like he usually did, but went straight to the locker room and put his maintenance man's uniform on. Joey mumbled something as he went past, something like "Grouch," with a laugh, but Lansing let it pass.

Morelli was waiting for him on the 15th floor, and yelled at him good-naturedly when he came off the elevator, for being late.

"Look at this, kid," Morelli said suddenly, turning and holding up his right leg. "Look what I did shaving this morning." There was a stump on the end, no foot— and then Morelli laughed and popped his shoe out of the pulled-down pants cuff.

"Got you that time, kid," he said, and laughed again. "Go clean up that mess on 18, the workmen'll be in early tomorrow to start. You okay, kiddo?"

"Uh, yeah, Nick." Lansing nodded curtly and left.

The eighteenth floor was completely gutted for renovation, and he went there gratefully, happy to be alone. But soon the emptiness of the floor and the strange shadows cast by the boxes and crates lying around began to get to him. He heard noises, and imagined a dancing foot, a legion of dancing feet, kicking things around, marching right up to him—

He swung around as the elevator door suddenly opened. Nobody got off. After a moment the doors closed again, and the arrival light over the opening went out. There was dusty silence for a moment, and then as Lansing turned to get back to work something moved.

He distinctly saw it, a severed foot scooting around a crate by the elevator, and out of sight. He began to shake and his body went numb, as if two giant icy hands had grabbed him. There was a scratching sound, and then the sound of a moving ballet slipper.

Lansing went rigid. The shuffling got louder, and then he saw a foot with a slipper on it appear from behind the crate.

Suddenly the elevator doors opened again, and the foot ran behind a box. Morelli stepped out into the room.

"Hey kid," he said, and then he saw Lansing standing frozen. "What's wrong?"

"The foot!" Lansing said.

"What?"

"Don't you hear the dancing?" He felt as if he would faint.

"Kid, go home early. Right now. Whatever's wrong, flush it out and come back tomorrow ready to work. I don't want a sick guy on the job, makes me look like a lousy foreman. Believe me, you don't look so good."

"I—" He nodded. "Okay."

He got in the most crowded subway car on the train and looked straight ahead all the way home. He was afraid that if he looked down he would see the foot in front of him. He thought he heard the rap-shuffle of it walking, but he refused to look. There was a light kick at the cuff of his pants just before his stop, but still he gritted his teeth and stared straight ahead.

He ran to his apartment and bolted the door, stuffing towels underneath the sill. He heard tiny footsteps outside. He slammed the windows shut, and double-locked the window leading to the fire escape, pulling down the shade. He sat on the bed in the corner of the room and pulled up his knees, closing his eyes tight.

There was the squeak-shuffle sound of a ballet slipper dancing.

He went to the window, sweating, and peeked out under the shade. An old man had set his hat on the ground in front of the building, and was doing a soft-shoe dance.

Lansing yanked up the window and screamed at the old man, who quickly moved off. He pulled the window back down and went back to the bed.

Shutting his eyes, he tried to think of the girl and the train. But only the image of his mother came to him, dancing her hand in front of him, waiting for his baby smile, then the fist—

Something was kicking around in the closet, and then the closet door opened.

The foot was in the room. Lansing opened his eyes and saw it skitter under the bed. It began to kick things around, moving shoes around, jumping up and kicking at the bottom of the mattress.

He screamed and stood quickly up as the foot leaped onto the bed. It disappeared under the covers; Lansing could see it moving around underneath them.

He pulled frantically at the bolts on the door, missing and then finally unlocking them. He threw open the door. He heard the rumple of bedclothes behind him, as the foot kicked the covers aside to follow him. He ran down into the street and toward the subway. Looking back once over his shoulder, he saw the foot walking leisurely, keeping up with him about a half a block behind.

He heard the soft shoe again. It was the old man; he had set his hat down by the subway entrance, and was dancing. Lansing ran past him, kicking the hat as he did so; the old man stopped his dance and yelled after him.

Desperate, Lansing jumped the turnstile, and turned back to see the foot running underneath it. He began to scream, and the startled crowd moved aside in a swath to let him pass. A transit cop, seeing him, began to follow.

THE DANCING FOOT

He ran down the stairs two at a time to the lower level, and along the platform of the express track. The foot was behind him. There was a roaring in his ears; he looked back to see the transit cop in the distance, an express train coming in, and the foot a few feet behind him, taking great springing jumps into the air. He tried to duck as the foot leaped onto his back, kicking him over the edge of the platform onto the tracks in front of the train. He landed on his back between the two tracks. Wild with terror, he looked over to see the foot stamping at him, and with a convulsive effort he rolled over the track to his right to safety as the train screeched toward him. But then, he realized with horror, the foot was stepping on his left leg, holding it down over the track, pressing it down as the train passed.

There was the shriek of steel on steel and then blackness.

He awoke in the hospital to the sound of Morelli's voice. The foreman was hovering over him.

"Thank God, he's coming around," Morelli said. "Hey kid, how you feel?"

"I...okay, I guess," he replied. He tried to push himself up to a sitting position and discovered that there was nothing to push with on his left leg but a stump.

Morelli moved quickly to help him sit up. "Hey kid," he said, obvious concern in his voice, "I'm really sorry about what happened. I keep thinking about fooling you that day with my pants leg pulled down over my shoe and it makes me shiver. That didn't freak you out, did it?"

"No. No, I'll be all right," he said. "You were just kidding around. That had nothing to do with it."

Morelli looked relieved. "That's great. I was really worried about it. You know, you were really lucky, kid. There was a cop right there when it happened, he said if you hadn't moved at the last second you'd have been cut in half or mashed to a pulp. In fact, they might have been able to do something with your foot if..."

Lansing immediately became alert with fear. "What happened to my foot?"

"They...well, they couldn't find it. It's really weird."

Lansing said nothing; and then suddenly the vision of his apartment left open, with the clippings of the girl, sprang to his mind. "What happened to my apartment? I left it open—"

"Don't worry about it, kid. I locked it up for you. It was dark when I went over so I just shut the door. And don't worry about your job, either, I'll see you get it back when you get rehabilitated. There's no reason why you can't come back to work with...the way you are."

Lansing's mind was racing. "Thanks, Nick. I mean it. I...think I'd better rest now."

"Sure, kid," said Morelli. "I'll come back to see you tomorrow."

In the quiet of his room a sudden peace came over Lansing. It was incredible how it all fit so neatly together. He almost shivered with pleasure. He had killed the girl, and she had gotten her revenge; she was dead and he was alive. She had taken his foot, but he could live without it; he would learn to work and do everything else with it. And he would always have that secret knowledge of what he had done and that he had survived it. He began to smile to himself and drew his knees up, resting gently on the stump of his left leg, rocking slowly. I've beaten them, he thought, and even the image of his mother's fingers dancing before him didn't bother him now.

And then he heard the shuffling.

It was very faint at first, very far away, as if it were way down the corridor or outside his window on the street below, but it began to grow in volume. A cold shiver went through him, but then he suddenly remembered the dancing old man outside the subway station, only a few blocks away. He gradually relaxed. It must be someone like that—maybe even the same old man—shuffling up and down the halls of the hospital serenading the patients. He thought of how foolish he'd been before, letting it all get to him. It was not bad sounding, although it needed a little work on coordination. It got louder; obviously the dancer was working his way down the corridor and would reach his door in turn. He settled back against the pillows and thought of looking through his trouser pockets for loose change so that he could give it to the old man. He began to get a little drowsy.

The sound was very loud now; the dancer had reached his closed door and was tapping a beautiful, slow waltz. A smile came to Lansing's lips.

"Come in, old man," he called as the door inched open; he would now be able to see who was dancing so he could compliment him. The door opened all the way as the waltz ended.

There was no one there.

There was a squeak-shuffle and Lansing began to scream hysterically as two severed feet came into the room. They stopped before his bed and began to dance again, a fast-paced tap dance this time. Lansing screamed and screamed but no one came to help him.

One foot, a graceful, feminine one, was covered with a ballet slipper and was doing most of the work, while the other, the foot of a man in a workman's boot, seemed to be getting better as it followed the other's example.

The dance ended, and after a short interlude for applause, another began.

Lansing, screaming and screaming, knew that the dance, the beautiful unending dance, would always be for him.

LIBERTY

THERE'S A STORY THEY tell in Baker's Flats that tells you everything you need to know about the town. It seems there was a Swede named Bergeson who moved in without permission from the town elders. He came from out East, and he was a little naïve because he assumed that since this was the United States, and that he was now a United States citizen, that he could go anywhere and do whatever he liked. Seems he believed all that business they fed him in Europe about this being the land of True Freedom and Golden Opportunity, and like any other poor fool who isn't getting what he wants where he is, he packed up and got on a ship that sailed through the cold waters and came to America.

This was 1885, the year those Frenchmen were putting up that Statue of Liberty in New York Harbor. I know because I was helping them do it, working for five cents a day and drinking four cents of it at McSorley's. I like to think that this Swede, Bergeson, got a good look at it half finished, because that's just about where Liberty stands in this country.

Anyway, to make a long story shorter, because I've got other things to tell, they found this Swede staked out on his land in the sun, naked, blue eyes wide with surprise more than fright, because he was a big man and wouldn't have gone down without a fight. They found his legal deed to the land he owned stuffed in his mouth, and a circle of bullet holes outlining his chest where his heart had beat. There were seven holes, just as there are seven elders of the town of Baker's Flats, and the story they tell is that these town elders went and killed the Swede Bergeson and made a solemn oath doing it, a pact if you will, that they would take it to their deaths and conspire against anyone who conspired against them.

That's the story they tell, and I know the story because I came out West with the Swede, running from the law and the half-finished liberty that statue represented, looking for my own freedom, and eventually, unlike the poor Swede, finding it, which constitutes the rest of my story.

As I said, the Swede was a naïve man, but he was a good man at heart, and when he told me the story of the land he'd purchased out West, the farm waiting for him in a town called Baker's Flats, a place so new and untamed that there wasn't a sheriff; was, in fact, no real law for three hundred miles to any compass point, only seven town elders who constituted the law and meted out justice; well, when he told me these things in McSorley's Bar, in New York, the night I met him, and I watched his blue eyes imagining the clear, hot plains, and the freedom they promised, we made a pact over the ale I bought him (because there is nothing in the world better than McSorley's Ale for pact making) that I would go out West with him, and that we would fulfill our dreams together. He would have his farm, and his wide-open spaces, and his America, and I would have—well, a chance at real liberty.

We laid out by freight that very night. The Swede insisted on taking a coach train and showed me his money, which would pay for two passages, but I told him no, and told him as much as I could of my reason for it, and he was wise enough (though so naïve in other things) to see my point.

Our car was a cold one, but the Swede was used to the cold, even to the point of giving me his coat when he saw the distress I was in, his big, open face splitting into a smile as he said in his thick accent, "Take it. If two men can share a dream, they can also share a coat."

The night passed slowly. We kept the car door slid open partway, because the Swede wanted to see the moon, which had risen white and stark over the east.

"The East," he said, "is where stars rise, and the moon too."

"But the West," I answered, "is where we're going, and where your face should be." So I threw open the door on the other side of the car, and we looked out there together.

We talked about a lot of things that night, about our hopes and dreams for a better life, and he showed me the Colt and the Winchester he'd bought "for the Wild West," as he called it, and somewhere, just as the sun was pushing the sky from purple to blue, he said the thing I had been hoping to hear, the thing that made me trust him as I'd hoped I could: "You don't have to tell me what you're running from. I don't believe you did it." And with that he lay down and turned his back on me and slept, and I sat looking out to the west, knowing my chance at liberty was safe.

We traveled a week by rails, till Reading, Pennsylvania, by boxcar, and then by first-class coach. The Swede insisted, showing me the roll of money he had saved and convincing me what I already knew: that the telegraphs weren't likely to have my picture up on the wall out here yet, and so, this far from New York, I was no longer a wanted man. I balked a little at him spending his money on me, but only a little, because to tell the truth, I was getting sick of the bum's life and craved a little cleanliness and a good cigar, and the Swede provided all this and good food to boot. And so on through St. Louis and then out to the territories, where the land got flatter but where, the Swede said, he could smell his new farm calling to him. I remember that day because it was the day he first showed me the picture he had of his wife and young daughter, and they were as blond as he was. The girl would be strong when she got older, and they would both join him when he was settled. I half wished, seeing the picture of that pretty blond girl, that she were here already.

It was another half week before we reached Baker's Flats, by short railway and then by stage and flatbed wagon, and when we got in there and the Swede made claim to his land, it was not a week later that the trouble started and the Swede was dead.

The day after the funeral, being as there was no law for three hundred miles, I began to hunt the town elders of Baker's Flats, one by one. It was not a quiet thing, and it got louder as it went along, and I have to say that in many ways I enjoyed it. I can tell you now I wasn't a stranger to killing when it was necessary, and hadn't been in New York. I kept the picture of the Swede in my mind as I went about it, and I kept the picture of his pretty daughter and wife in my pocket, and I thought about my own freedom, which made the killing easier.

The first was a man named Bradson, who owned the General Store. He had given the Swede and I a hard time right at our arrival in town and had made a remark that had told me all I needed to know about him. We'd walked into his store for some chewing tobacco, and maybe a cigar, since the Swede knew I liked them so much, and when the little bell over the door had tinkled, he looked our way, and a look filled his eyes when he saw us that I immediately didn't like, and he turned the bald back of his head to us and muttered, not so low that I didn't hear, "Foreigner," and went into his back room.

We waited fifteen minutes for him, the Swede with patience and me with growing anger, but he didn't come out. I had decided by that time that I wanted a cigar very badly, and was about to march into the back room after Bradson, but the Swede took my arm and quietly said, "Let's be going." I looked up into his broad face, and I knew at that moment that he had heard Bradson's remark, too, but had chosen to ignore it. This told me that he was sharper than I'd thought, but I was still mad, and finally he took my arm and said again, gently, "Let's go."

I went then, but I came back after the Swede's death, and I found Bradson where I'd hoped I would, in the back room of his store. It was after dark and the store was closed, but the lamp was lit on his little desk and he sat doing accounts. He didn't hear me slip open the front door and come in, and he didn't hear anything again after I cocked the butt of my Colt across the back of his ear and laid him out on the floor. I put a bullet in his heart, at the top, where the top of a circle might be, the start of a circle, just the way the Swede had been killed. There was a cigar humidor on a shelf behind the counter in the front of the store, and I filled my pocket with coronas before I left.

It was a dark night and stayed quiet after my shot into Bradson, and it stayed quiet after two more single shots, each continuing to advance a circle around two more hearts, rang out. There was the liveryman, Polk, who put up some fight and was strong but not strong enough, and the telegraph man, Cooper, who had a beard and was said to abuse his wife. He was in his office, too, with a bottle of whiskey instead of his wife for company, and I left him sprawled next to his telegraph, a bullet in the right of his heart, his spilled bottle inches from his cooling hand.

I hit the hills for a while after that, because I knew they'd be after me the next day. And I was right. I went high up, where it was cold and even colder at night, but I had the Swede's coat to warm me. Just as it had that first night in the freight car, and I made camp where they couldn't see a small fire and where I could hear the echo of their horse's movements a mile off. I waited two days and gave them enough time to get close, and then I fell in behind them and waited for them to splinter off, as I knew they would when they found the false clues I'd left for them that told them I'd gone one of two ways.

They split off just as I'd wanted them to. The two toughest stayed together, and the two weakest, who I wanted to take together, rode off down what they thought to be the least likely trail, which was where I waited for them. I had the Swede's rifle, and I waited in the V between two rocks, and I almost felt bad when

I picked them off because they rode right into me and never looked up. I took them out with two quick shots because the other two were the dangerous ones, and they weren't all that far away and were sure to hear the gunshots.

The two I took out were Maynard and Phillips, the bar owner and the fat banker, and I know I shot Maynard below the heart where I wanted, but I wasn't so sure that my shot into Phillips continued the circle up toward the eight-o'clock position, because he didn't go down right away and almost made me shoot again. But his horse was only carrying the dead body, and when momentum failed and Phillips fell, I took the time to check the body and found I had indeed hit him right on the eight.

I had a bit of a rough time of it for the next twelve hours. It turned out that Jeppson and Baker, the two remaining, were closer than I'd thought. Baker even got a shot off at me as I rode off, and he was a good shot and took part of my right earlobe off, which only added to my resolve.

They hunted me well, and for a while I thought they had me, but then they made a few blunders and I was able to play fox again. I left my trail in a stream, then falsified it on the other side, circling back to the water and running back past their position to fall in behind them. I was not stupid enough to try to pick them off then, but contented myself with letting them lose me, and I went back to the Swede's farm.

His body was long gone, buried out behind the farmhouse in the beginnings of his tilled field, but there was a bed to sleep in and a stable to hide my horse and some food in the larder to drive the hunger for real food from my belly. I even smoked a cigar after my meal, remembering the Swede, and took out the picture of his wife and daughter and looked at it for a while before I went to sleep for a couple of hours.

I was up before sunrise. I had breakfast, and then I went out and fed the horse so he wouldn't get hungry, and then I walked into town. It was Sunday. The moon was a thick crescent, waxing, much the same as it had been that night on the train when the Swede and I had looked to the west.

The cock was crowing when I reached Jeppson's church. It was small and empty, and I let myself into the back room where Jeppson bunked and waited. He had a nice collection of guns, and a bowie knife, and I admired the couple of Comanche scalps he had hanging on hooks over his shaving mirror. Services started at eleven, so I expected him around ten. I was disturbed once, about eight o'clock, but it proved to be a dog scratching at the door. I found a scrap bone for him and he went away.

There was a Bible on the desk, which I began to read, and I was so absorbed in my reading that I didn't hear the Reverend Jeppson enter his church a little while later and open the door to his office. He froze, and so did I, but he was more startled than I was, and that gave me enough time to get my gun up and drill him in the heart. His Colt was halfway out of his holster, and it fell to the floor as he dropped. He said, "Oh, God," which I thought appropriate. I walked over to him and was pleased to see I had hit him just where I'd wanted, around the eleven-o'clock mark.

I figured that if Jeppson was home, then so was Baker. He had the biggest house in town, because he was the biggest man, and naturally leader of the town elders, and the best shot. I had my healing earlobe to attest to that.

I figured rightly. I found him at breakfast with his family, ranged round their big oak table as if nothing had happened. His wife, a pretty little thing with dark red hair, was dishing out potatoes and eggs to three boys and a little girl, and there was Baker at the head of the table, dressed in his churchgoing best. I saw all this through the picture window. I could have broken the window, but I thought it would be better to go in the front door and make sure of my shot.

Again he proved to be the sharpest of the seven. He must have seen me move away from the window, because he was waiting for me behind the stairway banister when I pushed the door open. He winged me in the left shoulder, but I did the same to him, and then he panicked and ran for the stairs. I heard his wife and children screaming in the dining room as I mounted the steps after him.

We went through the upstairs of the house, and I got him to empty his revolver. I found him cowering in the room of his little girl, squeezed down in the corner next to her crib. He had his six-shooter on his lap, with the empty chambers out so I could see it. A scatter of unloaded bullets spilled from his shaking hand. "Please, don't do this to my family," he begged, but I took careful aim at his flushed face and then lowered the gun to his chest and put the last bullet into his heart at the twelve-o'clock spot, completing the circle I'd started with Bradson.

✦ ✦ ✦

I was tired then. I told Baker's wife to leave with her children and get the rest of the town together for a meeting at three o'clock. Then I bolted the doors and slept in Baker's big, comfortable bed. The Colt was loaded under my pillow, but I didn't think I'd need it, and I was right.

At three o'clock I got up and shaved and took one of Baker's fine cigars from his study and lit it and walked out into the street to have my say.

They were all waiting for me out there. I showed them the Swede's Colt, and his Winchester, and I told them how I had killed the Swede and the seven town elders. I told them about the story they would tell in Baker's Flats about how all this had happened, and I told them what would happen to any of them if they got it wrong. They were farmers and women and children, and they all knew what I meant. They knew there wasn't any other law for three hundred miles.

Just to be sure they understood me I told them about the man I had murdered in New York, throwing him from the scaffolding of the Statue of Liberty when he laughed when I told him that no man can be free under the thumb of any other man or government, that a man can only achieve true liberty by controlling all other men around him.

I knew they understood me, because they went home when I told them to. I stood on the porch of my new house and watched them go, and then I took out the picture of the Swede's beautiful wife and daughter and thought I'd write, in the Swede's name, to tell them to hurry out here, that there was a fine life waiting for them.

For the first time in my life I felt true liberty.

In Baker's Flats, they tell my story still.

DUST

They passed the signs, three in a row a half-mile apart, off Route 40 just after the sun went down. The first read:

G

It was white metal, with green lettering, just like all the road markers and speed limit signs they'd passed all the way through the Appalachians.

"What do you suppose it means?" Mary asked, and then they came to the second, which read:

2

followed by the third, which stated simply:

7

Mary strained her eyes ahead, looking for more signs, but that was all. She was propped forward in the front seat, in the same expectant position she'd held through the whole car trip. Though it had started out as a vacation, with a short side trip to Chapel Hill to pick up a few personal effects (a favorite serving dish, a bible, a picture book Mary had loved to look at when she was a child) of her Aunt Clara, who had passed away the year before, it had turned into something more: a revisit to her childhood.

She turned in the seat to regard her husband. "What do you suppose they were? I don't remember them ever being there when I was young."

"Beats me," Adam answered, shrugging. He was mid-thirtyish and open faced, a man who worked for an aerospace firm and looked it: there was always a semi-dreaming look on his features. He grinned. "Maybe they're like those old Burma Shave signs that used to line the highways—some kind of advertising. Maybe a come-on for another one of those antique places or phony country stores we've been stopping at for the last three days."

"We've gotten some good bargains!" Mary protested. "That old chest for the hallway, and—"

"A lot of other junk," Adam laughed, hitching a thumb at the back of the minivan, behind the kids.

"Oh, pooh."

They drove in silence for a stretch, listening to the soft rock station Mary had found on the radio, the road winding at the edge of the mountain down into a little dip, hiding the sky from them momentarily. Mary drank it all in. After two weeks at this rental-car driving they'd gotten so used to being in the Ford Windstar that it seemed like the natural thing to go exploring through the countryside she'd grown up in. Up until tonight they'd stuck religiously to the main roads; but the late afternoon had looked so gorgeous, with the promise of a high crescent moon later in the evening, that it seemed like the only thing to do would be to take a detour through the inner mountain passes she remembered. After all, Adam was from the Northeast, where they lived now, and the Appalachians were something he and the kids had never seen before. They'd even planned to possibly camp out, though they had hotel reservations a hundred miles further on Route 40. Adam wanted badly to take the telescope out of the trunk and do a little of the sky-gazing he hadn't managed yet. Such a clear sky. Such a beautiful Moon.

"You wouldn't believe it," Mary said, pointing up the dark mountain to their left, "but the hills and hollows around here are packed with people. There are cabins and cottages—"

A moment later, when they emerged into sky again, everything had suddenly changed.

"I don't believe it," Mary said, her mouth opening.

Swirling clouds of dusty fog had appeared out of nowhere. Adam cursed; now they'd have to drive on without stopping and find their way back to Route 40.

"Sorry, Adam," Mary said, putting a hand on his arm.

"Oh, well. I can always see the stars when we get back to Boston. I love that light pollution."

Mary smiled, and checked on the two girls in the back, who were gazing sleepily out the window.

Five minutes later a wind picked up, and what at first looked like rain began. It came on gently enough, and Adam immediately snapped on the headlights and wipers, but it increased in a steady, serious blowing way that soon alarmed him, to the point where he could barely see the road. The wind increased, and Adam realized that what was swirling around them was not rain but dust.

"What the—"

Dust or ash had completely blanketed the road in front of them, and suddenly, incredibly, when the car shifted to the side under him, and he knew that they were in trouble.

He stopped the car when he couldn't see anything at all. Rolling down the window, he put his head out to check how close to the end of the road the car was. With a sudden drop in his stomach, he discovered that not only couldn't he see the road but that the road was disappearing beneath them, melting in an upward build of dust. To their right was a steep slope that seemed to be growing closer.

"*Jesus*," he said, pulling his head back in and rolling the window back up, trying not to let his hands tremble.

"Adam—"

"Don't panic." He wanted to panic himself, but some deeper instinct than fear took over.

Gently, he tried to pull the Windstar to the left, away from the edge of the road. There was no response from the car. It was like being on an icy road in New England winter, only worse. This stuff was worse than ice. It reminded him of some of the dry lubricants he had used at work.

He put his head out the window again, and saw that they were sliding toward the edge of the slope.

He forced the wheel to the left, but it was too late to do anything.

Mary saw the cliff, too, and let out a strangled cry— but she quickly muffled it. She reached over the back seat to grab at the two girls, who had begun to wail.

"Hang on," Adam said grimly.

"*Oh, God,*" Mary moaned.

The car slid over.

Then stopped.

At that moment, as if by magic, the dust storm let up. Adam pushed out his breath evenly, gradually unclenching his hands from the steering wheel, and forced himself to look through the slashing wiper blades and dust-caked windshield.

The car was tipped forward at an ominous angle, but was anchored, at least for the moment. He gave silent thanks for the weighty antiques cluttering the rear of the minivan.

"Mary—don't move."

She looked wide-eyed at him, still clutching at the crying girls, but said nothing.

Slowly, deliberately, Adam rolled down the window and put his head out.

Just as he'd thought, the car was braced on the brow of the ledge. There was more of it on the road than off, but he could distinctly see the left front bumper dangling over a long, deep drop to the bottom of a shallow canyon.

The sky was an angry, sallow gray-yellow color, filled with swirling dust.

"Oh God," he said under his breath, and forced himself to begin breathing again.

He brought his head back into the car and rolled up the window.

The car glided forward a foot, then stopped.

"Mary," he said, forcing his mouth to say the words calmly, "we're going to have to leave the van."

She stared at him with animal fear in her eyes. "*No*," she said. "We can't. We'll fall—"

"We have to, Mary. I want you to move the kids over to my side; I'm going to get out and then open their door and help them out. I want you to slide across after me."

The wind was howling again, throwing a ticking hail of ash at the van.

"*Now*, Mary."

The car edged forward another foot, jerking a little to the right, and once more came to rest.

"Put your baseball cap on, Cindy," Mary said, trying to sound calm.

"No, Mommy, no! I'm scared!"

"It's all right to be scared. Just do what I say."

Adam pulled at his door handle, moving the door open a bare inch.

The dust swirled in at him—there was silt nearly up to the floorboards.

Sucking in a breath, Adam stepped out into it.

The viscous dust, like quicksand, took hold, tried to drive him subtly forward toward the precipice.

He put both feet firmly into the silty mass, sliding them back away from the softly insistent pull. It was like the waves they'd played in at the Massachusetts shore, a gentle but strong undertow. Calmly, with light, constant pressure, he pulled open the passenger compartment door of the van, sliding it back on its rail. He tried to keep all pressure out of his hold on the handle; he had the distinct feeling that any slight push from him on the side of the vehicle would send it tumbling off into the valley below.

"Come on, kids," he said evenly.

"I want to bring my Harry doll!" Lucy said, straining to reach under the seat for a floppy thing made of felt and buttons.

"Leave Harry, we'll get him later," Adam said. He reached in and pulled gently on her arm. She resisted for a moment and then stepped out into the mud.

"*Yuck*," she said, as her little sister, crying, followed.

Adam turned back to help Mary out of the front seat.

"*My God,*" she exclaimed, stepping into the silt and suddenly seeing where the front of the car was. "*Oh, sweet Jesus.*"

The car tipped forward, halted.

"*Lucy!*" Mary screeched.

Lucy had crawled back into the van and was reaching for her Harry doll.

The van began to move again and this time it wasn't going to stop.

Pushing Cindy down into the dust out of the way, Adam lurched into the back seat, catching Lucy by the back of her light jacket and yanking her out before she could get to the doll.

"My Harry doll!"

For a moment Adam lost his footing in the slippery dust and fell forward, half in the van and half out, still holding the child.

With Mary screaming hysterically, he felt the two of them being pulled over the cliff along with the vehicle. But then his dragging foot miraculously found a rock under the dust and he pulled himself backward, out of the van, bearing his daughter with him.

As he fell to his knees in the dust the van, with agonizing inevitability, slipped over the cliff and was gone. They watched its tail lights disappear like angry red eyes into the surging storm.

"Oh, Adam," Mary sobbed.

"It's all right," Adam answered. As he stood, his hand brushed against something in the mass of dust and he grabbed it; it vaguely resembled a chicken bone but then disintegrated in his hand. He pulled Lucy up after him. She stood unsteadily, crying over the loss of her doll.

He looked into his wife's eyes, but said nothing.

"Okay, kids," Adam said, "it's time to walk."

As they began to work their way through the silty dust to the lee side of the road, the wind came again, and the dust began to blow.

A flash of lightning, without thunder.

Ahead of them, down in a little hollow, in the midst of the roaring storm, stood a small cottage. Lightning came again, and in this second flash Adam grabbed Mary's arm and pointed the dwelling out to her.

"I don't remember anything like that being there," she said.

"Well, it's here now. Let's get the kids down," Adam answered, peering unsteadily through the whorls of dust.

Mary nodded, and then, in the next lightning illumination, looked behind them.

"*Oh, sweet Jesus.*"

A solid wall of silt was flowing down the mountainside toward them. There was no hint now that there had ever been a road where they stood. It was as if some mammoth volcano had reared up within the mountain and spewed a hundred thousand tons of ash down on itself, obliterating everything. They could see, up the mountainside, by the light of now almost continual, thunderless lightning, a few weather-beaten tips of pine trees, but nothing else. The dust, like liquid, flowed with silent determination down the mountain, toward what had once been the road.

"Quickly," Adam said, and this time he couldn't hide the fear in his voice.

There was a broken stone path down the hollow to the cabin, already slicked with viscous silt. They half walked, half slid their way down.

When they reached the front porch Adam saw with sinking hope how delicate and vulnerable the structure was. It was painted an odd dark color that might have looked quaint in summer sunshine but couldn't hide the fragility of the place.

Above and around it loomed most of the mountain.

The door opened easily. Inside, it looked like some sort of summer weekend place, one large room outfitted with the barest of necessities: a wash sink, cupboard, a few sticks of furniture including a small table with four chairs. Everything was painted in dark colors. There was a low ceiling of unpainted boards, and a picture window that looked out on the mountain and where the road had been.

Mary closed the door, took hold of Adam's arm and pointed through the window. There was awe and fear in her voice.

"Look."

Where the wall of dust had been flowing determinedly toward them, covering everything, it had stopped short of the hollow they were in.

"There wasn't any wall up there," Adam stated.

"It's almost as if it's waiting," Mary whispered.

They heard a loud creak and felt the cottage shudder.

Night came on, and stayed. The dust storm beat without mercy against the cliffs, drove in whistling tornados around the hollow. Intermittently, lightning flashed, without sound. By its light, they could see the wall of dust at the base of the mountain, hanging over them.

Inside, the small family, in the half-light of candles Mary had found in a cupboard, waited for sunrise.

"It sounds like it won't ever end," Adam said. He glanced furtively out the front picture window.

Mary stared at him without speaking.

The wind picked up with renewed fury, blowing its dry, moaning burden of dust against the fragile structure.

"I wish to hell daylight would come," Adam said.

His wife moved the blankets closer around the two children, who lay side by side on the cabin's single bed. They slept fitfully, their young minds drifting in and out of reality. "Mommee..." Cindy said suddenly, half asleep, then sank back into unconsciousness with a fitful breath.

For a few moments, there was only the moaning of the wind, the dry sound of ash washing against the front window.

"Are you sure we shouldn't have stayed outside?" Mary asked abruptly. "I keep thinking of that mass of dust above us. If it comes down..."

Adam took a shuddering breath. "We did the right thing."

"But—"

"*I said we did the right thing*!" He covered his face with his hands. "God, I hope we did..."

Outside, the wind and dust lashed mightily.

With a great rending groan, something above the ceiling was torn away.

The children awoke, screaming.

"My God!" Mary shouted, as Adam thrust himself up to go look outside. "Don't go near the window!" she pleaded.

But he was already there, peering into the foggy swirls of dust. "I can't see anything. It had to be part of the roof."

Mary set about calming the children down. Lucy began to cry, and Cindy, the older old, tried to go back to sleep.

"Adam, please, get away from the window!"

"I see…"

Another tearing groan from above.

"*Adam!*"

He shrank away from the window as something hard hit it. It rattled, but, somehow, it did not break.

"What was that?" Mary asked anxiously.

Adam moved cautiously to the window again. "I don't know. But I thought I saw something moving out there. A light."

"A *car?*" There was desperation edged by hope in Mary's voice.

"I don't see how it could be a car, with the road gone. Maybe some sort of plow or truck…"

Silence stretched between them, as Lucy again fell into a shuddering sleep.

"Mary, I have to go out there," Adam said finally.

"*No!*"

"This place won't last the night. I have to see what that light was."

As if in answer, there came a great rumbling sound from above them on the mountain. Something huge and heavy-sounding slammed into the cottage.

Mary looked with fear from the shuddering back wall to her husband. "You won't come back."

"I...just have to know if there's a safer place for us."
He looked down at the two fitfully sleeping children.
"You want me to take the chance of *not* going?"

Mary was silent.

Adam retrieved his parka and began to shrug into it.

The wind and dust whipped into a fierce cacophony of
sound, as if waiting hungrily for him to leave the cabin.

He hesitated a moment, looked back at his wife,
then unbolted the door and stepped out.

Immediately, the wind tried to yank the door from
his hands. Groaning with effort, he pulled the door shut
behind him. He stood with his back plastered to it for a
moment, trying to see through his dust-blinded glasses.

There *was* movement ahead of him.

Something...

Up where the road had been, the wall of dust was still
held in check. Adam tried to pick up some hint of why
so much silt could flow so fast so far and then suddenly
stop. He knew that was the spot where the car had been
washed over the cliff—he could see the vehicle canted
on its side at the bottom, its headlights like beacons,
dust duned slightly up one side—and he could swear
there had been no natural obstruction, a wall or dam, to
keep the wall of dust at bay.

Dry lightning flashed again.

In front of that wall, something did move. A lone
figure in a dark parka, barely visible against the black
background through the churning wind and dust, was
moving along the heaving backdrop, making its way
to the path down to the bottom of the valley and the
cottage.

The figure made its way to the bottom of the slope. It stood motionless.

"Hey!" Adam called, but he could feel the word ripped from his mouth and snuffed out by the storm. His lips were coated with dust.

The figure turned toward him.

Carefully, Adam stepped away from the cottage—and was immediately thrown down by the wind.

He nearly panicked. It felt as if hands had taken hold of him from below and were yanking him down into the dust, trying to suffocate him. There were little bits of something in the ash that broke apart—he remembered the chicken bone he had found before.

Then, abruptly, whatever had held him let go. He was up on his knees, panting into the wind.

Behind him he heard frantic tapping on a window and looked back to see Mary's frightened face at the picture window, gesturing wildly with her hands—

There were hands on Adam, helping him up.

"Wha—?"

He looked up into a dark, hooded face. He could make out no features.

"Thank you!" he shouted into the wind, regaining his footing.

The figure made a gesture and the two of them made their way to the front door of the cottage.

Mary pulled the door open, then slammed it closed behind them.

"Are you all right?" she said frantically to Adam, clutching his arm.

Adam nodded, spitting dust, beginning to regain his breath.

The children had stirred, and sat up, rubbing their eyes. Lucy sobbed out, "I want my Harry doll!"

The newcomer, turning away from them, shrugged out of his coat and began to shake the dust out of it.

"Some night," he said, matter-of-factly, turning around. He was tall, strong-looking, a weather-beaten, dark, almost cordovan color. His voice was deep and his large yet delicate hands looked as if they could pull a tree out of the ground without cracking any of the roots.

"That was your van that slid over the precipice?" the man asked. He was smiling, and he hung his parka over the back of one of the chairs at the small table.

"Yes, it was," Adam replied, realizing that even with the mud and rain and what he had been through, it was nevertheless time for social conventions, including chitchat, to be adhered to. "You're from around here?"

"You might say that," the man said, laughing softly. "This place belongs to me."

He thrust out his hand, so quickly that Adam nearly jumped.

"Please forgive me!" Adam said, taking the hand and noting the soft yet firm grip. "We just didn't know. We never would have barged in if we'd known someone was living—"

The man's laughter cut him off. "Did you have a choice?"

"As a matter of fact, no," Adam answered. He gave a short laugh himself, then asked, "Have you ever had a storm like this before?"

"Never anything quite like this," the man answered. He glanced out the picture window, then back at Adam. "Shall we have some tea?"

"I grew up here, and never heard of a dust storm in North Carolina before," Mary said suddenly, almost belligerently.

The man turned his eyes on her, and smiled.

"And for that matter," Mary continued, "I don't remember there ever being a cabin down here."

There came a loud banging, which made Mary gasp: it sounded like something living was being ripped away from the roof.

"Don't you think—?" Adam began.

The man waved a hand in dismissal. "Nothing can be done, now. Come, have some hot tea." He was already drawing water into a pot and laying out utensils and cups on the table.

The two girls had risen; Cindy padded over to Adam and tugged at his sleeve.

Her voice was small: "Daddy, are we going to slide away like the car?"

Adam was about to answer when Mary spoke up. She had wandered to the picture window, and was staring out through the swirling dust to the top of the valley where the road had been.

"Why hasn't the wall of dust come down on us?" she said, in a careful, even voice.

There was sudden silence in the room.

"Come, don't be bothered with that," the man said after a moment. He put his hand out to Mary, seeking to draw her away from the window. "Best not to think about it."

"Why not?" Mary replied quickly.

"It's just that, there's nothing to be done about it now," the man said, smiling.

"When we found this cabin," Adam said, "we saw that the dust that had come down from the mountain was in some way impeded from coming into this valley. You must have noticed it, you came down that way. Is there some sort of natural wall or outcropping up there that's holding it back?"

"No," the man said simply. "But I really don't think you should worry about it."

"The dust can't come pouring down on us?" Mary asked.

"It hasn't yet, has it?"

Something was ripped from the roof and whipped away by the wind.

"Come," the man continued, "have something hot to drink. It will calm you."

Mary was staring around, over the ceiling and down the walls. Adam couldn't help following her eyes with his own as another loud rip sounded somewhere up above.

"What were you doing outside?" Mary asked. A subtly suspicious tone had crept into her voice. Adam almost scolded her, but held his tongue.

He spread his hands wide. "This all belongs to me." He held out his hand to Mary again, but she stared at it and he gently lowered it.

"I don't like this," Mary said, turning to Adam. "I grew up here, and I know this cabin was not here."

"*Mary!*" Adam said, shocked. "How can you talk that way? The man lives here. This is his home." He was suddenly aware of his social obligation again. "Please forgive—" he began, turning to the man.

"It's nothing. Please." He gestured toward the steaming tea, set neatly at the table.

Mary stood with her arms folded staring out the picture window as Adam sat uneasily at the table, with the two girls in dainty chairs to either side of him.

Mary said quietly, "I read a story once, by Nathaniel Hawthorne, about a visitor to an inn on a mountainside. During the night, there was an avalanche, and everyone ran out and was killed. The inn was left untouched."

She turned her head slowly from the window to face the

four figures sitting at the table. Adam was staring at her as though she were mad.

"What do those signs out on the road mean—G, and 2, and 7?" she asked sharply.

"Mary—"

"Like I said," she continued, "there never was a cabin here. And the more I think about it, the more sure I am that there wasn't even a *valley* here." She turned back to look out the window. "I think this cabin is a trap."

The cabin's owner smiled evenly. "Then what about your story? If you leave, won't the dust come down on you in an avalanche and smother you?"

"I think if we stay that's what will happen."

"What if I told you it made no difference?"

Now Adam looked at the man, who only shrugged, smiling enigmatically. "Hawthorne was something of a philosopher. I've always enjoyed philosophy. It tries to explain so many unexplainable things."

There was a tentative rip at the roof above them, which cut off as the wind suddenly wound down a few notches. The dust storm was not beating quite as hard on the picture window, which now showed the first tints of a sallow dawn.

Mary turned back to look outside.

"*The dust is moving,*" she gasped, terrified.

"Is it?" the man said, still sitting at his table, smiling.

Adam got up. He could not be sure, but it did look as though the wall of ash was closer, roiling up, looming larger.

"I don't know—"

"We have to get out of here now!" Mary insisted.

She made a sudden movement toward the children, who began to cry. She thrust them into their coats.

She pushed the children toward the front door and opened it. Though it had abated, the dust storm was still fierce; the wind that met her nearly drove her back into the little bungalow.

"Mary, don't!"

But she was outside, the two howling, frightened girls in tow.

Adam looked at the man, who hadn't moved from his chair.

"You said it made no difference," Adam said, making it a question.

The man, who looked older, browner, larger and at the same time less distinct, said, "Your wife fears it has to do with this valley. It's much more than that. Read her Aunt Clara's bible." He added: "The G is for Genesis."

His smile was gone, replaced by something truly unreadable.

At his wife's sudden cry out in the storm, Adam turned toward her. Night had given way completely, the sky was filled with a sickly yellow cast, and he could see that she had fallen. The two girls were struggling to help her up.

"I have to go—"

When he looked back into the cabin it was empty.

He turned back into the storm, and soon reached Mary, who was back on her feet. Lucy had charged ahead, toward the fallen Windstar, whose headlights stabbed out of the swirling dust.

"My Harry doll!" she cried.

Mary gasped, "Catch up with her!"

Adam forged ahead, with Mary and Cindy close behind.

DUST

Lucy had mounted the van's grill and was climbing up toward the open sliding door, which now faced the sky.

Adam grabbed her, but she wriggled away from him and dropped into the interior.

As Adam tried to hoist himself up after her, he felt Mary's hands dig into him like claws.

"Oh, God, Adam! Look!"

Her voice held a note of terror he had never heard in a human voice before.

He turned toward the mountain, and gasped with disbelief. Nearly on top of them, moving like a tsunami, was a monstrous wall of dust. As it grew closer it grew higher, and there were things swirling in it that broke apart as they watched.

"Lord God Almighty..."

Mary was already pushing Cindy up and into the open door of the van, and now Adam helped Mary to follow. The ground began to tremble, and there was a sound like a freight train bearing down on them.

Adam pulled himself into the opening, and then struggled with the sliding door. The wall was right on top of them. Debris began to swirl in, dust and what looked to be bits of brittle bone, and just as Adam slammed the door shut the Windstar rocked as if a wave of water hit it. It nearly rolled over onto its roof, then slowly settled back into position on its side.

It became very dark in the van, and Adam switched on the interior lights.

Lucy was in the back seat, nestled next to the blanket chest they had bought for the hall, which was broken, holding her Harry doll, rocking it tightly against her, her eyes closed.

"Do you think—" Mary began.

"Find your Aunt Clara's bible," Adam said, leaving no room for discussion in his voice.

Mary looked at him for a moment, and then made her way into the back seat to rummage in the box of keepsakes they had taken from her Aunt's home.

The radio was still on, low, though there was no longer light rock playing. A voice was droning, and Adam, his fingers shaking, turned up the volume.

"Can we go home soon?" Cindy asked, with a young child's innocence bordering on incomprehension.

"...the entire planet," the voice on the radio was saying in a monotone. It sounded very tired, or drunk. "Reports from every corner of the globe of massive dust storms..."

Mary held up the bible. "What—"

"Look up Genesis, chapter 2, verse 7," Adam said. His voice was barely above a whisper, his eyes glued to the radio, its readout glowing green.

The car rocked, an underwater wave.

"...and this dust is not being whipped up by the wind—it is not dust from the earth or falling from the sky..."

Mary angled the bible closer to the van's dome light, which was to her back.

"Here it is," she said. "It says, 'And the Lord God formed man of the dust of the ground, and breathed into his nostrils the breath of life; and the man became a living soul.'" She looked up, perplexed. "Wha—"

Adam held up his hand; his eyes were on the radio with a fixed look.

"...humans. I repeat: the dust itself is composed of human bone and flesh. Every human on earth, apparently, one by one, is disintegrating into the dust from which we were made..."

The tired voice said: "I think..." and then there was a small gasp and then nothing but static from the radio.

Adam looked at Mary, whose eyes were impossibly wide with fright; she was clutching Cindy to her. She seemed to be fighting for breath.

"I—"

But already she was changed, turning to something brittle and dry before Adam's eyes, and Cindy, and Lucy, who was hugging her Harry doll in the farthest reaches of the rear seat, the same.

And then they broke into dust and bone and more dust, and were gone.

Adam reached out, and gave a choked cry, and watched his arm fall into dust from the fingertips back.

"But—"

He felt the breath sucked back out of his lungs, which went hot and dry and collapsed.

And then, at the last, he heard a voice, filled not with rage, or spite, or even wrath, but with mortification—

"*Go back.*"

THE PUMPKIN BOY

I

Jody Wendt, five years old, saw the Pumpkin Boy through the window over the kitchen sink, outlined against the huge rising moon like a silhouette against a white screen. Jody had climbed up onto the counter next to the basin to reach the cereal in an overhead cabinet. Now he stood transfixed with a box of corn flakes in his hands, mouth agape.

The Pumpkin Boy had a bright orange pumpkin head with cold night steam puffing out of the eyes, nose and mouth cutouts, and a body consisting of a bright metal barrel chest and jointed legs and arms that looked like stainless steel rails. Even through the closed window Jody could hear the creaking noises he made. He moved stiffly, like he was unused to walking: his feet were two flat ovoid pads, slightly rounded and raised on top, made of shiny metal. As Jody watched, one of the feet stuck in place in the muddy ground; the Pumpkin Boy, oblivious, walked on, and then toppled over with a sound like rusting machinery. He lay on the ground like a turtle on its back, making a hollow chuffing noise like *Saaaafe, saaaafe, saaaafe*. Then he slowly righted himself, rising to a sitting position and then turned slowly to search for his lost foot. Finding it, he fell forward and clawed his way toward it. He closed his hands around it. His head fell forward and hit the ground, rolling away from the body, and the hands immediately let go of the foot and grabbed the head, realigning it on the stilt body with a *ffffffmp*.

Then the foot was reattached to the leg and the Pumpkin Boy stood up with a groaning, complaining metal sound.

The Pumpkin Boy reached back down, creaking loudly, to pluck two fat organic pumpkins from Mr. Schwartz's field that grew in back of Jody's yard, and began to move off, away into the night.

"*Wow...*" Jody whispered against the window pane, making it fog. He quickly cleared it with the cuff of his shirt, and watched the Pumpkin Boy stiffly climb the fence that bordered Mr. Schwartz's pumpkin patch from another behind it. In the process the Pumpkin Boy lost hold of one of the pumpkins he held but paid no heed.

"*Wow...*" Jody whispered again.

Jody was alone in the house; it was the half-hour in-between-time when the afternoon sitter went home and his mother came home from her job in town.

He had been told repeatedly that he was not to leave the house during in-between-time.

The forgotten box of corn flakes lay spilling cereal into the kitchen sink as he climbed down, pushed his arms into his jacket and opened the door which led from the kitchen to the back yard.

THE PUMPKIN BOY

As Jody Wendt stood on the top step of the back stoop, the storm door closing with a hiss-and-bang behind him, he saw the Pumpkin Boy once again outlined against the moon, but moving quickly away. He was already two fields over, and would soon drop behind the slope that led down to Martin's Creek and the valley beyond.

Mouth still open in amazement, Jody was working at the zipper to his jacket, which wouldn't zip. His feet were already carrying him down the steps, across the yard, to the split-log fence.

He dipped under the fence, forgetting the zipper, and stood in Mr. Schwartz's pumpkin patch on the other side.

The Pumpkin Boy's head was just visible, and then the slope down made him disappear.

Jody hurried on.

Mr. Schwartz's pumpkin field was furrowed, bursting with fat, vined pumpkins that would soon be picked and sold for Halloween. Jody tripped over the first row he came to, and landed on his hands.

He found himself face to face with a huge oval orange fruit, its skin hard and strong.

It looked like a human head.

Jody pushed himself up and stumbled on.

He fell twice more. But still, in the distance, he could hear the metallic creaking sounds of the Pumpkin Boy. There were two more fences to manage, one again of split logs, which Jody scooted under, and the other of chain link, which he climbed with difficulty.

He nearly toppled over when he reached the top, but then, in the distance, he saw an orange flash in the moonlight: the top of the Pumpkin Boy's head. He held on and descended to the other side.

There was a rock wall, which Jody had never known existed, separating two more pumpkin fields.

Jody was now in unfamiliar territory. Even from his bedroom window, just before harvest, the fields surrounding his house were awash in taut orange fruit, and now, for the first time, he knew just how complicated the layout was.

At yet another rock wall he paused to look back. He could no longer see his house.

He heard a sharp metallic creak in the far distance, and hurried toward it.

The pumpkin field ended in a tangle of weeds and brambles and a ledge. Abruptly, Jody found himself teetering at the top of the slope. A tuft of brambles caught his foot and twisted his ankle and, with a short surprised gasp, he was tumbling down the damp, soft bank.

At the bottom, he came up short against an uprooted oak trunk, and came to a stop with one of its gnarled roots pointing into his face like an accusing finger.

He sat up, soiled and wet.

Suddenly, he realized what he had done.

He looked back, up the slope, and shuddered with the thought that, even if he could climb the steep incline, he would not be able to find his way back home through the tangle of pumpkin fields.

A quick, hot shiver of fear shot up his back.

But then: in front of him, like the sound of the pied piper's flute, there came the creaking sound of the Pumpkin Boy moving. The pumpkin head flashed through the trees, and Jody forgot his fear. His wonder renewed, he stood and ran after it.

✦ ✦ ✦

THE PUMPKIN BOY

The moon was partially hidden by a thick tangle of trees on the far bank of Martin's Creek, which made shafts of gray-white light on the ground. Jody splashed into the water before he knew it was in front of him. His hurt foot slid down nearly to his shin into icy tumbling water and lodged between two rocks.

Jody cried out in pain. For a moment he couldn't move, and panicked—but then, suddenly, one of the stones upended in the water and rolled over, and he was free.

Now, both sneakers were in the water, and the slight current tugged at his legs.

He tried to turn around, but the water hurried him out further.

He sank another half foot.

The current was trying to make him sit down, which would bring his head under water.

He gave a weak cry as he lost his struggle—and then there was water in his mouth and he could see nothing but the blur of moving wetness.

Almost immediately, his body pressed up against something long, dark and solid, and his forward progress stopped.

It was a half-submerged log.

Jody clung to it, and slowly pulled himself up.

To his surprise, the creek was only two feet or so deep here; the whooshing sound of water angrily churning around the log filled his ears.

He held onto the dry part of the log, and coughed water out.

He wiped his eyes with one hand, and had another surprise: not only was the water shallow, it was not half as wide as it had been just a few yards up-creek.

Holding the log, he pushed his way through the shallow water to the far bank.

He sat down, and his eyes filled with sudden tears.

I want to go home, he thought.

He stared out at totally unfamiliar territory: the creek, he now saw, twisted and turned, and he could not make out the spot where he had descended the slope, which was nearly a hundred yards away, and impossibly wide. At the top of the ridge, reflected in moonlight, were the green-vined tops of a few elongated pumpkins.

He turned, and saw that the line of woods was close, and darker than it had looked from the other side of the creek.

The trees were nearly nude, a carpet of yellow and red fallen leaves at their bases looking light and dark gray in the moonlight.

A few late leaves pirouetted down as he watched.

Deep in the woods, he heard the Pumpkin Boy move.

Jody looked once again behind him, and then back at the woods.

He got painfully up and hobbled toward the trees.

It instantly became darker when he entered the woods, a grayer, more sporadic light.

Almost immediately, Jody lost his bearings.

There were many strange noises, which confused him. He thought he heard the Pumpkin Boy nearby, but the sound proved to be a partially broken oak branch, creaking on its artificial hinge. There were rustlings and stirrings. Something on four legs scuttled past him in the near distance, and stopped to stare at him—it looked like a red fox, bleached gray by the night.

Jody tried to retrace his steps, but only found himself deeper within the trees, which now all looked the same.

Jody's ankle hurt, and he was beginning to shiver.

He stopped, even hushing his own frightened breathing, and listened for the Pumpkin Boy.

The sound of the Pumpkin Boy's movement was completely gone.

A soft wind had arisen, and now leaves lifted from the forest floor, as if jerked alive by puppet strings.

It had turned colder—above, the moon was abruptly shielded by a gust of clouds.

The woods became very dark.

Jody sobbed again, stumbling forward, and stopped in a small clearing surrounded by tall oaks. Again he heard scurrying in front of him and felt something watching him.

The moon blinked out of the clouds, and Jody saw what was, indeed, a red fox, regarding him with wary interest.

The fox became suddenly alert. As the moon's nightlight was stolen again by clouds, the animal bolted away, seeming to jump into the gray and then darkness.

Jody stood rooted to his spot, trying not to cry.

Something was out there.

Something large and dark.

The bed of leaves shifted with heavy, creaking steps.

Something ice cold and long and thin brushed along his face in the darkness.

"*I want to go home!*" Jody blurted out in fear and despair.

The cold air was suddenly steamed with warmth.

Cold braces closed around Jody's middle from behind.

He shrieked, and wrenched his body around.

He was blinded by something larger and brighter than the moon—a face staring down at him made out of a jack o'lantern, warm wet fog pushing from its triangular eyes and nose and impossibly wide, smiling mouth. A slight, mechanical *chuff* issued along with the sour, oily-smelling steam.

The slender mechanical steel arms tightened around Jody.

He shrieked again, a mournful sound swallowed by the trees and close night around him.

As he was carried away he saw, as the moon broke forth from the clouds again, on the forest floor, caught in gray light, the smashed leavings of a dropped pumpkin.

2

Another damn Halloween.

Len Schneider was beginning to work up a deep and real hatred for holidays in general, and this one especially. Halloween, he knew, meant nothing but trouble. He'd moved to Orangefield for lots of reasons—among them the fact that it had a real town with a genuine small-town feel—it was the only place he'd lived in the last twenty years that didn't have a Walmart and wasn't likely to get one. The people seemed friendly enough, but he'd found, as a police detective, that people were pretty much the same everywhere, from the inner city to Hometown, U.S.A. "People Are Funny," Art Linkletter used to say, and one thing Len Schneider had learned after eighteen years in law enforcement was that they were anything but.

THE PUMPKIN BOY

And now this *thing* came along—the thing he'd left Milwaukee to get away from...

"When was the last time you had a missing kid case?" he'd asked Bill Grant, the other detective on Orangefield's police force. Grant had been at it a long time, too, but all of it in this town. In the year and a half Schneider had been here, he'd found Grant polite but almost aloof. No, aloof wasn't the right word—it was almost like he wasn't completely there. The two packs of cigarettes a day he smoked didn't seem to help, and the emphysemic cough that went along with them, along with the booze he drank, had turned him almost sallow.

Schneider thought he was haunted himself, by what had happened back in Milwaukee—but this guy looked like he was haunted by *real* ghosts.

He'd tried to get Grant to open up a few times, once over a bottle of Scotch, but all that had happened was that he'd opened up himself, letting his own bile and anger out. He wondered if Grant even remembered, though he had a feeling he did. Behind the hollows of those eyes the cop-mind still worked—and Schneider had been told that Grant was very good at his job.

He had found out on his own later that Grant had begun to change after a case involving a local children's book author, Peter Kerlan. Something about Kerlan's wife being eaten alive by insects...

Grant was leaning back in his chair, his fingers idly drumming the neatly arranged desk in front of him. The man's skin looked almost jaundiced. Just as Schneider was about to repeat his question, Grant said, without moving his eyes or head, "We've had a few over the years. They almost always turn up."

"Ever anything..."

"Like yours?" Grant almost snapped. The confirmation that Grant not only remembered The Night of Scotch but had absorbed and catalogued everything that had gone on, startled Schneider.

"Yes, like mine," Schneider replied evenly.

"Not unless you go back a long way. Long before you or me."

Schneider waited for elaboration, but there was none.

"Any chance you'd like to take this one?" Schneider tried to keep his voice light, but knew he may have failed.

Another silence hung between them, and then Grant's voice came out of the emaciated face again: "None."

Schneider was swiveling toward his own desk with a sigh when he caught Grant leaning forward, his eyes finally giving him attention. He swiveled back, his hands on his knees.

Grant was staring at him, a bit too intently. His own yellow fingers had stopped drumming, and lay perfectly still on his desk blotter. Schneider suddenly saw the intelligence in the sunken light blue eyes.

"It's got nothing to do with you," Grant said, carefully. For the first time his gaze fell on Schneider as something more than a concept—Grant was actually *looking* at him. "It's just that this one has that...aura around it. And, frankly, I couldn't go through that again. There are things that happen around here that are perfectly normal, and then there are other things..."

"If you're talking about the Kerlan murders—"

"That," Grant shot back, "and other things. Usually around this time of year."

"All right then, Bill." Schneider moved to swivel back to his desk, but Grant's eyes held him.

"There are worse things than a kid getting killed," Grant said quietly.

Sudden anger flared in Schneider, but he saw that Grant seemed to be looking inward, not at him anymore.

Grant seemed to catch himself, and his sallow neck actually reddened. He fumbled with the small notebook that lay neatly on his desk, opened and closed it.

"I'm sorry, Len," Grant said, his voice lowered almost to a whisper. "I can imagine what that case of yours was like in Milwaukee. That kid's parents, especially his father going insane. Wasn't he some kind of genius or something?" He shook his head slowly from side to side; the flush of color had left his features. "There are some things you never forget. Sometimes I think about myself too much..." For a brief moment his neck reddened again. "Sorry..."

Then Grant leaned back in his chair again, his fingers drumming lightly on the neat desk.

The interview was over.

There are worse things than a kid getting killed...

"No, there aren't," Len Schneider said to himself, and loud enough for someone else to hear.

The kid might have been eleven or twelve. Without a face, it was hard to tell if he had been good-looking or not—sometimes by that age, you can tell how the features will set through the teen years. He looked like he was sleeping when they dug him up—resting his hand under his head; the face, or where it would have been, was turned into the dirt so that it looked like he had nuzzled into a pillow. The hand was covering a ragged hole in the boy's head where his brains had literally been beaten in. He was still fully clothed, except for his shoes and socks—later they found that he had been undressed and then redressed by Carlton, who had kept the footwear—along with one of the boy's toes—as souvenirs.

Jerry Carlton had almost boasted about it at his trial—his shaggy hair had been cut and combed, his red tie knotted, his eyes covered with mirrored sunglasses which, thank God, the judge had made him remove. He smiled through the whole proceeding, and played with his watch. He could fix a tractor, a television set, could build just about anything, and had murdered five boys in three states calling himself Carlton the Clown. He'd worn a different clown costume for each murder.

Len had never forgotten that: Carlton the Clown.

He'd wanted only three minutes alone with Jerry Carlton, but they wouldn't give it to him.

Just three minutes...

And nearly every night, because he made a mistake, Len Schneider dreamed of a kid with no face, turning his head from where it was nuzzled into his pillow and staring at him with empty eye sockets, trying to speak without lips...

This time, Len Schneider vowed to himself, he'd get his three minutes.

And he wouldn't make any mistakes.

Schneider was convinced the Wendt kid was not merely missing. Everything pointed to it. The kid's mother (another thing that made it worse: there was no father, he had died in a construction accident four years ago) swore her son had never left the house by himself before. Which led Schneider at first to conventional lines: that whoever had taken the child had learned the house routine, and knew that there was a window of opportunity every once in a while when the child was alone for a half-hour, between his afternoon sitter leaving and his mother getting home from work.

But there were no signs of forced entry, which led Len automatically to the next line of enquiry: that the child had unlocked the back door himself and let the abductor in.

Which could have happened—although, again, there was no evidence that anyone had been in the house. It had been a quick snatch, if that had been the case—which meant that the boy had probably known the assailant.

Which was possible, up to a point—the point being a weird one. It had rained a few days before the abduction, and the ground had been fairly soft—but there was only one set of footprints in the backyard, leading away from the house to the back fence.

Indicating that someone had lured him over the fence—*something he had never done before*—without actually stepping into the backyard himself.

When he asked Mrs. Wendt for a list of people, with the emphasis on males, who might be enough of authority figures in her son Jody's eyes to entice him to do such a thing, her face went blank. There were no clergy, no relatives, no real male role model who he would follow over that fence, she was sure.

He told her to think about it, and if anyone came to her to let him know right away.

AL SARRANTONIO

✦ ✦ ✦

At that point Schneider did the conventional thing: he followed the child's footprints as far as he could. And it was quite a job: behind the Wendt property was a patchwork quilt of pumpkin fields owned by various farmers. He nonetheless was able to follow the boy's movements through four of these fields to the edge of a fifth, which then dropped off down to a shallow valley and a thin ribbon of water known as Martin's Creek.

From the marks he found, it looked as though the boy had slid or fallen down the embankment.

There were indications that he had crossed the creek at one point.

For a moment Schneider's heart climbed into his throat, when he saw how deep the creek was at the point the boy entered. He followed the line of water downstream, fearing that the boy's drowned body might turn up at any moment.

But he found markings on the other side of the water at a shallower area where a fallen tree bridged the creek (perhaps the boy *was* in trouble until he came up against this spot) and these fresh marks led into the tangle of trees on the other side of water.

The odd thing was that there were only the boy's tracks. He broadened his search, and discovered that, a second, oddly shaped set of tracks led from the pumpkin field behind the Wendt house down the embankment into the woods, but they were nowhere near the boy's.

Which led him to believe that, perhaps, the boy had been *following* someone?

Out of breath and sweating a little, his slight paunch only one indication of how out of shape he was (*thirty years old and already starting to look like an old cop*), he found himself at a spot in the patch of woods marked by a broken pumpkin where both sets of tracks converged.

It was here, obviously, that the boy was abducted.

There were signs of a struggle. And then only the second set of prints—which were very odd indeed, not shoe or boot prints but large flat ovoids, which made him think that someone had worn some sort of covering over his shoes, to disguise the prints—led away.

And then, abruptly, in the middle of nowhere, among a gloomy stand of gnarled trees, so thick and twisted they blocked all light from above, they stopped.

At that point the hair on the back of Schneider's head (where there still *was* hair, a good part of the top of his head being bald) stood on end. He looked at the clearing he stood in, covered with leaves and dead branches.

Where...

He brought in dogs, of course, and along with two uniformed policemen he brushed the area of leaves and twigs, looking for an underground opening. But there was none. Even the dogs, who had been given a piece of Jody Wendt's clothing, had stopped at the same spot Schneider had.

One of them threw back its head and bayed, which, again, made the hair on the back of Schneider's head stand on end.

Jody Wendt had disappeared into thin air.

3

The poster, which read: *UNCLE LOLLIPOP LOVES YOU!* was upside down. He was glad his mom had taught him to read. There was more writing at the bottom of the poster, but he couldn't make out what it said because it was too small and it was also upside down. So was everything else. The sign was in bright colors, red and blue and yellow and green, as if the colors had been splashed on or finger-painted—they ran over their borders and looked still wet. The room smelled like paint, like the time his mother had painted his bedroom in March and left all the windows open. He'd slept on the couch in the living room that night (sneaking the television on at three in the morning, but there had only been commercials on for exercise equipment—some of which Mom had—and for calcium and vitamin supplements—he had soon tired and turned the TV off; even out here he could faintly smell the paint on the walls of his room) and when he went back to his room the next night he got sick to his stomach, even though the paint was dry and the windows had been left open a crack. A week later all his own posters and his bookshelf with *Mike Mulligan and His Steam Shovel* (his favorite book) and *The Wizard of Oz* and *Sam Hain and the Halloween that Almost Wasn't* were back, and the smell was gone. He'd forgotten his room had ever been painted.

But the smell wasn't gone here—it was stronger. It had a curious burning odor underneath the paint smell, as if someone was heating paint in a pan.

That was funny, heating paint in a pan...

He felt light-headed, and suddenly wanted to throw up.

Ahhhhh...

The discomforting noise he made caused another noise out of his vision, a shuffling like a dog had been disturbed. He could not see. Except for the upside-down poster and an upside-down coat hook next to it with a rain coat which was hung near the floor and ran up the wall (again: funny! And despite his queasy stomach he gurgled a short laugh) he could see little else. The wall was colored chocolate brown, and it was stuffy in the room.

Again he heard the dog-shuffle.

Something new came into his view, in front of the wall poster—something just as brightly colored. It was accompanied by the shuffling noise, which was caused, Jody saw, when he strained his eyes to look up (which hurt) by the slow movement of a pair of huge clown feet, which were red with bright yellow laces. His vision in that direction was impeded by a sort of cap that appeared to be on his head, though he felt nothing there. There was a sharp rim, and he could see no farther. What he saw of the ceiling under the clown's feet, was the same color as the wall.

Jody looked down, and his sight trailed over the figure of a circus clown dressed in blue pants, a red- and green-striped blouse with baggy sleeves and white gloves, and a white face with an impossibly wide, bright red smile, eyelashes painted all around his eyes, all topped by a snow-white cap with a red pom-pom.

The shuffling stopped; the clown was facing him now and Jody noted that the figure's real lips inside the painted-on smile weren't smiling. The eyes looked serious inside their cartoon lashes, too.

"*Ted?*" The clown whispered, in an impossibly gentle voice. "You're awake, Ted?"

Jody tried to tell the clown that his name wasn't Ted, but the feared throw-up rose hotly in his throat, out his mouth and ran up his face.

It was now, through the paint smell and dizziness and headache, that he realized *he* was upside-down, not the room.

The clown *tsk-tsked*, and a wet cloth was pressed to Jody's nose and cheeks, rubbed gently.

The bile was gone.

It was getting very stuffy in the room.

"Soon, Ted, soon..." the clown said, and then he shuffled out of Jody's sight.

"I—" Jody managed to get out.

The shuffling stopped. "Yes?" the clown asked, and there was a closed-in hush in the room.

"I...no...Ted..." Jody spit out, along with more bile, before his vision began to blur.

"I know, Ted. Yes," the Clown answered, in what was almost a sing-song whisper.

Then, Jody closed his eyes.

✦ ✦ ✦

When he opened them again, he was hungry.

The paint smell was still there, and the queasiness, and the headache, which was worse now, and he was still upside-down and couldn't move. But, somehow, he felt more alert.

He saw immediately that the poster—*UNCLE LOLLIPOP LOVES YOU!*—was partially blocked by a familiar sight: the Pumpkin Boy, or at least part of him. The Pumpkin Boy's chest, which was a thicker tube of metal than the articulated stalks that composed his arms, was open, revealing a cavity within with something red, suspended in a web of golden wire, that throbbed darkly. The web shivered noticeably with each beat. The cavity's door lay hinged back against the Pumpkin Boy's side. He seemed to be missing from the legs down (or up, to Jody's eyes) and his head was hinged open on the top. Now, in the light, Jody saw that the head itself looked to be made of some sort of ceramic or plastic or other hard surface; it was too hard-edged and brightly colored (a hue as bright as the poster colors, and the Clown suit colors) to be real. There were no seeds stuck to the inside of the lid, which looked smooth and clean.

A trail of golden wires led out of the Pumpkin Boy's head, the back part behind the eyes, nose, and grinning mouth (could there be a hidden compartment back there?) and were bundled together with white plastic ties. There looked to be hundreds of individual hair-thin wires. The bundle ended in a curl, like a rolled hose, on the floor.

Jody saw that the Pumpkin Boy wore a pair of ordinary leather carpenter's gloves, like the ones his mother used in the garden.

Jody now realized how quiet it was.

"Hel...lo?" he said. His voice sounded like a frog's croak.

There was no answer.

Feeling stronger than he had before, Jody tried to twist himself around.

Whatever he was trussed to, it gave little, but it did give. He turned a bit to the right, then swung back, as if he were suspended on a rope. He had seen the wall beyond the Pumpkin Boy and the poster: flat brown, unadorned.

He twisted again, harder. His legs were asleep, which at least meant that his twisted ankle didn't hurt anymore. His hands were also asleep, but he could feel enough of them now to discover that they were bound behind his back, tightly.

He tried for a time, but couldn't loosen them.

This time as he turned he saw the wall and something on the true floor: a table, a bright silver machine with a big black dial and the edge of a huge white clock-face with too many numbers around the edge.

He came stubbornly back to rest.

He was growing weaker.

The Pumpkin Boy hadn't moved, was staring straight through him.

Jody gave a mighty turn, with an *ooofff!*

This time he felt as if a lance had pierced his forehead. He cried out in pain—but he saw the whole silver machine, which was on casters, and other machines, one of which looked like the emergency generator Mom kept in the garage, and a door. No windows. The clown suit was draped over a single chair, next to a lamp—

The door was just opening.

Jody swung back to rest, the pain still driving through his head. He knew he was crying.

The shuffle sounded frantic.

"*Ted—!*"

He passed out with the man's hands on his head, or what felt like through it.

✦ ✦ ✦

A hum in his ears.

It sounded like bees, or millions of ants. He'd seen millions of ants once, two armies fighting in the forest, brown and black. He went back three days later and they were still fighting. His cousin Jim, who was fourteen years old, told him to make a cone out of the comic book in his back pocket and he did, and put the wide end of the cone near the massed ants and the other, the tighter end next to his ear. He heard a roaring, a scrabble and hum that sounded like the mighty armies he saw fighting in books.

THE PUMPKIN BOY

He thought Jim had played a trick on him, and took the homemade horn away from the battle, but there was Jim ten feet away from him, grinning.

"Somethin', ain't it?"

"Wow..."

It had sounded like this, only less so...

Jody opened his eyes. It felt, now, like his head had been split in two, like a melon. There was a dry burning behind his eyelids, and a circle of hot pain all around his head, as if a heated clamp had been tightened around it.

He heard a mewling sound, and realized it came from his mouth.

"There, Ted, there..."

A cool hand rested on his brow, above his eyes, and then withdrew.

The hot pain circling his head increased.

His eyes were watering, but he blinked and then could see, almost clearly. The Pumpkin Boy sat where he had been, staring mutely at nothing. To his right the silver machine with the big black dial and white clock face had been positioned at a slight angle; next to it, on another dolly, was a similar, smaller machine.

The thick bundle of hair-thin golden wires was now plugged into the side of the silver machine; another bundle was plugged into the opposite side of the machine and ran to the floor...

...toward Jody...

He cried out, in pain and terror—

"There, there, Ted..."

Again the soothing hand, the clown glove; as it withdrew from his face Jody saw the clown face close to his own, peering into him as if his head were a fish bowl. The lips didn't smile, nor the eyes.

"...*out!*"

"Yes, Ted," the soft voice sing-songed. "Yes..."

The clown hand came back to pat his forehead.

He writhed, tried to loosen his hands, his feet, to snake down from his captivity.

The soothing voice became almost scolding.

"Ted, you mustn't—"

The clown hand reached out to the huge black dial on the silver machine—Jody saw the hand grip it hard and twist it—

Pain came, and he went back to sleep.

4

Pictures of Jody.

She didn't know whether to take them down, put them away, turn them to the wall or put them in new frames. Nothing, Emily Wendt knew, would work. If she put them away it would be a defeat, an admission that he was gone, as well as giving up hope.

But having him staring out at her from every room in the house was almost unbearable. She had never realized how many pictures she had of her son: they were everywhere, framed on the hallway wall, in a gilt frame next to her bed, stuck under magnets on the refrigerator door, herded with other family portraits on top of the television, on the hunter's table behind the sofa, the last Sears portrait, from Christmas, on the phone table—

In the end, she put them all away except the one next to her bed.

That had been the first portrait she'd ever had taken of him, when he was one. Jack had still been alive, then. She remembered how much trouble they had keeping Jody still; the photographer had posed him in a chair covered with a blanket and Jody, who had recently taken his first steps, kept trying to dismount the chair. It was obvious he was fascinated by the camera and wanted to study it. Finally the photographer had to let him look it over, click the shutter twice and then promise him another look if he sat still for the picture.

You'd never know he had been any trouble by looking at the finished product. The portrait showed him staring quietly, with big eyes, at the camera; his face held a measure of interest that proved he was only thinking about getting his hands on that machine again. A lick of his thin auburn hair had fallen over his brow (later his hair would thicken, becoming almost coarse; unless cut very short it tended never to stay combed or brushed for long) and his pudgy hands were folded on his lap.

This would be the picture she wouldn't put away.

Later that day, after the session, she and Jody and Jack had gone to the taco place in the mall, the one and only time they had ever eaten out together. She still remembered what Jody had done to the burrito they had gotten him, how he had dissected it like a frog—

She found herself weeping—the first time, in the week since Jody had been taken, that she had cried. She had thought her life was over after Jack was killed, but now she knew just how much she had still possessed, even after the loss of her husband. There was a hollow place in her now that felt as if it had been scooped out with a trowel, and she knew it would never fill in.

This was *nothing* like it had been when Jack died.

She collapsed to the floor, hugging Jody's picture, and sat with her legs folded beneath her, rocking and crying.

"Oh, Jody, *Jody...*"

She thought she heard him call her name.

She froze in mid sob, and wiped her eyes with the sleeve of her sweater.

"Jody...?"

She knew how foolish this was, but she *had* heard him call to her.

Forgetting the picture, she pushed herself to her feet and stumbled to the back of the house. The noise had come from the kitchen.

A blast of cold air hit her. She saw that the kitchen door leading to the backyard was open.

Holding her sweater closed and shivering, she stepped out onto the back stoop.

"Jody?" she called, almost fearfully.

The backyard was awash in unraked leaves pushed into dunes by the wind. The sky was overcast, huge banks of gray cumulus clouds rolling over one another from west to east. The temperature was falling. The pumpkin fields beyond the fence looked ominous, cold, brown and wet. The far hills surrounding Orangefield were dark, the trees stripped of green.

It looked like the landscape of a particular kind of hell.

She shivered, still holding her sweater closed, and turned around.

She gasped, and put her hand to her mouth.

There, staring straight up at her, was the face of a pumpkin. Puffs of steam issued from the eyes, the nose. The surface of the face looked hard and glassy, and, from within, there was a soft orange glow.

There was a body below it, the size of an older boy or young teen, sharp angles and shiny metal. The thing had its hands on her shoulders, holding her. There were gloves on its hands, but she could feel sharp metal fingers within.

THE PUMPKIN BOY

The face came closer. There was a flat metallic smell, like 3-in-1 oil. The eyes stared into her, studying her, as if watching her from a far distance.

A long puff of metallic-smelling steam hissed forth from the mouth, which was smiling impossibly wide through its two angled teeth.

The jet of steam held a word, in the form of a question:

"Mmmmmom?" Jody said.

5

It was getting dark.

Len Schneider looked like a man who was thinking. He stood with his head down, hands in the pockets of his jacket.

He glanced at his watch.

Almost time to go.

His hands clenched into fists.

It had turned even colder. The last few days had each announced, with increasing earnestness, that autumn was here and winter wasn't far behind. A curt wind was dervishing dead leaves into some of the shallow pits they had dug. The deeper holes were filled with muddy water and blankets of leaves.

There was nothing else in any of them.

Where the hell are you, you son of a bitch?

His fists clenched tighter.

"Detective? We're gonna roll now."

Schneider looked up to see Fran Morrison, one of the fresh-faced uniformed cops, standing in front of him. Behind the tight cluster of trees, in a small clearing, a work crew was loading shovels and other tools into a truck: an emblem on its door, in orange letters on a black background, read TOWN OF ORANGEFIELD, PUBLIC WORKS.

As Schneider watched, one of the crew opened the door, climbed into the truck and yanked it closed behind him.

Morrison was waiting for him to say something, so Schneider let out a long breath and said, "Yeah, Fran, we're done here. You might as well go, too."

"You need a ride back?"

Schneider looked down at his shoes, which were covered with mud. "No, I'm good."

Morrison, almost sighing with relief, turned and was gone. A few moments later Schneider heard his patrol car spitting leaves from its tires as it followed the truck out of the road they had made and hooked up with a dirt road a quarter of a mile away.

He was alone, now.

But he knew he wasn't. He felt it.

"*Dammit!*"

His voice echoed through the forest.

He couldn't blame Morrison and the rest of them if they thought he was obsessed. He knew he was. But there was no way he wasn't going to do everything he could to find Jody Wendt.

And Jody Wendt was here, somewhere.

Whoever had taken him had a lair here, somewhere.

Schneider *knew* it.

For a moment, Jerry Carlton's smirking face rose into his memory, wearing those goddamned mirror shades.

"Not this time," Schneider said out loud.

"My party, this time," Grant said.

The bar itself was crowded, but the booth area, at three o'clock in the afternoon, was nearly empty. Bill Grant placed a fifth of *Dewars* gently on the table, as if setting down a piece of porcelain, and sat as he produced two eight-ounce glasses, one with ice, one empty. He hesitated as he pushed the empty one toward Len Schneider.

"This is the way you like it, right? Neat?"

Grant had already lit the first of what would probably be a hundred cigarettes.

Schneider nodded. "I didn't think you were paying attention last time."

Grant gave a slight smile and pushed the empty glass to the other side of the table.

Schneider was working at the cap on the bottle, and twisted it open with practiced ease.

He poured for himself, then reached across and studied the amber liquid as it trickled over the ice in Grant's glass.

"I thought we should talk outside the office," Grant said.

Schneider's ears immediately pricked up; already he detected a focus in the man he hadn't seen before.

Len replied, still looking at the scotch in Grant's glass, "You here to give me the fatherly pep talk? I'm sure Franny Morrison and the rest of them think I'm nuts."

He looked up from Grant's glass to meet the other detective's eyes. To his surprise, Grant had pulled his cigarette from his mouth and was smiling.

"You think I'm nuts too?" Schneider asked.

Grant's smile widened. "As a matter of fact, I do. But I understand. Thing is, I know now that this isn't... weird shit."

Schneider had downed one scotch, and refilled his own glass. Grant's new attitude had begun to irk him just as much as his old one.

"This isn't weird enough for you?" he said. "Did you hear what Jody Wendt's mother claims happened to her two days ago? That a pumpkin-headed robot appeared on her back stoop and spoke to her in Jody's voice?" Schneider let out a bitter laugh. "You don't find that *strange?*"

"Frankly, I find it charming. She told me the same story."

"*You interviewed her?*" Schneider said with sudden anger.

"On my own time," Grant added quickly. His smile faded a bit, and he actually looked apologetic. He lit another cigarette, blew smoke, and said, "It has nothing to do with you, Len. I just had to know."

"Had to know what?" Schneider's voice had risen— a few of the patrons at the bar, one of whom was a cop they both knew, looked around before turning away. Schneider finished his drink and poured a third.

Grant put his hand on Schneider's arm. Schneider looked at the hand, still angry—but his anger drained when he saw that the familiar haunted look had returned to the other detective's face. Grant's skin had the yellow pallor of the tepid cloud of smoke from his cigarette.

Schneider let a long breath out.

Grant had finished his own scotch and was pouring a new one. He drained half of this past its ice, which had mostly melted from the natural heat of the liquor, then put the glass down. He coughed.

"Remember when I said there were worse things than a kid getting killed?"

THE PUMPKIN BOY

Schneider's anger was back in an instant, but Grant pushed immediately on:

"I know how callous that sounded. Believe me, I do." He stopped for scotch and then a fresh cigarette, which he chain-lit from the remains of his current butt, only half devoured. "But I've seen things much worse than anything you can imagine."

"Like what?" Schneider replied, not hiding his mood.

"I don't want to talk about that," Grant said. His voice became a near whisper, and Schneider was once again reminded of the vague, haunted man in the office the day he had taken this assignment. "I don't ever want to talk about that."

He looked straight at Schneider, who was working on his own scotch. "But there are other things I will talk about. There was a local beekeeper named Fred Willims. He was involved in the Peter Kerlan case with me. That was the children's book author you've heard about.

"We had a closed-door session with the district attorney at the time, who sealed the case shut. His name was Charles Morton. He warned Willims never to say anything about what we'd seen happen on Halloween to Peter Kerlan or his wife. Me, he didn't have to tell, though I'm telling you now that Kerlan and his wife were both killed by hornets. As far as I know, Willims never said a word. But some time later Willims was found dead, hung from a tree with his eyes gouged out. The eyeholes were filled with hornets. Morton died, too, the same day, of anaphylactic shock from a hornet sting. And then there was a girl named Annabeth Turner—"

"I read that case after I got here," Schneider said. "Tried to hang herself in a park—"

Now it was Grant's turn to interrupt. "That's what the report said. There were two other suicides, both of them successful, at almost exactly the same time. There was more to it than just a bunch of suicides, Len."

Again, Schneider asked, "Like what?"

Grant shrugged, looking suddenly deflated. "Never mind. But here we are again at that special time of year in Orangefield, when the pumpkins get sold, Pumpkin Days come, the farmers get rich and weird shit crawls out of the woodwork. Only this year, my friend, for once it's just plain old crime."

Schneider said nothing.

Grant leaned forward and said earnestly, "What do you believe in, Len? What do you *really* believe in?"

Grant's question was so unlike him, so unlike his meticulous procedural ways and evidence building, and his manner so suddenly needy, as if some sort of dam had burst within him, letting out all the fears he'd tucked away, that Schneider said nothing. He looked at his scotch, then drank it. He started to get up.

"I believe in not fucking up a second time, Bill. That's what I believe in."

Grant grabbed his arm and urged him back into the booth. His eyes pinned Schneider in place, like a butterfly to a board. When he spoke again his voice was level and harsh. "Take me seriously, Len. The good news is that you don't have to worry about weird shit. At least not this time. The bad news is I think you just might fuck up again, if you're not careful. I think you should let me have this case, after all. It was a mistake for me to let you take it to begin with. You've got that mess in Milwaukee so tied up with this that you're liable to screw up. I've seen it happen. It happened to me, and just like you I was concentrating on payback instead of doing my job—"

It was Schneider's turn to be level and harsh. He leaned forward in the booth. "That bastard Jerry Carlton sat there during his trial taking his watch apart and putting it back together. He never glanced at the jury, not once. At the end of the trial, he looked up from his watch and mouthed the word 'Ted' at me. That was the kid in Milwaukee's name." His voice was shaking. "I could have saved that kid, Bill."

"Maybe," Grant answered.

There was another two fingers of scotch in Schneider's glass, and he drained it, poured again. Tears abruptly filled his eyes. "*I could have saved him.*"

"Like I said, maybe. Then again, maybe not. Maybe you still would have gotten there too late. Maybe Jerry Carlton would have killed him earlier, if he saw you coming. Maybe—"

Schneider drained his glass and gripped it so hard he could feel it getting ready to break. He looked at Grant, who was studying him; Grant's pallor had assumed its yellow, haunted tinge.

"Be careful, Len," Grant almost whispered. "Do your job and don't let things get out of hand." He paused to light yet another cigarette. "Advice from an old fart. Someone named Riley Gates, my mentor, once gave the same advice to me. He also saved my life by not shooting me when I was about to fuck up big time." He gave a short, bitter laugh that ended in a cough. "He also saved my career, such as it is."

The anger was back and this time when Schneider stood up Grant didn't try to stop him.

"This case is mine, Bill. Stay the hell away from it. And I don't need a goddamn mentor—especially not a burned-out lush who's seen the boogeyman one too many times."

As Schneider stalked off, Grant stared straight ahead, unconsciously pulling another cigarette from his pocket. He didn't look at it as he lit it from the one already in his mouth, which had barely burned.

"Careful..." he said.

6

Boring.

Here it was, almost time for the Pumpkin Days Festival, and Scotty Daniels was bored silly. He was sick to death of little kid stuff. In his kindergarten class, they'd already done their pumpkin cutouts for the windows, and made their "special designs" for the school projects display during the festival. They had already taken their bus trip to Mr. Frolich's farm to pick their own pumpkins.

They had tied yellow ribbons for Jody Wendt to one of the sycamore trees in the field behind the school, and Scotty himself, who had been one of Jody's best friends, had picked out a special pumpkin at Frolich Farm, which now sat on Jody's empty desk. There was a bulletin board in the back of the room with cards and balloons remembering Jody thumbtacked to it.

And now, there was nothing to do but wait for the festival to begin.

Or:

Think about hunting the Pumpkin Boy.

Scotty had first heard about the hunt from his older brother Jim, but the story had traveled like wildfire through all of the schools in Orangefield. One of Jim's friends, Mitchel Freed, claimed he had seen a boy made out of silver stilts with a pumpkin head walking through one of the fields at the edge of town; Mitchel's older brother was a police officer and claimed that the Pumpkin Boy had visited Mrs. Wendt after Jody disappeared. Soon there were Pumpkin Boy sightings everywhere, so many that the *Orangefield Herald* had carried stories about it, which Jim read out loud to him.

But when he asked if he could go with Jim when he and his friends went looking for the Pumpkin Boy tonight, Jim had only laughed and ruffled his hair.

"No way, little man! Mom would kill me if I took you." He looked suddenly serious and said, "And anyway: Mitch and Pete and I might get killed!"

Then he laughed and walked away to use the phone.

Scotty could hear him using it now, arranging for Mitchell to come by in ten minutes and that they'd go in Jim's car.

Bored.

Scotty wandered into the family room, where his younger sister Cyndi was watching the Cartoon Network. He sat down grumpily next to her on the couch and tried to wrestle the TV remote from her hands. She clutched it tightly and said, "Hey!" Finally he gave up and threw himself into the far end of the couch, among the sofa pillows, and folded his arms, feeling ornery.

He glanced out the window to the street, where a passing car's headlights momentarily blinded him. He continued staring, and when his sight came back he was staring at Jim's car at the curb.

The trunk was open.

A sudden idea formed in his mind.

At that moment he heard Jim get off the phone, yell down to the basement to tell his father that he'd be going out for a little while. After his father answered with a grunt, he heard Jim, loudly as always, go into the bathroom in the hallway, slamming the door behind him. In a moment there was water running, and the sound of Jim's bad singing voice.

Scotty got up off the couch and walked past Cyndi, who didn't even look his way, her eyes glued to the television screen.

Scotty went quickly to the hallway, removed his jacket from its hook and put it on.

He eased open the front door and slipped out, closing the door with a quiet *click* behind him.

It was chilly out, and there was a breeze. Scotty zipped his jacket all the way up to his chin, and ran to Jim's car.

The trunk was indeed open. Inside were the bundled old newspapers that Jim was supposed to bring to the recycling center. There were three bundles, thrown in carelessly.

Scotty pushed two of them aside, snugged himself into the trunk, and then worked the trunk lid partway down.

He hesitated.

From around the corner, someone appeared, walking briskly.

It was Jim's friend, Mitch.

Scotty held his breath and snuggled down.

Whistling, Mitch bounded past the car and up the steps to the front door of the house.

Scotty peeked out.

At that moment the front door opened, swallowing Mitch.

THE PUMPKIN BOY

Without further hesitation, Scotty closed the trunk all the way.

He heard the solid click of the latch, but immediately saw the glowing escape bar that Jim had showed him when he'd bought the new car. Of course Jim had showed him how it worked—then told him a few gruesome stories about older cars that didn't have the device, and what had happened to the kids who had been trapped inside. One of them, which Scotty didn't believe, involved a baby that had accidentally been locked in the trunk of a car one summer day in 1960: "...and when they opened the trunk that night they found the baby cooked alive, looking just like a roasted pig!"

Scotty began to think about that baby. His heart pounded, and he was just about to reach for the glow bar and sneak back into the house when he heard the front door of the house open. Almost immediately, the car rocked on its shocks as Jim and Mitch jumped into it.

In another second the car pulled away from the curb, the two older boys laughing.

Almost immediately, they started to talk about girls.

They made one other stop, and Scotty heard one other boy, who he guessed was Pete Henry, get into the car. The talk was still about girls, but then it eventually turned to the Pumpkin Boy.

"You think he's real?" Pete Henry's voice asked.

Mitch immediately answered, "It's real, man. I told you what my brother said. It's a fact that it went to Jody Wendt's house, scared his old lady half crazy. Dragged her into the house after she fainted, then left. And my brother said a couple of tourists from Montreal were picking pumpkins out at Kranepool's Farm and saw it walking through the woods. Just taking a stroll. My brother talked to them himself. He says there are at least ten other reports on file. One guy said he threw rocks at it, but he was drunk so the cops didn't take him too seriously. The Pumpkin Boy's real, all right."

"What if we really find it?" Jim said. There was uncertainty in his voice.

"If we find it, we kill it!" Pete Henry said. "Then we get the reward money!"

"There isn't any reward money," Mitch replied immediately. "Use your head, Pete! If we bring it in in one piece, we'll get in the papers. Then maybe somebody will write a book, and we'd be in that, too. If there's a book we could probably get some money out of it."

"I still say knock it to pieces!" Pete answered. "I ain't letting that thing near me!"

"You bring the camera, Pete?" Jim asked idly.

There was silence for a moment, then Pete Henry's dejected voice mumbled, "I forgot."

Jim and Mitch roared with laughter.

Jim said, "That's okay, Pete. I brought my kid brother's camera. You're covered. Here, take it. And don't lose it."

Scotty almost shouted out with annoyance, but kept his tongue.

"Good," Pete said. "If we get a picture, that would be almost as good as capturing him. I bet the *Herald* would pay us for that."

Mitch laughed. "I heard they've already gotten a bunch of phoney pictures. One of them was a scarecrow with a pumpkin for a head."

Jim chimed in. "There was a story in the paper today. Another photo they got was of some guy's kid with a costume on, holding a pumpkin in front of his face!"

THE PUMPKIN BOY

They all laughed. In the trunk, Scotty smiled. Jim had read him that story.

Suddenly the car moved from smooth road to a bumpier surface. It was harder to hear what the boys were saying with the added noise. One of them—it sounded like Pete—said, "How much farther?"

"Couple miles," Jim answered. "I want to get as close to the site as we can. You sure the police won't bother us, Mitch?"

"My brother said they packed up and moved out. Dug a bunch of holes but found nothing."

"You really think this Pumpkin Boy snatched Jody Wendt?"

Mitch replied, "Who knows? Most of the places he's been seen are around this spot. You got a better idea?"

Again there was silence.

"I still say we should kill him," Pete Henry said.

"Maybe he'll kill *you*!" Jim said, and then there was another, longer, silence.

Eventually the car came to a stop, after going into and then leaving a pothole.

"I think we ought to leave it here," Jim said, his voice clearer.

"Sounds good to me," Mitch said.

Car doors opened and then closed. There were sounds of fumbling and then Scotty heard them leaving the car.

The shuffling footsteps suddenly stopped.

"Hey, Pete, did you bring the camera?"

Amidst more laughter, Pete said, "Shit," and Scotty heard a car door open and then close again.

"Yeah, I've got it."

"And you brought a flashlight?"

Again the word: "*Shit!*"

Mitch laughed. "Stay with me, bozo. If we find the Pumpkin Boy, we'll let him eat you."

"Eat *this*," came Pete Henry's reply, and again there was laughter.

The voices, laughter and shuffling steps receded.

In a few moments, Scotty was alone.

And, suddenly: he *felt* alone.

He realized he had not brought a flashlight, either.

And where was he going to go?

He had no idea where he was, or where to look.

He knew his only chance to find the Pumpkin Boy was to trail along after his brother and his two friends.

Otherwise, he might as well stay in the trunk of the car.

He reached out and pushed the glow bar.

Instantly, the trunk popped open.

Scotty climbed out.

It was not as dark as he feared. There was a fat rising moon that peeked through the trees with yellow-gray light, and Scotty's eyes were already used to being in the dark from being in the car trunk. The car was parked on the side of a rutted dirt road, with thick woods to either side.

He could still hear Jim and his friends, though barely; there was a blurt of laughter and he went that way, to the left of the car, into the woods.

To his relief, there was a narrow path, half-covered in leaves and pine needles.

The laughter came again, a little closer, but still far away.

And then, suddenly, there was real silence.

It was as if a stifling cloak had been thrown over the forest—nothing moved, or breathed.

THE PUMPKIN BOY

Scotty became very afraid, to the point where he had no further interest in the Pumpkin Boy. All he wanted to do was go back to the car and wait for his brother to come back.

He turned around, but now was unsure which way he had come. The path had branched off and there were two paths in front of him, which split at a fork. He walked tentatively up one, looking for scuffmarks of his own sneakers, but it was smooth and untouched.

He turned back to find the other path, and now couldn't locate it.

The moon dipped into clouds, leaving darkness— then burst out with orange light like the light through Venetian blinds, cut into slats.

Scotty had no idea where he was.

He heard a single sound, a loud *thump*, and then stifling silence again.

As if the forest was waiting.

Then: a faraway snort of laughter.

He wanted to head in that direction—but there was no path.

Then he saw a flash of light, close-by.

"Jim?" he called out, loudly.

The light flashed again, just ahead and to the left of the path he was on.

He walked in that direction.

A third glint, and he broke through a rank of bushes and found himself in a clearing.

The moon glared down, higher now, filling the leaf-scattered bare spot he was in with orange-gray light.

He took a step and fell into a depression filled with leaves. He sank almost to his knees, then waded to the lip and pulled himself out.

Now he saw that he was surrounded by holes and depressions. It was like being on the cratered Moon. He remembered what his brother and Mitch had talked about in the car: a place where the police had been, full of holes.

Now he became very afraid.

There were muted sounds all around him now: rustlings, the break of a twig, scampering sounds.

He felt like he was going to wet himself, and closed his eyes, beginning to whimper.

A rasping voice said: "Scccotty?"

He thought he knew the voice, and opened his eyes with hope—

But it wasn't Jim.

Scotty yelped.

The Pumpkin Boy stood right in front of him, his huge orange jack o'lantern head glinting in the sallow moonlight.

"Ohhh..."

Scotty wet himself.

The Pumpkin Boy cocked his head to one side; his smile, lit dimly from within, looked almost comical. When he spoke again a slight hiss of steam issued from his mouth and eyes and nose holes: "Sccccotty, it's me. Jody Wennnndt."

A portion of Scotty's fear left him, but he was still trembling. The wet spot on the front of his jeans and down one leg began to feel cold.

With a series of little creaks, the Pumpkin Boy sat down on the leaves in front of Scotty. His thin metal limbs jutted out in all directions. "Sit down, Scccotty. Talk to mmme."

Scotty felt himself almost collapse to sit in front of the mechanical man.

THE PUMPKIN BOY

"Is...it really...you?" Scotty got out in a halting whisper.

"I...thinnnk so. I can see, and wwwwalk, and talk. It feels like I'm in a ddddream. And my hhhhead hurts all the ttttime."

"I..." Scotty didn't know what to say.

"And I nnnnever sleep, now. And my eyes are hhhhot."

"You went to your house—?"

"Yes, I ccccan't do that again. He won't llllet me. He ccccontrols what I do."

"Who—"

As if he had forgotten something, the Pumpkin Boy suddenly unfolded his limbs and stood up. The process seemed to take a long time. There was the faint odor of machine oil and heated air.

Scotty looked up; the Pumpkin Boy was now looming over him, his gloved hands opening and closing.

"I'm ssssorry, Sccccotty," Jody whispered.

"For what?" Scotty said.

With the sounds of metal sliding on metal, and a faint metallic groan, the Pumpkin Boy reached down and gripped Scotty around his waist. Scotty felt himself hoisted slightly up and then pressed tight to the Pumpkin Boy's cylindrical chest.

He heard a faint beating there.

The smell of oil was stronger.

The Pumpkin Boy walked with Scotty pressed tight against him with one enfolding arm.

Scotty, his own heart hammering, counted five long steps.

He let out a long weak cry.

Jody's voice said, very softly, "I'm ssssorry, Sccccotty, but he says I'm not a ggggood Ted."

7

Grant felt as yellow and dried out as he knew he looked. It was getting bad again—like it always did after Pumpkin Days began. He couldn't get through the mornings without that first drink at breakfast, and, by lunch, if he didn't already have a pint in him, his hands began to shake and he couldn't concentrate.

But, with the booze in him, he was as good at his job as he ever was.

He still knew he was a great cop—even if he was a walking car wreck.

And today, with the first pint already smoothly settled in his gut and veins, he could even face the Pumpkin Festival itself.

God, how he hated this town—and loved it. As Len Schneider had told him, people were the same all over, a healthy cocktail of good and rotten, and they were no better or worse here in Orangefield. There was greed, corruption, untamed anger, cheating, thievery, and, occasionally, even murder, just like anywhere else on the good green Earth. All the deadly sins, all in a pretty row. But Orangefield was one of the lucky communities of the rotten creatures called men who had learned to put a good face on it. They had dolled it up, made it pretty, which, somehow, made it bearable. The entire history of Orangefield was one long cavalcade of greed, one long pursuit of money, and the town fathers had finally, when they discovered—and then exploited—the serendipitous fact that pumpkins grew here like nowhere else on the planet, found a way to have their cake and eat it too. They could make money hand over fist, and, like Las Vegas, still pretend to be one of those "nice" places to live. Good schools, good facilities, good services, a mayor who always smiled and a police force who kept things in order.

As corrupt and rotten as anywhere else, only with a much better make-up job.

Grant took a deep breath, coughed, and chided himself; he knew damn well how cynical he had become, and knew that his problems came from something outside the normal proclivities of Orangefield itself.

From...the weird shit.

The weird shit that had begun that Halloween night when Peter Kerlan was killed, and then continued until that other Halloween, the one he wouldn't talk about, after Corrie Phaeder came back from California...

He shivered, a physical reaction, and ducked off the midway of the main Festival tent into an empty space behind one of the booths. He fumbled the new pint out of his raincoat pocket and twisted the top off with shaking fingers, putting the bottle quickly to his lips.

Two long gulps, another racking cough, and most of the demons went away.

This would be a bad day, and he would end up in his bed alone tonight, with the night sweats, and insomnia, and a hangover with all its own requisite horrors...

Still, he felt like he had a job to do.

One that Len Schneider wasn't doing.

He firmly screwed the cap back onto the bottle, and thrust it deep into his pocket.

No more until you're finished for the day, Billy boy. He took a deep breath. *You're still a cop. The best.*

He looked at his trembling hand, which eventually steadied under his willful gaze.

Go to work.

❖ ❖ ❖

AL SARRANTONIO

Grant was in the midway again, standing out in the lights under the huge tent, with the ebb and flow of the crowd around him. It was like being at a carnival, only a one-color one: everything, *everything*, was in shades of orange. The tent was orange- and white-striped, the booths hung with orange crepe paper, the display tables covered with orange table cloths. Light was provided by hanging lanterns shaped like pumpkins.

And everything displayed was pumpkin-related—pumpkin toys, forty different foods made from pumpkins, books on pumpkins, school projects made from pumpkins, the biggest pumpkin, the smallest pumpkin, one-and-a-half inches wide—

The sweet, cold, slightly cloying smell of fresh-carved pumpkin hung in the air like a Halloween libation.

Music drifted in from outside the main tent—there was a bandstand in the auxiliary tent, and tonight, thank God, it was forties dance music. He did not want to be here when it was rap night...

The lights overhead flickered, there was a gust of chilled October air...

He was entering the entertainment section of the midway: nickel and dime games of chance (proceeds to charity), a local magician, a balloon-toy maker. The hiss of helium brought an oddly nostalgic tinge to Grant's mind: he remembered when television was in black and white and on Saturday morning there was a guy who twisted impossibly long balloons, which he first inflated with that same insistent hiss, into impossibly intricate animals—a giraffe, a rabbit, a dachshund that looked like a dachshund. He paused for a moment at the booth—this guy was not as good. His latest creation was something that looked like a duck but which the balloon-twister proclaimed an eagle. He presented it with a flourish to a little girl, who promptly declared, "It's a duck!"

Grant snorted a laugh, and moved on to other booths and displays:

Someone selling rug shampoo, who had managed to procure a bright-orange rug to demonstrate on, a pumpkin cookie stand, a pumpkin-colored pretzel stand, a dark, long, well-enclosed booth with flaps over the cutout windows. Inside there were rows of benches in the dark, and an ancient 16mm movie projector showed black and white cartoons against the back wall. Grant peeked in. Popeye and Olive Oyl on the screen, and, sadly, only a few children with their parents watching.

Grant turned away—another reflection from his own childhood, only then the benches would be packed, and popcorn merrily thrown at the screen...

A wide, high booth near the end of the midway caught Grant's eye. Immediately, and for no reason he could put his finger on, that sixth sense that he knew made him a good cop tickled and came alive.

There was something about it, about the guy who was in it...

The booth was brightly lit, deep and wide, and had attracted a crowd. Behind a rope barrier covered with crinkly black and orange crepe paper, on a white wooden platform far away so that he couldn't be touched, a clown solemnly performed. He was dressed in orange and black mostly, head topped with a white hat with orange pom, his face painted flat white with a huge orange smile and black lashes completely circling his eyes. He was juggling three balls, two orange, one white.

Behind him, plastered on the back of the wall, was a huge, grotesque poster of a more vivacious clown dressed in brighter clothing, which proclaimed, UNCLE LOLLIPOP LOVES *YOU!*

On the bottom of the poster, in small letters, was written: Brought to You from Madison, Wisconsin.

The little tickle of awareness in Grant's head turned to a buzz of recognition.

Wisconsin...

Grant studied the clown for a moment: he was of medium height, medium weight. He barely looked at the crowd. His lips were thin inside the painted smile. His eyes were empty, staring at nothing.

Grant moved past the remaining booths—an orange juice stand, a table selling gardening tools: "Make Your Pumpkins the Biggest in Orangefield!" a homemade sign proclaimed—and pushed through the tent flap to the outside.

Crisp night air assaulted him. The band music, "Don't Sit Under the Apple Tree," not played very well, was louder. Rainier Park was filled with strollers, a lot of teenagers milling in groups, the occasional policeman put on extra duty since the second child abduction.

He hurriedly lit a cigarette.

Butt firmly between his lips, Grant buttoned his raincoat as he walked around the tent to the back facing the booths he had just observed.

A cloud darker than the night sky came toward him, and he held his breath as it resolved into what looked like a swarm of hornets.

It fell to the ground and swirled past him: a tornado of tiny leaves moved by the wind.

No weird shit this time, he thought, with a strange peace.

This time it's merely real horror.

THE PUMPKIN BOY

Again he briefly thought of Peter Kerlan, and Corrie Phaeder who came home to Orangefield from California...

There were vehicles parked in a ragged line— Winnebagos, SUVs, a couple of old station wagons, at the far end a semi with BIFFORD FOODS painted on the truck in bold letters. Grant counted down from his end to approximate the back location of the clown's booth, and found a large white panel truck without markings bearing Wisconsin rental plates.

The hair on the back of his neck stood up.

He studied the back of the truck: there were two outwardly hinged doors, closed at the middle, and locked through a hasp and staple with a large, heavy, new-looking padlock.

The front of the truck was empty; the door locked, no key in the ignition.

He walked to the back and put his hand on one of the doors.

In a fierce whisper, he called out: "Jody? Scott?"

There was no answer.

He slapped on the door with the flat of his hand, and put his ear to it, but was met with only silence.

What he wanted to do, and what he was supposed to do, were two different things. He wanted to borrow the nearest crowbar and pry open the back of the panel truck. But if he did that, no matter what he found, none of it would be admissible in a court of law.

Even "just cause" wouldn't cover it.

Then again, if he did nothing, he would not be able to live with himself for much longer. If that truck held what he feared it held, and he did nothing, and his hesitation was the difference between those two boys being alive and dead, he knew that the demon memories

275

that chased him, the things he wouldn't *think* about, never mind talk about, would catch up, and that would be the end of him.

He thought of Len Schneider briefly—this was, in essence, Schneider's dilemma: *I waited too long...*

"This one's for you, Len."

Grant tramped farther down the line of vehicles, avoiding thick electrical lines which led from the tent to ground outlets farther off, till he came upon two men sitting on the dropped back end of a pickup truck and smoking. He showed them his badge, angling it in the faint light so they could see it.

"You guys have a crowbar?"

One of the smokers flicked his cigarette away and nodded. "Sure thing."

In a moment Grant had what he needed. Gripping the strong metal bar, he went back to the panel truck.

Throwing his own cigarette aside, he angled the crowbar into the curl of the lock's closure and gave a single hard yank.

With a weak groan, the lock snapped open and fell away with a *clank*.

One of the doors, uneven on its hinges, swung slowly towards Grant, opening.

Light filtered into the back of the truck, illuminating the interior.

"Shit almighty," Grant whispered.

8

Len Schneider dreamed. Except for the one about the kid with no face, he didn't dream much. But when he did they were significant.

THE PUMPKIN BOY

In this one, he was flying like a bird. He had wings of long blue feathers, white-tipped, and he soared high into the clouds and then dived, his mouth open in exultation.

And then: in the manner of dreams, things changed, and he was in a balloon. His wings were gone. He was floating, at the mercy of the wind. The basket, which was constructed in a loose weave that let him see through the breaks in the bottom, shifted precariously when he moved, threatening to break apart. But he was unafraid, and held tightly to the ropes that secured the gondola to the balloon. He peered calmly out.

He was passing over a huge green forest that spread out below him in all directions. At one horizon was a line of mountains, impossibly tall and thin, their peaks like snow-capped needles. The sun was either setting or rising. A glint of something that might have been a vast body of water shimmered in the direction opposite the sun.

But he studied the trees.

Suddenly (as in the manner of dreams) he held a spyglass in one hand. He peered through it, and the tops of the trees looked close enough to touch. While still looking through the glass he reached down and *did* touch the tops of trees, feeling the light brush of healthy leaves vaguely redolent of moisture against his fingers.

And then something rose large as a whale into his vision, and he felt the flat, hard touch of an artificial structure slide under his hand.

When he stood up gasping, and threw the spyglass away, the thing had already disappeared behind him. When he looked back anxiously he saw nothing but the receding tops of trees waving their leaves at him, going away—

"Jesus!"

Schneider opened his eyes. For a moment he was still in the dream, which he needed no interpretation for: he could smell the rushing high air from the gondola, and the faint hot breath of the balloon overhead; he moved his arms and for the briefest second thought they were ridged in feathers.

"*Jesus,*" he gasped, fully awake now, and jumped out of bed and began to dress quickly, strapping on his shoulder holster.

9

"That's right: Carlton. C-A-R-L-T-O-N," Grant said. The voice on the other end of the line said some words, and then Grant answered: "No, the panel truck was empty, but I still think he's the guy who took the kids. Call it a gut feeling." More words from the other end, and then Grant once more: "That's right, he was gone when I went back into the tent."

The phone receiver pressed tight to his ear, Grant tried to shake another cigarette out of the pack but found it was empty. Grunting in displeasure, he crumpled the pack with his free hand and fumbled in his raincoat for another. He coughed. His hand found the pint bottle but moved impatiently past it. Amongst loose change he located the new pack, and grunted again, this time in pleasure, as he drew it out and expertly opened it, tapping a butt out and lighting it.

While he waited on the phone he turned to regard deputy sheriff Charley Fredricks, who he had grabbed from his post at the entrance to the music tent in Rainier Park and brought to the station with him. The kid was bright and willing, and hadn't opened his mouth about this not being sheriff's business. Charley was young, but he had seen his own share of weird shit in Orangefield.

Grant said to him, "Anything on who rented that panel truck?"

A second receiver pressed to his own ear, Charley made a face. "On hold."

"Dammit. You tell them this is an emergency?"

Charley looked hurt, then gave a sour grin. "Guess that's why they didn't just hang up."

Grant scowled, then pressed his receiver tighter to his ear. "Yes? You sure?" There was a pause. "Well, thanks, Warden."

He hung up the phone and traded puzzled looks with Charley Fredericks, who was still on hold.

"Jerry Carlton is safe in his cell at Madison State Prison, reading an old copy of *National Geographic* as we speak," Grant said.

"Maybe an accomplice?" Charley asked, trying to be helpful. "Someone he worked with who didn't get caught?"

"Carlton killed five boys, all on his own. He was a loner." He gave a heavy sigh. "I've got to talk to Len Schneider, find out if there was someone else..."

Charley nodded absently, giving sudden interest to his own phone. Grant suspended his own punch-dialing expectantly.

Charley said, "Shit," and looked at Grant. "They just changed the music, is all."

Grant shook his head and jabbed in Schneider's number.

It rang until the answering machine took it.

"Isn't Schneider off tonight?" Grant said to no one in particular.

Charley Fredericks shrugged, then said, "Yes?" into his receiver and began to nod. His pencil went to work on his notepad.

Behind Bill Grant the voice of Chip Prohman, the night sergeant, fat and laconic and nearly useless, chimed in. "You looking for Schneider? He called in a little while ago. I just sent two black and whites out after him. He sounded out of his head—claimed those two kidnapped kids were out in the woods after all."

Grant was about to answer when Charley Fredericks hung up and waved his notepad at him. Grant squinted forward to read what it said.

"Holy God." Grant turned viciously on Prohman and spat: "Where the hell is Schneider?"

The sergeant answered, "Out in the woods—"

"*Where?*"

Prohman was almost yawning. "Same spot he dug all those holes. You ask me, he's just plain out of his gourd—"

Grant was already half out the door, with Charley Fredericks, perplexed, studying the name on his notepad as if it was an ancient rune telling him nothing, behind him.

10

Grant could see the roof flashers of the cruisers ahead of him. He felt as if he was in a dream. Charley Fredericks had talked all the tire-screaming way out, but Grant felt as if he was alone in the car.

It all came down to this.

To this: the most horrible thing of all, at least in this world.

For a tiny moment he almost wished it was the other business, weird shit, that he was dealing with.

With a shiver, he let that thought go.

His only hope was that he wasn't too late.

The car bumped in and out of two successive dirt ruts, and he slammed the brakes behind the first of the lined-up patrol cars.

There wasn't a cop in sight—but flashlight beams danced in the woods off to the left.

His gun was already out of its holster as he pushed himself out of the car.

"Hey, Bill!" Charley Fredericks shouted behind him, unheard.

Grant pushed through the brush as if it wasn't there; dried vines and branches slapped at his arms and across his face.

Behind him, Charley, his own flashlight on, made his way carefully along the path into the woods.

Grant heard voices now, one of them loud and irrational:

"*Hold those lights on the front of it, dammit!*"

Grant broke into the clearing—into a tableau from a nightmare.

Like a nightmare, there was a strangely ethereal beauty to it. Three uniformed police officers stood stock still, holding their flashlight beams on a single spot up in the trees. The gnarled mass of denuded branches there at first showed nothing to the eye, they were so tangled and uniform—and then the eye resolved a section of them pinpointed by the triple beams into a manmade opening, a brown door set neatly into the branches.

In the doorway, frozen in place and looking confused and lost, staring straight into the lights pinning him like a butterfly, was the orange-and-white motleyed clown

Grant had seen in the tent at Rainier Park. His pompomed cap was gone, showing a thinning head of light-colored hair; there were rips in his orange and black motley costume and his makeup was smeared, pulling his smile into a high, grotesque grin on one side. The blacking around his eyes, which had been used to line his lashes, had run together.

On the ground in front of the three police officers, Len Schneider, looking disheveled himself, a pajama top peeking between his shirt and pants, stood in a two-handed firing position, his eye sighting down the barrel of his .38 police special trained tightly on the figure in the doorway.

Grant, holding his own revolver at his side, but in a tight grip, said, in as reasonable a voice as he could, "Len, put your gun down. It's all right. He's Ted Marigold's father, Lawrence Marigold."

There were tears streaming down Schneider's face, but his hands were rock steady on his revolver. "He's Jerry Carlton!" he screamed. "And this time I got here in time!"

Grant kept his voice level, but slowly brought his handgun up. "Jerry Carlton is in Madison State Prison, Len. I talked to the warden there twenty minutes ago. The man you're aiming at is Lawrence Marigold, the father of the last kid Carlton killed. Ted's father. Remember him, Len? The genius biotech engineer? How he went insane after his son was murdered? He escaped from his institution. You couldn't save Ted, but you can save Ted's father. Just lower your gun."

Schneider ignored Grant. "*I told you!*" he screeched at the figure in the doorway. "*Send them down now!*"

The clown turned away for a moment, and then a long rope ladder rolled out of the doorway like a red carpet, its end swinging to rest just inches from the ground. The clown stepped aside, and Jody Wendt appeared in the doorway and carefully descended the ladder.

"Jesus," Charley Fredericks, who had stopped beside Grant and was aiming his own flashlight at the opening, said.

"*Now the other one!*" Schneider screamed.

The clown moved aside and said something that sounded like a sob. "Ted."

There was darkness in the doorway and then something else, not a boy but boy-sized, with impossibly thin, bright metal limbs and a head made of a pumpkin, climbed out and began to descend the ladder with practiced ease. Little puffs of steam issued from the cutout holes in its face as it came down, gazing mechanically back and forth.

Charley gasped and said: "*Je-sus!*"

Grant's own gun hand began to tremble, but he steadied it with the realization that what he was looking at was something real, something that had been made by a man.

The Pumpkin Boy stood at the bottom of the tree, next to Jody Wendt. He continued to stare back and forth, with a look almost of fright on his cartoon face. His gaze finally settled on Jody. "I'm sssssscared..." he said in a horribly distorted, faraway voice.

"*Where's the other boy! Where's Scotty Daniels!*" Len Schneider screamed, his attention still riveted on the doorway in the trees.

"I—" the clown said confusedly, his voice swallowed by the night.

Then he turned back into the doorway and disappeared.

Grant took the opportunity to say, "Len, please listen—"

"Shut up! Shut the hell up!" Schneider wheeled on him for a moment with the gun, his eyes wild. Grant could see the muscles standing out like taut cables in his neck. "If you shoot me in the leg, Grant, to try to stop me, I'll blow the bastard's head off!"

There was movement in the tree-house doorway and with an almost animal growl Schneider swung his aim back that way.

"Here…" the clown said.

Charley Fredericks gave a shout of horror: there in the doorway was the body of a young boy, trussed upside-down and suspended from some sort of wheeled rack. On his head was a silver cap with a thick arm of wires leading from it.

"Oh, God, what did he do to that poor kid…" Charley Fredericks said, reaching for his own revolver.

Even Grant hesitated, starting to move the aim of his gun from Len Schneider to the doorway of the tree-house. "Son of a—"

The boy moved. He twitched in his bonds, looking like Houdini trying to make an escape.

"Let him go, Carlton! Now!"

Lawrence Marigold made a confused motion, and then his shoulders sagged. He looked down at the pumpkin-headed robot at the bottom of the rope ladder, who turned his face up to regard him.

Marigold sobbed out, "Do you remember…what I used to say to you when you were a baby, Ted? When it was just you and me and mommy, and I stopped at the store after work and bought you the candy you loved? Do you remember what I always said after you squealed and held your hands out, laughing, when I gave you your candy? *Do you remember what I used to say? Uncle Lollipop loves you!*"

Still weeping, he disappeared into the opening, then reappeared, reached down and did something to the bundle of wires on the boy's metal skullcap.

And then something happened which caused even Len Schneider to open his mouth in wonder—

The steam issuing from the Pumpkin Boy's facial cutouts increased in intensity, until an orange fog engulfed its head. A thin trail of something that resembled fire and smelled like electricity curled out of the cloud, rose up the bole of the tree and snaked into the tree-house opening.

Two flashes of tepid lightning lit up the doorway. Grant could see the edge of another poster inside the hut like the one the clown had mounted in the tent in Rainier Park.

The boy suspended from the rack began to writhe and cry out in pain.

On the ground, the Pumpkin Boy stood mute.

Len Schneider again had his .38 trained on the tree-house doorway.

"*Cut him down! Now!*"

In another few moments the boy was loose and rubbing his hands and legs.

Lawrence Marigold, his face a nightmare of streaked makeup and tears, stood dumbly as Scotty Daniels climbed slowly down the ladder.

"Get the kids out of here, Charley," Grant said.

Fredericks nodded. When Scotty reached the ground he herded the two young boys, Jody Wendt limping slightly, away from the Pumpkin Boy and down the path to the cars.

Grant thought, *At least they won't see any of this.*

Out loud he said: "Len, you've got to put the gun down right now. It's all over. You did a great job."

"*I won't make any mistakes this time, Carlton!*" Schneider screamed, ignoring him.

"I just borrowed them!" Lawrence Marigold said, throwing his arms out in supplication. "I thought you would let me!"

Grant saw Schneider straighten his aim. "*Not this time, Carlton!*"

Oh, God, Grant thought, his own finger tightening on the trigger of his police special. In the next split second he thought, *Goddammit, Len, don't make me do it—*

Two shots that sounded like the echo of one rang out.

Two bodies crumpled.

Shit!

Grant saw that, by the length of the time he had allowed himself to think, he had been too late to save Lawrence Marigold.

Len Schneider was down, unmoving, and in the doorway of the tree hut Marigold collapsed with a huffing grunt. He sat tilted on the sill of the tree hut for a moment, then fell forward.

He hit the ground a moment later, groaned once and was silent.

Grant walked over and knelt down to study his face.

It had the same lost, mad look on it it must have held for many months and years, since the night his boy had been taken.

"I'm so sorry," Grant said.

"Ted..." the clown whispered, staring past Grant at nothing, and then was silent forever.

Grant stood up. Two of the uniforms were working on Len Schneider, but Grant knew it was a waste of time. He hadn't missed.

He was good at his job.

Hands shaking, he lit a cigarette, coughed, and thought about the bottle he would have to open later.

Another nightmare for the menagerie.

And Jerry Carlton sat snug and warm, reading a magazine in his cell at Madison State Prison.

Idly, Grant wondered if the Warden would let him visit with Carlton, for just those three minutes Len Schneider had so badly wanted.

It wasn't until much later that Bill Grant discovered that the Pumpkin Boy was missing.

11

The Pumpkin Days Festival came and went.

Halloween came and went.

Newspaper headlines came and went.

Years came and went.

But:

Some nights of some years, out in the fields behind the house where Jody Wendt used to live in Orangefield, when the moon was just rising like a huge sickly white lantern, and the ground was covered with fattening pumpkins, they said you could see something outlined against it in black, like a hand puppet silhouette against a wall:

Something that looked like a pumpkin.

Something that looked like a boy.